Reign of the Dragon Queen

Cadence Connor

Contents

Chapter One

The dragons always know.

That was a saying circulating this place at least a dozen times during their stay. The riders believed it as if it was some kind of law. If that was the case, then maybe one of them could help solve the mystery of that blasted voice that wouldn't leave her alone.

Meilene!

Not again.

It's called to her for hours with no end in sight. What she wouldn't give to have it silenced, and her thoughts be her own again. She cracked an eye open and groaned at the darkness that greeted her. Judging by the lack of light coming in from her window, morning remained hours away.

If she ever wanted to sleep, then she would need to find that voice. A small part of her wondered if someone was playing a trick on her.

She threw aside her cover, made of a thick canvas that made her skin itch, and winced at the cool breeze.

Could this place get any more barbaric?

The cold floor stung like ice against her bare feet. The stone pattern covered every inch of this vexing place, including the dreary walls and high ceiling. It was clear the dragon riders had no taste for decor.

She retrieved a pair of slippers from her travel chest and tossed a soft cover over her shoulders. It would barely hold against the harsh weather here, but it was something.

With a swift movement, she tightened the knot around her midriff and pushed the door to take her first steps outside.

It was late, and she shouldn't have been out wandering . . . but that voice . . .

The Fordde's odor made her wince, reminding her of the old stokes they had used when visiting the countryside, outside of their castle. That felt like so long ago.

Why did the dragon riders' home have to smell so primal, like . . . well . . . like dragons?

Meilene sighed and pinched the bridge of her nose.

One more day until they could fly home. One more day until she could leave this dreadful place for good. She dreamed about the comforts of her room every night. The silken sheets, the warm rooms filled with her clothes, and the expanded rooms full of workers to attend to her every need.

Meileeeeeene.

The sound bounced off the hallway's walls and rattled her bones. She clamped her hands over her ears, hoping that would put an end to it.

I'm hungry.

How was she the only one out right then? The noise should have woken up half of the place by now. This Fordde. It was what the riders called these giant stone cities built on the base of the old magic lands, using the ancient word for an old fort. They had built several on the old lands where the two kinds finally called peace and crafted the blood bonds between dragons and humans. They always said that a hint of the ancient magics still flowed through this place, but she'd yet to see any evidence of it.

The next set of doors led to her father's room, the lord of Valchar. She could have woken him, but he would be of no help. He was as unfamiliar with this strange place as she was and always held a strong disdain for the dragonfolk.

Long stone hallways stretched in every direction, lit faintly by hanging lamps. Someone must have been keeping them restocked. Where were those workers?

She had to find that voice. Didn't that voice know she had a long flight home the next day? She already had a long week of traipsing after her father, smiling pretty, and making small talk with the mundane dragon riders around here.

An enormous ornamental saddle hung from the stone wall beside her. She paused to admire it. It revealed no creases or lines, as a real dragon rider's would. This one had never seen the back of a dragon or felt the wind against its leather.

The day she could finally put this Fordde behind her could not come soon enough. She'd never have to pretend to appreciate the hospitality of these common-folk and listen to their trite plights. She never should have agreed to come with her father in the first place.

As his only living child and heir to the Valchar kingdom, she had to come and play nice. The riders needed them more than her father needed their dragons. The Valchar kingdom was the wealthiest and the most powerful on the planet, devoid of competition.

The dragonfolk desperately needed her father's help in the coming days, and as much as they pretended otherwise, Meilene knew the truth. All this pageantry of late, pretending they were equal partners in the war, meant nothing. They were not equal and had not been for a long time.

A queen dragon had not existed in years and a Reina in almost a century. Their numbers dwindled to less than a thousand across all the lands. Power the dragonfolk used to hold meant nothing by then. They were only as good as the manpower they could give to the lower kingdoms, and lately, that wasn't enough to keep their enemies at bay.

The riders were a joke.

Other than the dragonfolk, everyone else knew that.

Meilene.

"What?" She covered her mouth with her hand as the words echoed back. She didn't mean to shout. Where was she, even?

Again, she was on her way. On her way to a destination that only her feet knew.

After several deserted hallways throughout this behemoth of a stronghold the riders lived in, she came across a guard in his high-collared uniform at a set of doors. The oak doors were twice as tall as her, a large dragon etched onto them. Someone had carved the intricate lines, ensuring every detail was correct. Something amazing must have been beyond those doors.

The guard was young, with shaggy brown hair that fell into his blue eyes. Handsome for a dragon rider, not that she'd get caught saying it aloud. The rider surveyed her with his piercing eyes.

"What are you doing out at this hour?"

An overwhelming desire to get past filled her, but he blocked her way.

I am starving.

Meilene was hit with hunger pangs more intense than anything she'd ever experienced. She never wanted for anything back home, so this was a new sensation. If she didn't eat soon, she would waste away.

All that consumed her was her overbearing hunger and the urge to eat . . . now!

"What are you doing?" The rider sounded angry this time. "You shouldn't be here."

Meilene ran her hand through her tangled mass of hair, aware she only wore her nightclothes. "I have to—I can't." She pushed past the rider and through the double doors of what she now knew was the hatchery.

They should get better security here. Anyone could walk in . . . and she was so hungry right now.

As she made her way down the rough stairs into the large hatchery, she was vaguely aware of the rider following close behind. The room was several stories high and larger than any of the entertaining rooms they had back on Valchar. Another dragon emblem was emblazoned on the far wall. This one was adorned in spikes and wearing a warrior's armor.

Even though it was night, the room sparkled with brilliance. Beams of light reflected off the glass ceiling and formed shining crystals around the eggs. This place was clearly valued above the rest of the downtrodden ones she had seen this past week.

An annoying noise buzzed from behind her. The rider was speaking, but his words jumbled together in a mess, and she didn't care for what he said.

All that she cared about was silencing the darned voice. She was so close now. She felt it down to her core. This was it.

The first egg she passed was neatly tucked in its corner, surrounded by piles of old hay. The oval shell, waist-high on her, had been there for years, if its shield of dust was any indicator of time. It was hardly the oldest one, if she remembered their guide on the first day correctly, as their magic protected the small dragon within until it was its time, sometimes taking hundreds of years to awaken.

Dozens of large eggs lay in front of her as she passed. Several gleamed brown and green in the light, whereas others were muted reds, blues, yellows, and oranges. Whites and blacks were scarce among the group, but they weren't the rarest.

One would grow to be the fastest ever and even outpace an Anver; one would take its time and eventually mate with a queen for years, and another would die quickly but save many of its kin before it did.

All of them had fine destinies and would find rider partners to help complete them. They all waited . . . like she did.

Meilene didn't stop to wonder how she knew all those details. As she trailed her hand along each dormant egg, she could almost hear each of them, see their future, and know who they were destined to be with.

How did she know all of this?

"Are you sure I can't take you back to your quarters?" The voice was less aggressive this time, more uncertain. That rider was unimportant for now.

Hay crunched beneath her feet as she made her way past these dull eggs. She ascended the stairs toward the ancient sections. The eggs here were old, but they had no dust on them like the others. They were placed prominently by the windows to get the best sunlight.

Where the other levels had crowded eggs of all colors huddled next to each other for room, up here, the hay was fresh, and the eggs spaced out to allow for ample nurturing. She passed a particular egg hatched by the last queen and another blue egg, who would wait centuries more for its bonded partner.

These eggs weren't waiting on just anybody. Each one was created for one specific soul and no one else.

A second Fordde rider came crashing in through the doors. He paused at the sight and didn't try to stop her, joining the other, who was watching her from a distance. They spoke among themselves, muttering nervously.

They didn't try to stop her again.

Meilene strode past all those eggs toward the one who would not let her rest. That annoyingly persistent voice. That annoyingly familiar voice. That warm, familiar voice calling to her and her alone. It pulled and tugged her forward as if called by a bond deeper than blood and magic.

Up her feet went. One step in front of the other until she stood on the silver dais. She passed a large egg from the first breeding queen, Anarillia, and another from the Reina

Alianthe, who led the dragonfolk to their first victory against the Anver creatures.

A shudder came over her, unbidden, while the tips of her fingers tingled. She felt nothing but familiar coldness at the thought of their ancient enemy. The dark magic that powered those beasts was old and brutal.

When she was young, Meilene used to have dreams of a dark, formless creature flying through the skies with only the intent of blood fueling it on. Blood and the search for the ancient magics.

Many dragons and their riders had been killed over the centuries in the fight to keep their home safe from the dreadful creatures. Aletzia knew she'd destroy any who were foolish enough to cross her path, even though they'd been defeated years ago.

Aletzia. That name was so familiar and yet so strange. It was as if she'd known that name all her life.

Once she was in the middle of the dais, she finally saw it.

It was larger than the others, as it should be, reaching past her torso. The egg stood out with its golden sheen, dancing brightly in the light.

Tonight, it brightened the room.

A ripple went through the shell when Meilene touched it, shocking her at first. Then the egg pulsed with warmth, and she felt movement inside.

Meilene.

Relief permeated throughout the voice. Relief and warmth and love. Finally, she was here. Why did she not hear her cries earlier? She's been calling for days.

"I came as soon as I could."

A crack formed at the top of the golden shell. Small at first. Then it reached out like a spiderweb until covering the entire egg. The cracks deepened and spread until they eventually gave way.

Meilene pulled her hand back at the sudden shock as pieces of shell spattered outwards, revealing a large, golden head with angular ears that were pinned back. She had never heard of gold-colored dragons before, they must have been a rare breed. Thick scales covered the creature's body, with spikes sticking out along its spine and a long tail wrapping around its clawed talons.

Obsidian eyes stared back at her. The longer she stared into those hypnotizing eyes, she saw the shades of purples, golds, greens, and browns in them. Beautiful.

The small dragon unfurled its wings and shed the remnants of its cage. She was stuck in there for a hundred years and was so glad to be out.

Aletzia preened and made a low throttling sound from the back of her throat.

Echoes of other dragons answered the call, but she paid them no focus. She only had eyes for her dragon.

Aletzia was perfect.

She tilted the creature's head to examine it. That stabbing pang of hunger was back. They would have to find something to feed her. She couldn't let her dragon starve.

A noise across the hatchery snapped her attention away from the young dragon. More riders ran into the room. Meilene locked eyes with the first guard who first tried to stop her. His mouth hung open in horror.

The dragon nudged at her and demanded to be fed.
What had she done?

Chapter Two

C racks trailed along the dark stone wall, reaching out like a claw toward the low ceiling. Inches of dust and old shavings covered the beaten-up floor. There were no windows to look out of and nothing but a stiff bench to sit on. This room, like the others, was lacking attention.

"This is completely unacceptable. I demand you make this right." Her father's voice boomed in from the next room. The heat in his voice was palpable from here.

These old walls were no match for the lord's rage, even the light from the wall lanterns seemed to cower from it. The lord of Valchar was not used to hearing the word *no*, and today was no exception. Meilene stared through the wall and tried to picture the image of her father pacing the room. Tried to imagine the look of pure fury that must have been on his face.

"As I've explained, my lord, there is nothing that can be once the blood bonds are sealed—"

"Stop! I do not want to hear one more word out of you. I demand to speak with your boss. Where is he?"

"As I told you before, sir . . ."

The small head nudged her elbow. Meilene ignored the argument and focused on pouring love and attention into the creature next to her. She scratched the top of Aletzia's head, marveling at how it felt beneath her fingertips. She paid extra care to the scales behind her ears, the spot she knew the dragon loved.

When could they leave?

There was nothing in this room to keep her attention besides her dragon, studying the cracks in the wall, and listening to her father's heated voice. The riders who brought her here said it was a holding area they used to help clean the new hatchlings and get them ready. They could have at least afforded her a blanket so that she didn't have to sit on that rough bench.

Don't stop.

She scratched along the jawline and found a spot that made the small dragon hum in pleasure. She ran her hands around the rough scales and played with the small spikes on her back. It felt weird against her skin but not unpleasant.

Such strange creatures.

Another nudge against her side, and she resumed scratching with vigor. Even though they flew in for three days on a pair of dragons, she'd never taken the time to properly appreciate them. Such magnificent creatures they were.

How did she never take the time for them before?

If she wasn't so sleep-deprived and in awe of her dragon, she'd be as worried as her father was right now. Somehow, she wasn't so concerned. There would be a way out of this, and she could leave the details to her father to figure out. They'd be back at home as planned before the week was over.

Surely, the warmer climates of Valchar would be much more agreeable for Aletzia. She'd love to dig in the beaches and play in the giant waves during high tide. Meilene would never have to set foot in the blasted Fordde again. She'd be home.

Home?

"Yes, dear." She caressed the delicate head. "You'll love it there. Our lands are the largest, and you'll have no worries about scrounging around to feed yourself. You'll be taken care of, like the queen you are."

We will go home together?

"Yes, we will." She scratched at the joint below the translucent wing. Strange to think this thing would eventually grow large enough to carry a full rider. They'd have to figure out where she could sleep back home. "It's your home now, too. You belong with me. I'll make sure you never want anything. How much do you eat anyway?"

I'm so hungry.

"But you just ate, silly."

The gold dragon finished off a small hare when they left the hatchery. It was unsettling at first, all the blood and guts everywhere, but it made her dragon satisfied, so she kept her comments to herself. The riders here knew what a new hatchling required, down to the quiet of the room they were currently sequestered in.

That was good, as she had no clue how to help the starving dragon and bumbled around for aid at first. Aletzia had grown fussy in the crowded hatchery, and her squawks of hunger threatened to wake the entire Fordde, those that hadn't already come down at the commotion.

The dragon calmed down when they brought her to this room for food and some much-needed cuddles.

That was so long ago. I may starve soon.

"We'll figure something out." She swiveled her head around the room as if an answer would pop out at her. She should get one of those riders to help her.

The voices next door got louder until the door burst open. It ricocheted off the wall with a resounding thud. Her father entered with a burly dragon rider on his heel and froze when he took in the scene in front of him.

The small dragon peered around her shoulder curiously, wondering what had taken her partner's attention away from her.

The lord managed to dress in his formal attire this early hour. He was rapt with attention, even if the bags under his eyes told a different story. His jaw was clenched tighter than she'd ever seen.

Meilene stepped back.

"We are leaving." Her father nodded at her. He was usually stoic and calculated, never allowing his emotions to show. She'd never seen his face such a shade of red before. "Meilene, get your things. Now!"

"My lord, we have been over this—"

"No." The muscle on his cheek twitched, and he pointed his finger at the rider's chest. "You talked. You did not listen . . . and we are not in agreement. Tell your dragon lord our negotiations are finished, and he will get no support from Valchar. We are done with this place."

Meilene nodded. Relief warmed her blood at the prospect of finally leaving.

"My lord, Eoibard." The mustached rider tried to calm him down as a bead of sweat dripped down his forehead. "Emotions are high from these unexpected events. Let's not make any rash accusations."

"I'll make any accusations I want." The Valcharian lord towered over the dragon rider. A formidable enemy with his official royal uniform on. His dark hair, similar to Meilene's, was plastered against his head, and his olive skin was flushed with emotion. "We came here based on your good intentions. First, we dealt with substandard negotiations and now this duplicity." He waved his arm wildly. "I'm taking my daughter."

"That's not possible, my lord." The rider licked his lips. His eyes glazed over as if listening to a voice in his head. "Wait here. The dragon lord is coming and will explain everything."

"You can't hold us hostage here," Eoibard Velum shouted. "Meilene, get away from that thing and pack your bags."

Meilene furrowed her brows. She paused in the middle of scratching along Aletzia's jaw and searched for the source of what he was talking about. "What?"

What's wrong?

Her father never got the chance to answer, as four large dragon riders entered the room, two of them looked half asleep. Meilene recognized the head dragon rider from their previous events at the Fordde. He was a thickly built man with wispy blond hair that receded away from his surly face. He puffed his chest, as if he thought to intimidate the Valchar lord.

The first time she met the dragon lord, as they called him here, Tork Streno, Meilene was less than impressed. She always heard dragon riders were a fierce and cunning kind. The stories made them out to be great people who cowered from nothing.

This man was none of those things.

Eoibard Velum strode up to Tork. He didn't seem to care that the man was twice his size in width. "I demand this be rectified and for those guards to be punished. This never should have happened."

Meilene remembered how worried that one guard was when she entered the hatching grounds. At least the young rider didn't buckle when the Valcharian ruler screamed in his face, promising to have him hanged for what happened.

"The hatchery guard did try to stop your daughter," the dragon lord said calmly, "but it was already too late."

What did that mean?

I'm hungry.

Another pet to the scaly head. Hopefully, the ravenous dragon would keep her whines down. Now was not the time for a scene.

"No." Her father shook his head violently. "This is not happening. Let's go." He grabbed Meilene's arm and made for the door. The small dragon squawked at the abrupt end of her scratches and lost her balance.

A silver-haired rider stood in their way, a senior commander, if the stripes on his arm were accurate. He had a scar under his cheekbone, but even with that, his wrinkled eyes were soft and seemed less menacing than the others.

Meilene's father once mentioned how the dragon lord had several commanders who helped him run the Fordde and commanded several wing battalions of riders each. They were a formidable force, accountable for all the riders within this place. This must have been one of them.

The man, Commander Yannet, had smooth tones as he spoke. "We all need to take a moment to calm down. Think about what you are saying, my lord. You can't expect to take them back. How would you care for a fully grown dragon? You don't have the resources or the knowledge. We have taken care of them for almost two thousand years."

Eoibard stared at Aletzia, who was struggling to get back on her feet, as if she was an annoying insect he wished to kick away. His gaze returned to the commander. "You can't expect me to leave her behind. This is my only child and next in line to rule. I will not allow this. She's coming back with me. I'll pay what you want if that's what this is about."

Finally, someone made sense.

All Meilene dreamed of was her own warm bed. Far away from this cold, alien place. She bent to pick up the gold dragon.

"Leave that thing." He gestured wildly at her side.

"What?" She expected to see something else at her side. There was only Aletzia.

"That creature is not coming with us," he said dismissively.

"I'm not going to leave her," she said, taking a step back. She clutched a hand to her chest, trying to calm the battering of her heart against her ribcage.

No! The dragon's distress was palpable from here. Meilene felt those feelings seep into her own and caressed the scaly head in reassurance.

If the lord of Valchar wasn't prone to any sort of humor, she would have thought he was joking.

"I'm not having that—that *thing* ruining our castle. It's got to stay here."

The commander opened his mouth to speak, but Meilene cut him off. "That thing has a name, father, and she's coming with us." The small head brushed against her side.

"No." His face was like stone, unmoving and unyielding. "That absolutely will not happen."

Meilene glanced between her father and the gold dragon that she'd barely met a few hours prior but felt like she'd known it forever. "Then, I can't come with you."

"Sir," Tork said kindly. "She's right."

A deafening silence filled the room, punctured only by the young dragon licking at its claw. The lord appeared to be at battle with himself.

"Let's figure this out, father."

The dark-haired lord shook his head slowly. "There's nothing to figure out. You've made your choice. I won't forget what you've done here, dragon lord Tork. Our negotiations are done, and you'll find no support from Valchar in the future."

"Father, wait." She wanted to move. She had to stop him but couldn't think of the words to make this right.

With a disparaging look at the gold dragon, her father turned on his heel and left, leaving her alone.

Meilene's legs were rooted to the spot. The cogs of her brain were frozen, and she couldn't formulate a coherent thought. What just happened?

Surely, he would be back. She was turning eighteen next year, and he was preparing her for taking over some of his duties. He can't leave her in this place. Her eyes darted around the dark stone room, hoping for an escape.

The panic must have shown on her face, for the scarred commander looked at her kindly. She hated it.

"Maybe you'd feel better if you got some rest and changed out of your nightclothes." Meilene realized she was still wearing her original dressing gown. "We can help you get her more food and then she'll sleep for a while. Most hatchlings do."

The dragon tilted its head. *More food?*

Her throat was dry, and she couldn't find the words, so she nodded. Was it her or did the room become smaller? She had to get out of here.

"Here, my lady." A mousy worker handed her a bundle of materials. It was rough against her fingers, made of the same material she'd seen riders wear. The worker curtsied and backed away with the others to give her privacy.

The walls of the room seemed to shrink as her father's words repeated in her head. *You've made your choice.* What choice did she truly have in all of this?

Her hands tightened on the pile of clothes in her grasp. None of this was her choice. None of this, she had any say in. All she wanted was to go home, back to where she belonged, and where she should have never left in the first place.

Meilene was truly alone.

Chapter Three

SIX MONTHS LATER

"Don't you have anything else besides this terrible tanned skin?" Meilene held the beige riding jacket up to the light and winced. The thick blanket on her bed was littered with similarly hideous ones made from the tough material.

How did anyone ever think this color was wearable?

"I'm afraid not, my Reina," her mousy-haired helper, Maeve, said. She grabbed another jacket from the pile, nearly identical to the last one, and ran the material through her fingers. "These are the best materials for flying. They'll protect against the wind and debris. Anything less wouldn't be feasible."

"But they're disgusting." Meilene paced the oval stone room that she came to call her own these past months. Her boots echoed against the worn floor. How many other boots followed the same path throughout the years?

These rooms were built more plainly than she was used to but served their purpose well. They were built to withstand thunderous shakes from dragon landings and keep their riders warm throughout the cold seasons. What they lacked in decor, they made up for in practicality, suitable for any normal dragon rider.

Maeve scrunched up her face. "I'm afraid it's all we have."

"Fine." She snatched the least offending garment from the bed. A leathered jacket, probably from a guinea buck judging by the thickness, with bright stitches and lined with extra paneling on the sleeves and torso. "It'll have to do. Are you certain there isn't anything else, perhaps in a different color?"

"We can try dying them. It's not traditional, and I'm not sure what that'll do to the fabric. I can do a few tests to see how the material handles it."

Meilene turned the jacket over to examine the high collar, imagining it wringing her neck in flight. "That would be wonderful. How about a nice black—and do you have any trimmings that can be added to help with the cold? Something fur-lined and fashionable?"

"And—black?"

"Yes."

Black was fitting for her mood.

After all this time, the Fordde and everything in it still felt so foreign to her, down to her dark stone room. Even with a fire lit, she still froze in this room that felt like a cage. Perhaps having something of her own would help her feel more at home and less like a prisoner.

But we are at home?

"That's not what I meant," Meilene said. Maeve raised an eyebrow quizzically. "Sorry, that was for Aletzia. So, do you think you can spruce this up a bit?"

The small helper's face filled with panic at the request, but she nodded. "I'll see what I can do, my Reina." She gave a half-curtsy and backed away.

"I guess this will work for today," Meilene said to herself. She crumpled the beige jacket into a ball and tucked it under her arm. "Wouldn't want to give that man another reason to delay our flight now, would we?"

I am a Reina dragon and should be allowed to fly when I want. No one should be able to ground me.

"I know." She walked outside to comfort her dragon. "They aren't concerned with *you* going out flying, my dear."

Aletzia unfurled her membrane wings and stretched before curling back into a ball. The dragon had been resting in the stone berth of her quarters, or as these riders liked to call it: her Maise. The one redeeming part in the Fordde's design was how the riders' living quarters were fashioned, with a large outside den for their dragons to rest.

It brought her comfort having her dragon close and within view, especially since Aletzia was all she had here.

Meilene ran her hand along the thick scales, each the size of her palm. Gold scales. A mutation of sorts the likes of which hadn't been seen since the first Reina dragon.

Aletzia had been growing so fast, it was hard to keep up with her cleaning and feeding some days. She already stood taller than Meilene in height and was large enough that she could support her rider while flying, if the dragon lord declared so.

These rules were insufferable. Not suitable for the heiress of Valchar. Well, not the heiress anymore. She was . . . Meilene didn't know what she was anymore.

A light nudge to her shoulder. *You are my partner.*

"Yes, I am," she said fiercely. She wrapped her arms around the golden head, breathing in the scent and matching her breath to that of her dragon.

Meilene may not have had any friends here, and she may not have had her father's support anymore, but at least she had the best dragon.

Of course, I am. I'm a Reina.

Dragons were the farthest things from being humble.

And why should I be?

"You're right. There's no reason for that." She rubbed Aletzia's long neck, stopping to examine the dirt underneath her rough nails.

They made her cut them within the first few days at the Fordde. Longer nails would get caught and break, they said. No riders here kept them so long, they said.

So, she cut them.

They tried convincing her to cut her hair to help when she started flying, but she refused. No one would touch her long locks if she could help it. If she had to spend hours untangling the brown mess after, so be it.

Footsteps signaled the approach of the dragon lord. Meilene closed her eyes and rested her head against Aletzia, praying for strength.

Right on time.

If she could go one day without seeing his annoying face, she would thank the skies. So far, she'd been unlucky in her six months here.

She plastered the fakest smile on her face she could muster up at this hour, even though her blood ran like ice through her veins. "Dragon lord Tork. Commander Brawne. So nice of you to stop by again."

The two dragon riders entered Aletzia's den, stepping around a bundle of blankets she had left out from last night. The dragon lord wore his usual too-small uniform and had his wispy blond hair slicked back in a way that did him no favors. The graying Commander Brawne also wore his official uniform, displaying the commander's brand on his jacket arm, as if it were a treasured prize.

"I thought I'd check how Aletzia is fitting in." The dragon lord's eyes ran over the golden dragon, who scratched her claws on the cool stone floor, before settling on Meilene. She flinched. "Do you have everything you require?"

As annoyingly persistent as he was in making certain she was settling in, there was something off with the dragon lord. She couldn't quite pinpoint it, but his forced joviality didn't always reach his eyes. Those cool, calculating eyes sent shivers down her spine on the best of days.

Did he make others feel that way, or was it just her feeling out of place again?

If only she had someone she was close enough with to ask. She was out of place here, and everyone knew it.

There was little point in making friends, as no one cared enough to get to know the foreign rider. No one thought she deserved to be bonded with their precious queen dragon, who's veins ran hot with the old blood magic and the hold it had over the others.

Nobody here would give her the time of day if it weren't for Aletzia.

"Everything is fine. Those new fabrics you sent over served well, along with your other presents." She rubbed her palms together. "Aletzia is growing quickly, and we're ready to move on to our flight practice."

"Hmmm." The dragon lord walked closer to the young dragon, his boots echoing with every step. It was too close for Meilene's comfort, but she knew better than to say anything. "I don't know. I'll have to talk to the lead instructor."

Again?

Meilene was eager to finish with her current lessons. As most riders matched with their dragons at an early age, she was forced to take the beginning coaching with riders nearly ten years younger than her.

Children. She had to take lessons with children.

This wasn't the first time this happened in the Fordde. There were always riders who matched later in life and needed to learn the basics of dragon care and flight along with the rest.

Older riders advanced quickly through the initial lessons, usually. Meilene had to wait for approval from the dragon lord at every step, and he was always hesitant in moving her forward. He'd pushed this off the last three times she attempted this conversation.

It didn't help that her instructor seemed to despise her. All she did was call his teachings archaic one time, and now, she's been labeled as difficult.

"Aletzia is ready for me to fly with her," she said, still smiling pleasantly. "I know she is."

Aletzia extended her wings and shook them out. Muscles rippled underneath the layer of hide and scales. Her thin tail flicked back and forth as golden scales shone in the sunlight.

I am the strongest and fastest flier. Why wouldn't I be ready?

The mustached commander backed away to avoid getting hit by a wing. "She has grown faster than the newest batch of hatchlings, sir. Perhaps the queen is ready."

Meilene sent the commander a dazzling smile. At least one person saw things her way.

"I'll have to see," dragon lord Tork said slowly, his eyes dark and clouded as he reached out to touch the golden dragon. Meilene clenched her fist at the sight. Tork stared into her golden scales for a while before turning back to them. "Let's review this tomorrow, Brawne."

"Absolutely, sir."

"If I do allow it, I'd like her to have at least two full wings as an escort. We wouldn't want anything to happen to our Reina."

There he went again, talking to the commander like Meilene didn't exist. It took everything in her to bite her tongue and keep smiling like a fool. *Remember your place here*, she repeated to herself. Causing a scene would get her nowhere with these riders.

If people weren't busy falling over themselves, trying to get her attention, then they treated her like she was a piece of property that belonged to the Fordde. No one gave her a say in anything, and the dragon lord was the worst of them all.

She wanted to learn how the Fordde ran, but he kept her at a safe distance from any real decision-making. Typical. Didn't they know she trained for these things from an early age with her father?

Running a Fordde with dragon riders shouldn't be any different than a kingdom. She could handle it but just needed them to see it, too.

After checking over her dragon and determining she was satisfactorily healthy, the commander and the dragon lord took their leave of the pair. Leaving them alone, as she was used to.

The moment they were out of sight, she allowed her mask to drop.

Are you all right?

"It's nothing, dear."

Meilene rested her head against the golden dragon and listened to the heavy heartbeat. Aletzia. Her only source of comfort and affection in this dreary place.

Words could not describe how much she despised being here.

Chapter Four

The lessons she was forced to take were the worst form of torture in this place. She'd rather clean up after an entire wing of dragons at feeding time then spend another hour listening to this man drone on and on.

"Does everyone have a list of requirements for the quartermaster?" the graying instructor asked the group at large, rolling back the sleeves of his tan jacket.

The small classroom had a single board at the front, filled with the day's instructions, and dozens of small wooden desks that threatened to fall apart if sat on in the wrong way. The walls were a color that reminded her of an old book, dull and fraying.

The instructor's eyes wandered over the rows of desks filled with eager-eyed riders and settled on Meilene for a second too long. That look was far too familiar now. Instructor Alian didn't think she was ready for this.

It didn't matter, though.

After several more pleas to the dragon lord, Meilene was able to advance to her next phase of lessons and would finally take her first flight with Aletzia. She'd only been pushed off by him for the past two months.

A greasy-haired student occupied the instructor with a question about his dragon's eating habits. Meilene sighed and stared out the window, hoping to spot Aletzia on the giant concourse. The outside grounds were humongous. Built for the dragons to lounge, play, and train on, and spread almost as far as a small village.

It was always a tease to be able to watch the dragons outside but not be allowed to join them as they prepped to take to the skies. Anything would be better than here.

These classes bored her. Most focused on how to care for your dragon or preparing riders for their future duties throughout the Fordde and how the report structure worked with the wing leads and commanders.

It was less relevant for her, as Meilene would never have to perform the same functions as the rest. She had a Reina queen.

But being a fully-fledged Reina still felt so far off.

Not until her first mating when Aletzia would select her first mate. That one tradition frightened her the most in all her months of uncertainty at the Fordde.

As much as queens matured faster than the others, Aletzia still wouldn't mature for her first mating for years to come, and Meilene had Tork to deal with until then.

After a queen mated for the first time, she would be able to control all the dragons through the ancient blood bonds. That magic hold would pass to her mate as well. That's how it was always done and how the chain of command was enforced.

Would Tork let that happen? Would he just give up power to her or had he envisioned a different future using her dragon and her magic for his own purposes?

He must have something up his sleeve, as he seemed determined to slow her progress at every stage.

Not that any of that mattered today.

Today it was only about her and Aletzia and getting to fly together for the first time. That made up for most things she'd endured since being abandoned here.

Finally!

"I know," she whispered.

"Meilene?" the instructor asked.

Meilene winced. Her desk creaked in protest. No one used her name anymore. It was usually "my lady" or "my queen" or "Reina." Her latest instructor clearly didn't think she deserved any of those titles.

"I have it right here." She waved her paper of instructions to outfit her queen with. The instructor gave it to her in case she forgot.

Queens grew larger than regular dragons, with wingspans that could grow up to double their size. They were built longer and leaner, making them nimble and speedy in the air. This made for a ferocious beast that would almost never stop growing in size.

It also meant it would be hard to find reins and a saddle that would properly fit her unique partner.

"Thank you, Meilene. Please make sure you make haste with the quartermaster, as the dragon lord requests your presence after."

There were several murmurs and giggles at this comment. Meilene had to stop from rolling her eyes at the immaturity. She could not wait to be rid of this class.

Before anyone could stop her or ask annoying questions, she ran out and made her way to the quartermaster. She was the first to arrive, but he looked prepared for a large group of rider requests.

"Ah, Reina Meilene." The quartermaster was bent over a pile of leathers, hard at work when she approached. "I heard you were coming down. What can I help you with for your dragon?"

"Quartermaster, ah—?"

"Gaelen." The stocky man brushed the dust off his pants and extended his hand. A measuring rope hung across his shoulders, and the belt at his waist drooped under the weight of tools.

"Thanks." She ignored the hand and smoothed out her paper in front of him. She would be happy to be rid of this place as soon as possible. It smelled like a barn here. "Quartermaster Gaelen, Aletzia, and I will have our first flight together shortly—"

"An exciting milestone for any rider."

"Yes, very much." She pointed at the paper. "We have our first flight, and I need her outfitted for a proper saddle, harness, and all the other things listed here."

"Absolutely. Whatever I can do to help our future Reina." He clapped his hands together and grabbed a metal strap from a shelf. The entire place resembled an overgrown shed. Bundles of leather and metal hung from every inch of ceiling. "Can you call your dragon to the concourse, so we can take some measurements?"

I am coming.

"She's on her way."

Four riders worked on a series of long stirrups in the back of the shop. He waved the tallest one over and handed him the measuring rope.

"Ryland! Come help the Reina outfit her dragon while I work on those orders for the dragon lord." He steered the young rider forward by his shoulder. "If you have any problems, come and get me, but I think you can handle it."

"Thank you, Quartermaster," she said. "I appreciate your help."

"Anytime you require new gear, feel free to come directly to me in the future and not through the dragon lord."

"I'll keep that in mind." She turned to the rider assigned to attend to her. He was maybe a few years older than her, with brown hair and blue eyes, but still a junior judging by the bands on his uniform. It took her a moment until she recognized him as the guard who was at the hatchery the night she bonded with Aletzia. It was hard to forget that night, as much as she wanted to some days.

At least he managed to survive both the dragon lord's wrath and her father's threats of disembowelment and beheading.

"What all do you need?" the rider asked wearily, keeping a careful distance between them.

Was he not happy to help? Most riders would have given anything to help and would have fallen over each other for this chance, but not him. Instead, he seemed annoyed.

"Everything," she said with a smile. "And I'm in a hurry, if you will."

"Works for me," he said briskly. "I have things to do. Where's your dragon?"

"Outside. She's the gold one."

The rider chuckled, almost as if against his will. "Thanks for the tip."

Meilene's mouth dropped open at the jab. He brushed past her before she could utter any proper retort.

"The gold one," she mumbled to herself, stomping after him onto the grassy concourse where her dragon lay ready. Tail flicking in barely-contained excitement.

Her boot caught in a small dip, and she nearly lost her balance, catching herself before toppling face-first into the grass. If she had a mirror, she was certain her face would be bright red by now.

"The gold one. So stupid." Aletzia was the only gold dragon here. Everyone knew who she was.

"Hurry up," he said without looking back to her. "I thought you were in a rush."

This was going to be a long day.

By the end of the hour, it became clear that the rider would have given anything to not have to help her anymore. It may have been around the fifteenth time she sent him back to find a different color for her saddle that she saw the light leave his blue eyes.

"What's wrong with it now?" he asked in a tired voice. "I found a darker version as you asked. This one is less *strappy* like you wanted."

I think the rider is eager to leave you.

"I preferred the stitching on the prior version, plus it's slimmer on Aletzia. Do you have something closer to that but in this color?" She nudged the fourth option laid out with her toe.

The way this was going, half of the concourse would be littered with her rejected options. Judging by the look on his face, he was starting to come to that realization as well.

"Slimmer. *Slimmer*," he muttered, not bothering to hide his eye roll. "I'll be right back with that, Reina."

Meilene knew she was being fussy but didn't care. Everything had to be perfect for her first time flying with Aletzia. She was a queen and deserved only the best, no matter how much she may annoy the young rider here.

Eventually, she settled on a saddle fit for a Reina, one that even Tork could find no fault in. The rider looked like he could pass out from relief when he brought out the winning option. It was black leather with ornate gold stitching that was perfect for bringing out the beauty of Aletzia's colors and a smooth seat that would fit her petite frame.

Perfect for a Reina.

Perfect for *her* Reina.

It seemed like the rider wanted to leave. He hovered for a moment then settled on asking, "Do you know how to put it on properly?" His voice was kinder this time, without the prior judgment.

The ground underneath her feet became suddenly interesting. She stared at it as she shook her head, refusing to meet his gaze.

He sighed. That prior annoyance was back in full strength as he beckoned Aletzia closer, not afraid to get too close to her sharp claws. "Come on, then. I'll show you."

"Thank you," Meilene said in a quiet voice. As annoyed as this rider was with her, he had shown her more about how to equip her dragon in a matter of minutes than her instructor had taught her in months.

It was frustrating to be looked at as the stupid foreigner all the time. It was hard when nobody took a chance on you.

Aletzia was eager to ride with Meilene and willingly moved her wings when he asked and crouched so he could reach around her torso to fasten everything. His attitude changed when he spoke directly to Aletzia, it was hard for anyone to stay annoyed with such a lovely dragon.

As the rider painstakingly demonstrated how to tie up her harness and saddle for the third time so that Meilene could do it on her own, a familiar voice interrupted their work.

"How is everything going for our young Reina today?" The dragon lord peered around Aletzia's head, somehow managing to sneak up on the pair.

The rider jumped away faster than she'd seen him move all day. "Just finishing up here, sir." His voice hitched in a nervous way, and he lost any of that prior casual arrogance.

"I was speaking to the Reina," Tork said in a dangerously low voice. "Don't you have duties with the quartermaster to return to, Ryland? You shouldn't be here."

The rider got the hint and quickly excused himself, throwing one last look over his shoulder before he disappeared

That one was kind and I liked the way he complimented the shine of my scales too. She rustled her wings for emphasis.

"Did he bother you?" Tork asked in a sickeningly sweet voice. "I've had problems with that rider in the past."

"Not at all, dragon lord," she said pleasantly. "Quartermaster Gaelen had him carry the saddle out for me, as it was too heavy."

"Either way," he looked over his shoulder, "I'll have words with his leader about this. They need to know the proper protocols."

One thing she noticed in her months at the Fordde was that the dragon lord didn't like her conversing with other riders, especially the males. He made sure she was never alone without one of his commanders or wing leads supervising. He almost always found an excuse to interrupt her those few times she did strike up a conversation.

What was he afraid of?

Meilene finished tightening the strap like the rider had shown her and stepped away to admire her work. She was painfully aware of Tork watching her every move.

"Beautiful work." He ran his hand along the underside of Aletzia's neck and checked the tightness of her straps. "She's a fine specimen." His shrewd eyes trailed over to Meilene as he ran his hand through his thinning blond hair.

Meilene clenched her jaw. "I like to think so, too."

"Perhaps Vylor, and I should escort the two of you on your first flight tomorrow. Help ensure everything goes to plan."

"I don't think that'd be proper." When he looked at her, she added pleasantly, "I wouldn't want the other students to think there was any favoritism, and I'm sure you have lots to do instead of escorting young riders around."

He shook his head, as if catching himself. "Yes, of course. If you need anything else prior to tomorrow, please let me know. I'm at your service."

"Absolutely, dragon lord."

He bowed to Aletzia and excused himself.

I don't like him.

"That makes two of us." Meilene watched Tork make his way to the quartermaster, undoubtedly to give him some harsh words for whatever wrongdoing he thought was done. She was painfully reminded of her father's old aide and how condescending he was to Meilene, all because she was a girl. "But we're stuck with him for now."

For now.

Chapter Five

S treams of air caressed her on all sides as Aletzia took to the sky with her rider on her back for the first time. The force of the wind sent her hair flying in all directions, covering her view of the grounds below. She didn't care. She only cared for the creature whose muscles flexed beneath her. The only word that she understood cohesively was *enemy*.

This was the first time they flew as one and Meilene had never felt more alive. Aletzia radiated with pleasure as she narrated her every movement.

Look how strong my wings are.

"They're lovely."

And see how nicely I take my turns.

"You are doing rather well." Wind buffeted her in her seat, and she tightened her grip on the leather reins.

The wind is nothing against me.

"Nothing can stand against you, darling." She reached over and thumped the thick hide of scales. Aletzia hummed and pumped her wings even harder. Taking them further into the crystalline ocean that hung in the skies.

Can we fly together every day?

"I want nothing else."

Nothing could stop that now.

Half a dozen riders flew a few dragon-lengths below her and a full dozen to either of her sides. The dragon lord came through on his promise to make sure she always had an escort.

Such an unnecessary rule.

Still, she shouldn't complain. At least she was finally allowed to fly with Aletzia.

There was no better feeling than the one she experienced now, riding hundreds of dragon-lengths in the air with no one to judge her or complain. Not saying they wouldn't provide ample feedback after her first flight, but how could anyone find fault in her dragon?

They are flying much too slow for my liking. May I leave them behind?

"If we ditch our escort the first time we're allowed out together, we'll never get to leave the Fordde again."

Let them try to stop me. No one can command me, not even the one who calls himself leader.

"I know. Now is not the time for that, lovely."

Aletzia rumbled beneath her legs. Meilene felt the same but didn't want to press her luck. This was the happiest she'd been in months, since her father left her behind without any word.

While she had yet to feel at home at the Fordde, when she was here, flying above them all with only Aletzia and their bond, nothing else mattered. The thick muscles moved under her with every pump of Aletzia's wing, as if they were her own.

She pulled her new fur-lined jacket closer against herself to keep out the wind. Maeve did a fantastic job with the dye, as it was now a darker shade than the others.

It was fitting, as she didn't ride any dragon or even an ordinary queen. Aletzia was a Reina queen, the head of all dragon wings.

When the dragon lord explained it to her, it sounded like a hive pack, with one queen who reigned above the regular wing leaders, higher than any regular queens . . . not that there were any of those around, either. Not yet.

Reina queens were the sole continuing lifeforce of all dragons and the blood magic. All other dragons had to follow the Reina's lead, both hers and that of her mate, whenever she was finally ready to mate and come into her full powers.

"The first egg a Reina lays will become the next Reina," her historian had said during one of her lessons. "Ready to hatch years after that one is gone. That is how the bloodlines continue."

Weird tradition to wait years for a new Reina to hatch, never knowing when that chosen human would show up or who it would be. It could be months or years in between Reina queens, yet the riders never seemed to worry since *the dragons always knew.*

Dragon riders were a strange, superstitious people.

Well, they were technically her people now.

That is how it has always been done.

"It's still strange. Especially to someone who is not used to it. You've known nothing but the Fordde. I grew up far from here."

There were a lot of things about rider customs she wasn't used to. Some days, she didn't think she'd ever fully assimilate to their ways.

Aletzia banked left and dove below a series of clouds. The circular shape of the Fordde was barely visible from here. Nestled on the edge of a cliff and overlooking the rolling hills, it was the perfect stronghold for the head of dragons and the hundreds of dragon riders residing there, even if it was freezing half of the time.

The Fordde was a monstrous building by all standards, even dwarfing Valchar's castle stronghold. It had to be gigantic to house all the dragons and their riders.

Meilene never truly appreciated its size before now, being able to see it like this. From this angle, it was clearly larger than any city she'd ever seen, its true size well-hidden from those approaching on foot or mare.

The large turrets were still visible, and she could make out the hundreds of circular divisions for each wing's Maise. The Fordde was well-built like a labyrinth, with its sections built upon sections to confuse any potential attackers.

Meilene couldn't even pick out her own Maise from this angle.

They dove past a group of trees, nothing but play toys from this distance, and near the lake that Meilene spent many an afternoon bathing Aletzia in. It sparkled turquoise even without direct sunlight on it.

Meilene let her hands drag behind her as Aletzia flapped her wings joyously. Six months ago, being this high up terrified her on their trip to the Fordde.

Now all she was filled with trust and joy. Her dragon was most at home here in the skies . . . as was she.

"Let's go higher, Aletzia." She clenched her straps and pushed herself closer to her queen, as if they were one. "Can you?" she asked, unsure of her dragon's limits.

Of course. Meilene thought she sounded irritated. She should never doubt her.

Golden wings beat against the air, pushing them further up in a few swoops. Aletzia stopped when she broke into sunlight, hovering as if suspended above the clouds. Meilene loved the feel of the sun on her face.

With a beat of her wings, Aletzia took them toward the north.

Faster. She was determined to test her wings at their full potential. *I love flying with you.*

"Same with you."

Aletzia took them away from the others and caught an updraft, which she let herself glide along. Eventually, she settled into a low glide near the smoky peaks. They must have flown for miles now as the mountain tops started to resemble rolling waves from this height.

The other riders were not behind her. She didn't realize they had gone this far.

"Maybe we should go—"

Whomp. The force of the hit nearly threw her off her dragon. Aletzia dropped several lengths before regaining control of her flight while all that Meilene could do was clutch tightly to her dragon.

The ground looked sickeningly close from this angle. Had they always been this high?

Something else is here.

"What is that?" She twisted in her seat, trying to see what hit them but it was hard when her dragon continued to move in every direction, looking for what had attacked them.

Hold on!

For the second time, Meilene was almost thrown from her dragon by a force hurtling into them. She wasn't prepared for the speed at which her queen took off. Meilene caught a glimpse of something black and scaly, almost like scabs, before Aletzia dove back into the clouds. Her dragon twisted and turned to try to get a better view. Meilene could barely see a few feet in front of her; she'd have to rely on Aletzia's sense of direction.

"Where did it go?" She was surprised by the panic in her voice. Seconds felt like hours as each pump of her dragon wings sounded like the beat of a giant heart.

Meilene's own heart raced, and she could feel the blood pumping against her ears. Where were the others? They should not have gone so far without them.

The others come to help. I have ordered them.

A snarl from above preceded the next attack, followed by an overwhelming stench of rotting flesh. A black creature with four tattered wings dove at her dragon, mist from the clouds framing it, as if it wore a cloak. Aletzia turned on her tail and narrowly missed the sharp red talons.

The creature shrieked and pivoted, pursuing its prey.

Aletzia dove at the creature with her claws outstretched. She collided against the beast and scratched at its belly, trying to catch its head in her teeth. The beast snarled and kicked, catching just beneath Aletzia's hind leg. Meilene barely managed to duck as a spiked tail whipped at her.

Her dragon hissed in anger and snapped her jaw, catching a small pinion wing in her mouth. She tugged, and the wing ripped. The black beast screamed in agony as black liquid spilled into the skies.

The two went into a freefall before Aletzia released it from her jowls and pushed away. Meilene struggled to catch her breath as whatever it was disappeared into the clouds.

"We have to get back," she gasped.

They hovered in place for a moment before the white dragon escorting her finally made its way to them. The rider's panic was visible from this distance. He shouted and waved them over, but was too far to be heard clearly.

Meilene snapped her head around, still searching for their attacker. The newest addition must have scared it off.

"You're hurt, Aletzia. Are you all right?" She noticed blood running along her poor dragon's golden scales. Aletzia leveled off her flying, and her wings slowed to a less frantic beating.

I am fine. Her dragon's voice was laced with heat and anger. She'd never heard her like this before and tried to send soothing thoughts her way.

"What was that?"

What she got in response was a series of emotions and images. Some felt old, as if from another person or entity. She was overcome with the feeling of pain and anger and a lot of sorrow.

Chapter Six

The moment Aletzia touched down in the safety of the Fordde grounds, she was confronted by a furious dragon lord. Her legs shook and almost buckled from first flight exhaustion, but the blood rushing through her veins managed to keep her upright for his barrage of reprimands.

"How dare you! Get down from your dragon right now. What do you call that stunt?" Tork waved his glove wildly around the grassy landing pad. He must have come from the command center, as he was dressed in his formal attire. "In all my years as dragon lord, I've never seen a rider with so much contempt for the rules."

The man is upset with you. He should be praising my—

"We were flying, and something came after us." Meilene managed to dismount with some grace while shaking from head to toe and tripping over Aletzia's straps. Her brain was still trying to process what had happened.

Why was Tork so mad at her?

A few of the riders originally escorting her had dismounted and came to check on the pair. They edged close cautiously. She regretted leaving them behind like they did, but didn't realize they had gone too far until it was too late. She didn't expect anything to happen as it did.

What even was that thing?

Meilene reached out to undo Aletzia's strap with trembling hands. Before she could get the first knot untied, Tork grabbed the leather from her and threw it on the ground. It lay like a mess of tangled weeds on the grass.

"This is exactly why I expressed concerns before." Spit flew out of his mouth with every word. "We have rules for a reason, even if you think they're not for you. You've managed to rile up half the dragons here with your little stunt."

He waved at the grounds. Several nearby dragons flapped their wings irritably and flicked their tails, as if something had agitated them. She didn't realize the dragons were so attuned to each other.

"That wasn't my—"

"I've had to endure dragons shouting at me for the past fifteen minutes and can barely hear myself over Vylor."

His blue dragon, Vylor, stood beyond on a large boulder, peering at the group curiously. He looked perfectly calm now.

I called to them but at first they wouldn't listen. I had to force them to listen.

Aletzia's words only further confused Meilene.

"I want an explanation," the dragon lord said sternly.

"We—we were flying over the peaks. Aletzia liked the strong currents there and wanted to practice in the clouds. That's when whatever *it* was attacked us."

"There was nothing spotted by our scouts," the dragon lord said. He looked back at one of his riders for confirmation.

Meilene wrung her hands together, a bead of sweat dripping down her neck. "I don't know what it was, but there was something."

Aletzia eyed Tork curiously with one of her large, multi-faceted orbs. He ignored her.

"Why did Aletzia raise an alarm and send everyone into hysterics?" He whipped his head toward the young wing lead escorting the Reina. "Did you see anything?"

The young man shifted his feet. "I didn't see anything when we got there. It's possible whatever it was had left by then, sir."

"Whatever it was had scared Aletzia," Meilene said. "It was fast, too."

One of the commanders, the gruff Calenth, had come down at the commotion, concern etched across his face. "Could it have been—?"

"No," Tork said quickly. "They haven't been seen in these parts in a century. Aletzia must have gotten spooked by a large animal."

"She wasn't spooked," Meilene said forcefully. She clutched her hands to her side. "We were in the air above the mountains—"

"Alone." Tork's hands flew around haphazardly. "Without your escort."

"Only for a few moments. I thought the other riders were right behind us."

It is not my fault they were unable to keep up. This was our first time together and I wanted to see how far we could fly.

"You put your dragon in danger. You put our entire blood-lines in danger to prove a point. I always knew you were a selfish brat but didn't expect this."

Meilene didn't understand the issue. Aletzia was fine. Her dragon was focused on cleaning her talons and examining the new group that formed. "But there was something there! You are completely missing the point."

Why would no one listen to her?

"I swear I saw a creature." Her voice broke as she continued. "It was hidden in the clouds. I remembered reading up on the Anvers, and this thing could have been . . ." she trailed off after seeing Tork's face.

A stocky rider that had flown with her tried to speak up but was silenced by his friend. It wasn't hard to know why.

Nobody wanted to speak against the dragon lord. The hold he had over the place and its riders was frightening. She wished she had one person on her side, even one friend in this Fordde who could back her up.

In a low voice, the dragon lord said, "Calm yourself, young Reina. You forget where you are and who you are. I wouldn't want to have you sent to the infirmary for hysterics."

Murmurs spread among the crowd, and nobody would meet her eyes.

This could not be happening. Her body felt numb, but Meilene understood completely. She would not let him take her down for this.

She ran her hand through her hair and took a couple of deep breaths. "You're right. This was Aletzia's first time flying. She may have gotten disoriented in the ranges."

Instructor Alian pushed his way toward the queen. "My apologies. I knew it was too early to allow her to fly."

"It's all right, Alian." Tork waved him off. "We can't keep our Reina grounded forever. She had to test her wings."

"Perhaps the queen was attacked by a particularly large avian," one of the wing leads supplied. That terrible Simeon again. "There are reports that the feasts were large this year, and they've become brash. It also could have been a griffin that ventured south."

"Perhaps," Meilene said coolly. On the inside, though, her blood boiled. "This won't happen again. My dragon is tired. May I have your leave to take her back to our quarters?"

"Of course, my queen." Tork bowed in an over dramatic way, meant to be insulting. "I'll make sure to have someone check in to ensure you are all right. You shouldn't be alone after your episode."

It took everything she had to bite her tongue. It was clear what the dragon lord was doing. She wasn't stupid.

It was clear now. Tork didn't care about what attacked her. He didn't even want to investigate if it was the Anvers and the threat they posed. He was only worried about keeping his position. His power.

If Anvers had truly ventured this far into human territory and attacked their Reina, it would not reflect well on the dragon lord. It was easier to blame her for this mishap. She was a fool to think he wouldn't use this against her.

It was apparent she would never be able to lead as the Reina she was meant to be. He would never give up power when it was time. She was to be a well-kept prisoner under his close eye until Aletzia's mating, maybe longer.

Tork Streno was no proper dragon lord and needed to be removed.

Chapter Seven

The jacket hit her table with a smack, knocking papers onto the worn floor of her Maise. The plump would-be-assistant ran out of the room in tears, not even bothering to close the door on her way out.

How rude.

What was wrong with that one?

"What wasn't wrong with that one?" Meilene's patience was drained from the constant pestering questions and how much what's-her-name followed her around. She was glad to be alone again in this large cavern she called a room.

She wasn't a child, as much as Tork insisted on treating her like one.

The departure of this most recent aide was just another item on the list of many she'd have to discuss with the dragon lord. She kicked at a nearby stand and a decorative vase with wildflowers crashed to the floor.

"Aargh." Meilene hopped on one foot. Her cries echoed across the empty Maise, bouncing off the stone walls. Why did nothing go right for her?

This was the sixth helper she had been through since the dragon lord decided she needed more *one-on-one attention* after the incident. Each one was more terrible than the last. They only cared about whatever agenda Tork gave them and didn't listen to any of her requests.

Meilene was used to people trying to manhandle her from her previous life. She knew how to handle people like this, but every time she managed to get rid of one, the dragon lord had a replacement waiting.

It had been a month since Aletzia was attacked while flying with Meilene. A whole month, and the dragon lord had become even more unbearable. He constantly checked in on her every move, demanded reports every time they left the Fordde on a flight, and made sure no one in the Fordde took her seriously.

Meilene cradled her sore foot and slumped into the nearest chair.

If she didn't think they'd be turned around the moment they got there, she had half a mind to take Aletzia and fly home to Valchar. It was fun to dream. As if Tork would let her get far from this place and as if her father would take them in with open arms.

Meilene was truly on her own here.

As if on cue, Tork came storming into her room. His wispy blond hair was plastered to his red face. He must have come from a flight, as he wore his formal riding gear, with a strap on his shoulder to indicate his precious status as leader.

"I hear that you have dismissed yet another one of my helpers."

Meilene didn't bother to stand for the dragon lord. She peered up at him with her best doe eyes and clutched at the arms of her chair. "I don't know what you are talking about, sir. Eileen stormed out of here, complaining about inhospitable working conditions."

"Yes." Tork paced the room, pausing to check that Aletzia lay safely in her den. "Conditions that were caused by you."

"Hmm." She picked up a text on dragon flight patterns from the table and flipped through the pages. "First time I'm hearing of it."

"Don't play those games with me, young lady."

"I'm not playing at anything." She focused on the diagram related to wind tunnels and what speeds to best approach them. "I let your stupid worker come in, and she was terrible. I told her as much."

"You can't keep scaring away everyone I send over here."

"It's not my fault your people are easily spooked," she said, peering over the edge of her book.

"Fine. If that one was not to your liking, we'll try something different," the dragon lord said with a terrible glint in his eye. He stopped his pacing and towered over her menacingly. "I have the perfect person."

"Are you certain this is necessary?" she said in a smooth voice. "Our recent flights have gone without an incident, and Instructor Alian has been singing Aletzia's praises."

"I wouldn't want anything happening to our Reina now. We'll stick with the current regiment for the time being."

"We'll see." She returned her focus to the pages in front of her. "I thought the dragon lord would have better quality workers to choose from."

"We'll see how easily you get rid of this one, my Reina."

Based on his tone and the unusual sparkle in his eye, Meilene had a sinking feeling she would pay for her remarks.

She wasn't left waiting to find out for too long.

Before the day was over, a knock announced the arrival of her new helper. Meilene braced herself before opening the wooden door.

In front of her stood a surly-faced rider well past his prime, with a receding hairline and weathered face. He had a purple birthmark that spread from his cheek down to his neck and below the line of his faded uniform.

He eyed the Reina curiously with a look she did not like. It was obvious he would give her nothing but problems.

"Did the dragon lord send you?" she asked.

"Why else would I be here?" He brushed past Meilene and into her chambers. His eyes passed over the broken ceramic and pile of unwanted straps by the entrance to Aletzia's den.

Compared to her old rooms in Valchar, this was nothing, but it was one of the larger and more updated ones in the Fordde. At least the dragon lord afforded her that much comfort, even though the Maise was far too close to his own.

"This place is a mess," the man said, kicking aside the pile of leather. He favored his right foot, as if he had a prior injury. "Didn't they teach you proper upkeep in your training?"

"There's a lot of things a Reina doesn't need to do." Yes, she could stand to tidy this place a bit more, but surely there was someone paid that could do it better?

"Is there now?" He circled her like a feline hunting its prey. "I've been tasked to keep you in check."

"I don't need anybody's help." She grit her teeth as she spoke, allowing the anger to show through her usual mask of calm indifference.

"And I have much better things to do than follow a coddled, uninformed rider around, even if she is a Reina." Without asking permission, he sat at her long table, designed to seat a queen's wing of at least a dozen, but still strikingly empty.

"How'd you get so lucky, then?" She sank into a seat opposite the man. He was different from the others Tork had sent, less jumpy.

"Let's say that Tork and I have a history," he said with a smirk. "Sounds like you do as well. I know he wants detailed reports on you, which I'll have to provide on a daily basis. Annoying. What did you do to set him off so?"

Meilene laughed bitterly. "Besides having a Reina that can depose him from his precious position and hold a power over the dragons that he covets, nothing of note."

"Hmmm." He nodded slowly. "The dragon lord also said you are prone to hysterics and should be watched closely, especially when on flights with your young queen."

"I. Do. Not. Require. Watching."

Tell him I am more than capable of flying on my own.

"I would hope not. You don't look like an invalid to me unless it's something in the head." He tapped the side of his temple.

"There's nothing wrong with me."

"Maybe not. Time will tell." He tilted back in his seat and whipped his head to get a good view of Aletzia. "If you were senseless, I doubt your queen would have chosen you. Excuse me." He lifted his hands in apology. "Your Reina, I mean."

"You're the only one around here that thinks so." She tapped her fingers on the edge of the table.

"I heard about your first flight," he said casually.

"Everyone did."

Dragon lord Tork made certain the entire Fordde knew she had gone off on her own and nearly killed her dragon on the peaks of the smoky mountains. He liked to leave out the details of whatever attacked her in his narrative.

The man nodded. "What a good excuse Tork has for why you shouldn't be left on your own."

"It seems so."

"I also heard you were attacked by something large, not an avian—as Tork would like us all to believe. Do you still stand by your story?"

"It doesn't matter. No one believes me."

The dragon rider grabbed a cup filled with a dark liquid leftover from her morning breakfast. He downed the drink as Meilene watched in disgust. "True. Why would someone ever listen to a warning from Reina?"

Silence filled the room for a few moments. "You didn't say your name. Why did Tork send you? I don't understand what's in it for you."

"My name is Namail Ronna . . . and I wouldn't say he sent me as much as he is punishing me for a recent transgression. Believe me, I want to be here much less than you want me here."

"Sounds like he found a way to punish us both."

The rider surveyed her with unyielding eyes. "It would seem so."

Chapter Eight

I f the dragon lord wanted to find a way to punish her, he couldn't have found a more perfect vessel. This new rider mentor was insufferable, rude, and hated everything and everybody in the Fordde. He refused to help Meilene clean after Aletzia and was adamant about checking in on how her flying and other lessons went.

Namail Ronna had been a rider to his dragon, Mennon, for over eighty miserable years. Eighty years spent being a deplorable wretch, no doubt. Thanks to the ties with their dragons, riders tend to live elongated lives, unfortunately for some.

The week Meilene had spent with the sour rider was the worst since arriving here. Worse than getting attacked with Aletzia or being abandoned by her father. Namail had something to say about the way she cleaned her dragon and had choice words with her instructor about not letting her skivvy off her weekly duties, as she had in the past.

This man had to ruin everything good she had going on just because he thought she should learn what it *really* was like in the Fordde.

I like him.

"You would." She paced around her stone Maise, glaring at the messy bed she had yet to make and the rumpled clothes she had thrown across the floor. She threw back the curtains to let the sunlight in and so that she could fully view her dragon. "He's forced me to give you extra cleanings . . . Not that I don't mind, but that's what the help is usually for."

The help?

True. Since living at the Fordde, Meilene didn't have any help as she used to at home in Valchar. She wasn't a full Reina yet and wouldn't be able to command any riders to do her bidding. That's not saying riders weren't already drawn to do as she asked whenever Namail wasn't there to stop them. She wasn't in charge of anything officially.

If Tork had his way, she'd never be in charge like she should've been. That man was insufferable. He hated the fact she was brought up in a rich kingdom instead of working her way through the Fordde from an early age, like he always bragged about. He didn't think she deserved to be here. None of them did.

"Argh."

A small gasp brought her attention across the stone Maise. "I'm so sorry, Reina. I thought you heard me come in."

Meilene whipped around to scold the intruder and froze. A uniformed rider, barely ten years old, stood in front of her with a brown package half her size. The poor girl's face was drained of blood and every inch of her body trembled in fear.

"I was supposed to deliver this package from the dragon lord," the girl said in a small voice. "He told me not to come back until I did."

"What is it?"

"A present for Aletzia." She bowed her head. "It's an ornamental headpiece." She gasped at the sight of the gold dragon lounging in her outside den, and the package fell from her hands.

Meilene sighed and picked up the parcel. "Here, let me take that off your hands."

"I, uh, I . . ." The girl's eyes widened as Aletzia curled her back and stretched, her jowls spread wide to show off her pointed teeth.

It must be quite a sight for someone so young.

"It's all right." Meilene touched her shoulder. The girl jumped at the contact, as if remembering where she was and who she addressed.

"I'm so sorry." Her face turned bright red. "I didn't mean to stare."

Meilene crouched, so she was eye level with the young rider. "How old is your dragon? He must be very young."

"He's not ten months yet, my lady."

"Then he's a bit older than Aletzia."

"Yes, but nowhere near as big as her." Her eyes wandered back to the large windows.

"Queens mature extremely fast. What's your name, rider?"

"Oksana," she said with a small bow. "My parents work in the bakeries here. I'm the first to be chosen out of our family in years."

"That's exciting." Meilene smiled. "I'm sure they must be so proud of you."

"Yes, ma'am. Even though my father hoped I would one day follow in his footsteps, he's ecstatic for me and Bernal."

Meilene's smile faded. "You're lucky to have your family's blessings."

"But, but . . ." She looked around the empty Maise and dropped her voice. "I'm afraid I'll disappoint them, my Reina."

"I don't think a parent to someone like you could ever be disappointed."

"I hope so." The young rider kept looking between Meilene and Aletzia, unsure which was more worthy of her attention.

"You know," she stood up, "she's not so scary up close. Do you want to meet her?"

"Am I allowed?"

"Absolutely," Meilene said with confidence. "You can do anything you want, rider."

With an encouraging nod, Meilene led the young rider toward her dragon's den. Aletzia was always happy to have someone new sing her praises, and a distraction from her own troubles was welcome.

A break was much needed before her meeting this afternoon.

※※※※ ※※※※

Hours later, Namail dropped a tangled mess of straps at her feet with a resounding thud.

The pair occupied an old stable room, preparing their equipment for flight. Meilene never liked this area of the Fordde, as it smelled disgusting and was always filthy. The wood panel walls felt as if they would fall on her at any minute.

"If you want to practice some of the formations," Namail said, "I suggest you get your dragon ready. Aletzia is waiting for you outside."

"That's nice, but I don't like doing her harness straps. Can you grab one of the juniors that usually helps me? They're always so eager."

Meilene's joints were sore, and she was exhausted from bathing Aletzia earlier in the morning. That wasn't counting the time spent on the countless passages her new *mentor* had assigned her to read late into the night. He was starting to seriously annoy her.

The man froze in the middle of picking up his own equipment. "They're all busy right now. I'm afraid you'll have to do it yourself."

"That's not going to happen." She planted herself on a wooden stool and crossed her legs, glaring across the dim room. "Would you be a darling and get Aletzia ready for me?"

Namail grabbed a pile of fraying straps from a hook on the wall. "I've got my dragon to get ready, so you'll have to do it yourself."

When the dragon lord said he had a new helper for her, she didn't know he meant a cynical old man who hated everything at the Fordde more than she did.

"No . . ." she said slowly. "I said that I need you to help me with the straps on the harness. That means you *help me with my straps.*" She threw Aletzia's straps at his feet. A pile of dust rose around his boots. "Is that so hard to understand?"

The rider froze and sent her an icy glare. "You should learn how to do it yourself, as I'm not here to be your manservant. Now get to it."

"I don't have to do anything. You have to do what I say. I'm your Reina."

"I'm not here as your personal servant, my lady." He pushed the thick straps back at her. "You are a dragon rider and should know how to gear up your dragon. I don't care if you are a Reina."

"I am from a noble bloodline, and you can't speak to me like this."

"Oh, are you, your highness?"

"Don't take that tone with me. I was bred for better things than this. I was bred to rule."

"Rule what?" He looked around the decrepit stables. "Not this rundown place. You're a long way from Valchar, and nobody cares about your foreign bloodlines here. Most people would even say it's a disadvantage."

"I am a Reina and that means I—"

"Your dragon hasn't risen to mate yet. She won't for years. Until then, you're not in charge of anything around here, least of all me."

She let out a strangled noise. She preferred the simpering, frightened riders Tork tried to pair her with over *this*! She should have been nicer to the last one.

What was her name? Marjorie? Mariam?

"Isn't there anything you like, or do you just hate the world?" She glared at the man, annoyed by everything about him down to his stupid birthmark and stupid frayed uniform. "I thought this place had turned me into a terrible hag, but you, sir, you are much worse. I pray I never stoop to your level of apathy."

For a moment, there was silence.

Nothing but the sounds of heavy breathing and the steps of workers far away in the Fordde. It was apparent that she had gone too far.

Namail let out a long, deep breath, as if trying to steady himself for what was to come. "I know that you are used to getting your way around here, *Reina*, but things are going to change."

Meilene bit her tongue and watched the rider with avid attention.

"I was warned you were bad. I didn't expect this," he said. "Why are you here? Why don't you take your dragon and leave?"

"I can't," she whispered.

"But you can. You know it." He picked up her dark saddle and held it out. "No one would be able to stop your dragon if you wanted to. Not even the dragon lord. The dragons have to listen to Aletzia and they have to do what she commands. The hold will only grow stronger as she matures and especially after she mates."

"Don't you think I'd leave if I could?" She snatched the heavy saddle out of his hands and almost buckled under the weight. "We're stuck here. I'm stuck here, and you are stuck with me. I didn't ask for any of this."

As much as it pained her to admit, Meilene couldn't go home anymore. Her father made it clear that she was useless to him the day she bonded with Aletzia. She also couldn't leave the Fordde, as much as she hated it. They were safe here.

This was where she and Aletzia were meant to be.

"And we didn't ask for you, either. Yet here we are." He dusted his hands on his pants, never taking his eyes off her. "Do you know what they say about you? Our Reina queen from the foreign lands."

Meilene stared at a crack in the wall behind him, studying the lines, as if they were the most interesting piece of artwork she'd ever seen.

"You know." The man nodded, taking her silence for a response. "Nobody wants you here as much as you don't want to be here. They'd rather anybody else. But Aletzia chose, and we are stuck with you. Eventually, she will rise to choose a mate, and they're all terrified of you, with more power, along with whoever that unfortunate mate is."

"You don't need to tell me about this. I already know what everyone thinks of me."

He stepped closer to her. "But do you know what else they are terrified of?"

"No." Her voice was hollow, emotionless.

"They're also terrified of our joke of a dragon lord who has been in charge for way too long. Right now, they'd rather him over you. As much as he has let us down time and time again, we know him. And the way things are going, he'll be able to keep his powers after Aletzia chooses a mate."

"I know that," she said through gritted teeth.

This wasn't news to Meilene. While Aletzia would get to choose her mate, the current dragon lord had all the power over which dragons would be there during the mating to present themselves as viable options for her to select from. She shuddered to think of the kind of men Tork would choose, or even worse, if his Vylor somehow managed to mate with Aletzia.

Running away was starting to sound like a good idea again.

"I know what you saw that day with Aletzia. I believe you."

"Wait, what? You do?"

"When Aletzia bonded with you, everyone was hesitant to have an outsider match with a queen, one who shares the gold color of our very first Reina dragon. Within that hesitation was hope, however small. Surely the dragons wouldn't choose wrong? But soon enough, everyone realized you were not the savior we were promised. Instead, we got a weak, selfish, self-absorbed queen who would become our biggest failure."

"I am not a failure," she said, her voice blazed with determination. She felt blood pump through her veins as Aletzia echoed her sentiments. "I am a Reina, and I am not weak. I'll show you."

"Good." Namail's eyes held a strange fierceness. "If you want to make it through this, you can't be weak. Running the Fordde is not easy."

"I'll never get to run the Fordde."

"Not the way things are going. For what it's worth, I don't believe the dragons choose wrong. Want to know why I'm helping you, truly?"

"Yes," she whispered.

"My dragon is lame, I have the karupe sickness. My time is spent as a rider. I'd like to make a difference with the small time I have left . . . it helps that I deplore the current dragon lord and would rather see him at the bottom of an enchial pit than leading us for thirty more years." He paced the dusty floor. "I would like to make sure the next leader isn't an imbecile who will lead us to certain death. Don't you want that?"

"Yes." She was surprised at how small her voice was. "I'd give anything to not have to choose from Tork's pick."

"Then, let's make certain that doesn't happen." He stopped in front of her with an odd glint in his eye. "There is a way we can both get what we want. To have Tork removed from this Fordde and to have a strong Reina ruling us instead. We can't afford anything less in the coming years. To do that, you'll have to follow my exact orders. Do you understand?"

"Yes."

"Every single detail has to be exact or else it will not work. We cannot make one small slip up, or it'll all be in vain. Are you prepared for that?"

"I am," she said in a strong voice. Aletzia echoed her thoughts.

"Nobody can ever have a hint of what we are doing. Not even the smallest suspicion. Understand?"

"Yes, sir."

He clasped his hand together, looking happier than she'd seen him yet. "Then let us begin."

Chapter Nine

THREE YEARS LATER

"Meilene, will we have the pleasure of you actually joining us in the formations today?" the head instructor asked patiently.

All two dozen heads of the junior riders in the stuffy room turned to her. The fraying beige walls seemed to have gotten worse over the years and several of the desks were practically decrepit now.

Most of her class had been with their dragons for at least ten years, given that riders bonded with their partners around close to the age of ten, unlike queens. They mature faster and usually bond with adults in their maturity, like Meilene.

The attention from the riders didn't bother her. She continued lounging in her seat at the back of the oval room and stared out the window at a wing that just landed back on to the grounds.

The wing lead outside was one she recognized from her visits to the command center with the dragon lord. She could see the patch on his arm and recognize his slouched stance from here, Simeon.

It seemed like a personal mission of his to get unnecessarily close to her under the guise of explaining the Fordde accounts. His eyes always lingered uncomfortably, and his breath smelled terrible up close. The mere thought of it almost made her gag in the middle of her lecture.

It seemed like basic hygiene escaped a lot of the older riders at the Fordde. When she was Reina, that would be something to fix.

"My Reina?" Head Instructor Liam persisted. The short instructor was much kinder than her previous ones and treated Meilene like a rider and not a foreign outsider, which was rare these days, thanks to Tork. No one else took her seriously.

Without bothering to sit up or look at the instructor, Meilene answered. "I don't think we can today. I have a headache and Aletzia needs to be fed before she can do anything. She's not up for it."

"Very well, my lady. You may take the rest of the afternoon to attend to your dragon."

As much as he wanted to, Liam wouldn't say anything to his special student. None of them ever would.

She discovered it early on and Namail hated it when she used it for personal reasons. The dragon riders were beholden to their queens, especially a Reina queen. It was part of the hold dragon magic had on all riders, to keep the formations.

They couldn't disobey an order, and it was built in them to want to impress their Reina, which suited Meilene perfectly.

Not even the dragon lord held that power over them. But then again, the dragons did not choose him to lead.

Instructor Liam dismissed the rest of the junior riders to prepare their dragons for flight patterns. A pang of jealousy formed in the pit of her stomach.

A small part of her yearned to join, but she couldn't.

At least this new instructor understood his student's needs and didn't press or judge when she told him she couldn't attend a lesson due to some ailment or other excuse. It was hard to get creative with them some days, so she usually just said that Aletzia was fussy. That shut most people up, as nobody wanted a grumpy Reina dragon snapping at the others.

The moment she left the classroom, that familiar disgruntled rider waited for her, leaning against the wall. He scratched at the birthmark on his neck and held out his arm for her books.

"Aletzia said you have a headache today," Namail said bemusedly. "Again? Thank you, Liam. I'll make sure she gets back to her quarters safely."

The head instructor smiled, relieved he wouldn't have to arrange for a guard to escort the Reina back. That was all Tork still. He thought it wasn't safe for his Reina to go anywhere without protection.

The dragon lord called it protection, but it was meant to keep an eye on her. Make sure she wasn't doing anything rash or getting up to any schemes.

Meilene scoffed. "You would have a headache, too, if you had to listen to that man drone on for hours about the proper looping techniques we should use when traveling through the smoky mountains."

Namail grabbed her bag and gestured for her to lead the way down the curved hallway. The crowd of junior riders parted ways, not wanting to get in the Reina's way.

Yell at a rider once for blocking your path to get to a hungry dragon, and everyone runs out of your way after that.

"Yes. Yes. Very well," Namail said in even tones. "Is Aletzia back at your Maise, resting?"

"She'll meet us out in the fields to eat," Meilene said quickly. "She says she's not completely famished but could do with a light snack of several hares or a shrew if there is one."

"Want to drop off your stuff at the Maise first?"

"It can wait."

Her new Reina Maise was large and dazzling, fit for a senior queen. A ruling queen. Tork had those quarters cleared out last year to better accommodate the Reina dragon, who continued to grow in size and had to be moved.

The dragon lord wasn't happy to move her away from him and into her official Reina's Maise. After some persuasion from Namail, he relented, not without reminding Meilene how much she owed him after the move.

If he thought the new Maise would keep Meilene content, he was mistaken. It was built for a Reina and her mate to live comfortably, along with both of their wings. Two dozen sections remain unused for those riders whose spots had yet to be filled but not until Aletzia found her first mate.

A shudder ran through her body at *that* prospect.

What has upset you?

"It's nothing, dear," Meilene said out loud.

Namail didn't bother questioning her. It was common for dragon riders to randomly burst into speech when conversing with their dragon partner. The first few times it happened around Meilene, she thought the riders had gone insane. Over time, she understood.

There was much she understood now.

Like how her new quarters meant to keep her trapped instead of giving her the space for practices and hosting, as Tork said. They both knew that was a joke, as she had no one to have over. If they weren't already bought into Tork's story that she was a terrible half insane Reina, then they assumed she was an entitled foreigner not worth their time.

The rooms themselves were spacious, with several areas for eating and entertaining. The decorations were considered extravagant by the Fordde's standards, but still not like where she grew up in Valchar.

Meilene hated it. The empty rooms served as a constant reminder of how alone she was here.

"Here we are." Namail opened the metal door that led outside. Radiant sunbeams blinded them for a moment.

A pair of guards joined them at the entrance to the grounds. While Tork was fine with Namail escorting her to most places in the Fordde, he didn't like the Reina appearing alone while out in the open. What a ridiculous rule.

In the distance, a group of dragons flew in tight formation to practice drills, while another wing ran perimeter scans to the south.

A smile escaped her tight expression as Aletzia flew above them. She was a gold diamond sparkling in the sunlight. Her shadow stretched long over the grass concourse of the Fordde.

The sight of her partner in her full glory, expertly slicing through the air, would never bore her. Aletzia was over three years old and already as large as most full-grown males.

Several young riders paused in their lessons to watch the dragon. Meilene waved at them.

Judging by their size, their dragons would take at least seven more years before maturity. Her Reina outpaced all others easily and would be ready for her first mating at five years of age at the latest, as per the current dragon lord.

Meilene knew that some queens will mate as young as three years or as late as seven, depending on what history book you read.

As the last Reina died a hundred years ago, there was barely anyone around who could remember firsthand. Those who flew during Reina Alianne's time could not be counted on for any factual information anymore. That time was even before Namail became a rider.

Namail held his hand to his eyes to block out the sun. "Her coat shines bright today. She is healthy and well."

"As she should. She's perfect," Meilene said with fierce pride in her voice.

They stopped atop a hill and watched as the gold dragon hunted for a snack. Her large scales picked up the light from the sun to form quite a sight. Her head was as large as Meilene was tall, and she had to bend her forelegs for Meilene to use as leverage to climb on her back for riding now.

It was strange to think that this creature once barely measured past her waist. Look at her now. She'd soon be bigger than all the dragons here.

Aletzia flew near a large red dragon. Its rider gave Namail a wave before turning away from the Reina. No one acknowledged her.

"When we are done here, I would like to take you back to your Maise, and we can ah—review—some of the history books again." He glanced toward their two escorts. "Instructor Liam said you did not show up for the passing tests."

"That's correct. Aletzia was unwell."

"Nothing serious, I hope."

"I think she overindulged and made herself sick . . . and you know how much she hates to fly with her stomach like that."

He nodded to himself. "He's not recommending you advance to the next levels with the current juniors because of how far behind you are?"

Unnecessary for a Reina, in her opinion.

"Also correct."

She didn't want to give the dragon lord the chance to assign her wing riders. Knowing Tork, he would be displeased with this turn of events as he was wanting to assign her some of his closest riders, to keep her safe, of course. Never to keep her in check.

"Liam said he volunteered to help you catch up before the next tests, but you declined."

"Seems like a lot of wasted effort."

"So, you'll stay with the juniors until the next season, at least."

"I guess so."

"Perfect." He stuffed his hands in his pockets. "Maybe next time you'll find some rider friends among them."

Meilene focused on the grounds where Aletzia was currently preening, having stuffed herself to her satisfaction. "I doubt it."

She didn't need anyone.

"From what I hear, several juniors are declaring for independence at the next opening."

"Mm-huh."

"The dragon lord is not pleased there are so many attempting the trials."

"He never is."

Tork preferred that all riders joined the ranks with a wing of their own, under his leadership. Declaring independence meant a rider was unbeholden to the current dragon lord. Not just anyone could declare. There were requirements and trials to prove the rider was ready to be on their own.

Those trials were near impossible . . . and a rider was only ever given one attempt to complete.

Namail brought her out of her thoughts. "Are you sure about this?"

Aletzia swooped past and blasted them with air as she passed. Any other dragon would have been reprimanded for such actions, but not a Reina. "I don't have a choice, do I?"

"No, you do not."

Meilene felt tears in her eyes and turned to her mentor, the only friend she had. "Namail," her voice cracked ever so slightly. "I want to thank you for your help these past years. Without your guidance, I don't know where Aletzia and I would—"

He put up his hand to stop her. "Enough of that. It's not becoming of a Reina."

Meilene snorted. As closed off as she was, it was nothing compared to her crotchety mentor. That must be why she had taken such a liking to him, especially since they both had the same goals.

"I'm not a full Reina. Not really."

"Not yet."

Meilene smiled as her dragon took off from the grounds, spooking a pair of hatchlings barely a month old.

Not yet.

Chapter Ten

The dragon lord leaned against the oak table as if he owned the entire place, looking as self-important as ever. "Are you quite certain I can't step in and help progress the Reina to the next levels?" As usual, he addressed Namail and not Meilene herself.

Meilene sat at the long table and focused on the cup of tea in her hands. Even though this was her Maise, she may as well not even be there as far as the dragon lord was concerned. She would be glad for the day these stone walls no longer felt like a prison.

"As grateful as the Reina is for your offer," Namail said delicately from his spot by Meilene's shoulder. "We believe she's not ready for the next levels and to do so would put her even further behind. The Reina's dragon has quite the needs with how quick she's growing and requires the extra time devoted to her."

"Hmm. If you say so."

"We do," Namail said. He clasped his hands on the back of Meilene's chair.

She pursed her lips and focused on the pattern of swirls coming from her cup. One took the shape of a lovely flower, followed by small puffs of cotton balls.

"I have some journals from the old wings you requested." Tork tapped the pile of books next to him. "We, unfortunately, didn't find anything from the queens or Reinas."

"That is kind of you to check for us." Namail slid the books over to Meilene with a warning glare.

"Very kind," she said dryly. She held back the shudder her body wanted to emit when the dragon lord trained his eyes on her.

Kind of him to not provide her with the queen's books that were her right to have, which he had been keeping from her thus far. She saw past his pitiful attempts to placate her with this garbage.

"Anything else?" Tork asked.

Namail kicked her chair.

"If it's not too much," she said. "I'd love to order in some more materials to outfit the rooms with and to have new outfits commissioned."

"Anything for our Reina." The dragon lord peered toward the lounging Aletzia in a way that made Meilene's skin crawl. "She's looking magnificent. Is she eating well?"

"She's exceptionally ravenous of late," Namail said.

Meilene studied the wispy bird rising from her cup of tea.

"A sign of a healthy dragon." Tork tapped his fingers on the table. "And the Reina?"

"Same as always," Meilene answered pleasantly. She straightened up in her seat. "Our new rooms have worked out well. Aletzia enjoys the space."

Her helper, Maeve, circled the table to refill her cup. Meilene insisted on bringing her along to their new quarters, and the girl was more than happy to leave her current assignment, which used to work closely with the dragon lord.

"It will be perfect for her to, ah, grow into later." Again, the dragon lord had those dark eyes focused on her. "Are you certain I can't be of further assistance?"

Meilene's spine tensed up, and she refused to meet his eyes. The shapes coming from her tea reminded her of a lake near their home in Valchar. She loved going there with her mother.

"Thank you for your generous offer." Meilene rose from the table. "Now, if you'll excuse me, I must tend to Aletzia. She is asking for attention."

Meilene left without a backward glance at the pair. She could trust Namail to get rid of the dragon lord. She didn't have the patience to play dumb in front of him.

Not tonight. She needed the quiet and rest to get through her day tomorrow. It was a big day for them.

"Riders, don't forget to meet tomorrow at first light for our final practice on the combat formations," Instructor Liam said as he walked through the rows of youngsters. "This will be the last one before your tests."

There were a few mumblings about this throughout the class. One of the riders cast a look at Meilene; no doubt she was trying to determine if she would turn up for this lesson or not.

She most definitely would not.

Meilene smiled and waited for the last rider to file out. They eagerly left to attend to their duties around the Fordde or go flying with their dragons.

Not her. Not today. She held her papers in a death grip and winced as her chair squealed when she got up.

Why did her stomach feel like stone?

Her legs wobbled as she walked up to the instructor. She tried to keep an outlook of cool deference. No one could know how terrified she was inside.

"What's this?" Liam asked pleasantly as she slid the papers over to him. The exact ones she and Namail meticulously combed through for hours.

Nothing could be out of place.

There was so much counting on this. They couldn't afford for one single detail to be wrong. Her spare hand shook, so she tucked it against her side so that no one would notice.

The only thing getting her through this was the thought of Namail waiting for her right outside.

"These are papers for my application for independence from the Fordde and the dragon lord."

"Uh—pardon me?" the teacher sputtered. His eyebrows furrowed as if still processing what she said. "What are you wishing to do, my queen?"

"Reina," she corrected. "I want you to file my paperwork with the Fordde. I'd like to declare Aletzia as an independent queen before her first mating selection."

"I'm sorry. What?" Liam ran a hand through his sandy hair. "I think I misheard that. Are you certain?"

"Absolutely." She pushed the papers closer. "I'd like you to file this with the Fordde. Everything should be in order."

"My lady—my Reina." A bead of sweat formed on his brow. "Do you know what you're asking?"

"Yes."

"I can't file this for you."

"You have to file any requests that come to you. I'm in time before this season's cut off."

"The dragon lord won't accept your application. A Reina cannot—"

"There's no law saying a queen can't do the same. She's a dragon, and I'm her rider, like the others. He will have to accept it. All of the paperwork is there."

"Reina Meilene," he lowered his voice, as if afraid the empty room could hear. "I don't think you can apply. There are certain rules for any queen to declare independence. It's so uncommon. I don't think you meet the requirements. You're on track to run through the Fordde lessons and join a wing. You can't just—"

"I am not on track to advance to the final levels, so I don't think there are issues."

"But the requirements—"

"The Fordde will only allow independence so long as the rider hasn't met their hourly flying commitments, which is less than a thousand overall hours with the Fordde. I know the rules. They don't allow anybody who's committed to a wing or who has the flight hours with the Fordde. It's all there." She tapped the sheets again. "You've signed off on all of my hours, and we've missed quite a bit of flight time. I meet the requirements."

Her poor instructor opened and closed his mouth a few times, but no sound came out.

She clasped her hands together. "Will you please sign these and submit them to Tork this afternoon? I would hate to miss the deadline."

"You can't possibly ask me to give these to him. Do you know what he'll do?"

"I'm well aware. You're merely fulfilling your duty as my instructor. He can come to me with any issues he has."

"But, but . . ."

"I've included all the requirements, plus all my flight records. If anything is missing, please do let me know."

"I can't—"

"And let me know about the times for the trials. I heard you've scheduled them for the others next week. I expect to be included in that. The day you book me in does not matter, for I have full availability."

With that, she turned on her heel and confidently strode out. Namail was still outside and joined her as soon as she was out the door. Her nerves were a mess, but she kept a calm and steady demeanor for anyone that came across them.

"How'd it go?" he asked.

"Brilliantly." She braced herself against the wall. When would her heart stop racing?

"Good," he said. "Now we wait."

There was a small twinge of guilt she felt for Instructor Liam. He was a kind man, and she did not envy the madness that would happen in the command room when Tork received those papers. She wouldn't have to wait long to find out when he was served.

"I need a drink." She lifted her hand to show how it shook. "That was nerve-racking."

"If you thought that was difficult," he said harshly. "You're not ready for what's coming. But agreed. A large glass of mulled wine would be perfect."

"Shall we go to one of the cafes by the grounds? Catch the last few rays of sun while we wait for the mayhem."

"Great idea." He gestured dramatically. "Lead the way, my Reina."

"Not quite a Reina yet."

Chapter Eleven

"**C**heers."

Namail clinked his glass against hers. The red liquid teetered dangerously near the edge before Meilene downed the rest of her glass. The man had the foresight to order an entire bottle upon seeing how Meilene shook while trying to take her seat at the small cafe.

At least the views of the Fordde grounds were pleasant this time of the year. One could see the full expanse of the circular building from this viewpoint, along with the grounds that stretched for miles. The building stretched over the grounds like a powerful behemoth, covering everything within eyesight.

"You're up." Namail pointed at the wood board in between them.

They were seated in one of the small cafes dedicated to the higher-ups in the Fordde, decorated as the rest of this place was, in strange dark colors with ornaments that were better suited for a war room than a place to relax. But it was how the riders seemed to prefer things around here.

Meilene hated coming here, as that meant she would have to entertain some of Tork's commanders. These places were usually full of them, but luckily, today was empty.

A worker brought out a small vase and wildflowers, knowing how much the Reina loved them. Meilene leaned over the board of tiles to contemplate her next move against Namail, holding a small tile between her fingers. She had thoroughly enjoyed the game of Callavan ever since Namail taught her how to play it.

It had been a strange game to first learn. Each opponent had to display their entire hand of tiles for the other players. There wasn't a lot of room to hide your plan, which made it interesting. You had to try to trick your opponent into thinking you were planning something else.

Meilene moved a blue pair of tiles and sighed. "The wait is killing me."

"It's not that bad. There could be worse things." Namail scratched at the birthmark on his neck. He switched out her blue river tile for his own, a dainty-flowered one worth no points. Strange choice, but she was no expert at the game.

"How's Mennon doing?"

Namail's old dragon had a bad hind leg from a years-old injury that never healed properly. The poor beast couldn't do flights longer than twenty minutes or so. Namail had to put a special ointment on his dragon daily and force him to do stretches against his wishes.

Mennon enjoyed complaining the entire time Namail tried to help him.

Meilene smiled. The things they did for their partners.

Namail wasn't paying attention, so she played down two more to complete her row: a dragon and a moon piece.

"His leg was bothering him more than usual, so I took him to the lake for a long soak."

"You should have it looked at again. I don't understand why Tork hasn't given you leave to try some of the menders down south."

"Mennon would never make the trip. Besides." He smiled. "I have important work to do here." He found a spot where she almost completed a set and swapped out a tile to stop her.

"I don't think we'd make it a week without you."

Namail sighed and surveyed the empty skies above them.

"There haven't been any attacks lately."

"That we've heard of," Namail corrected.

"True." She tilted her head. The dragon lord would want to keep any instabilities quiet. He didn't want panic or give cause for any potential upheavals.

The blue board was almost complete, but somehow, Namail set up his defense to counteract her without her seeing. There wasn't a lot she could do to win. She'd have to be smart. She picked up a sword tile and contemplated her next move.

"You!" a familiar voice bellowed.

Their game would have to wait.

"Here we go." Namail stood and dusted off his jacket.

"You lunatic. You absolute—you complete—complete—" The dragon lord stomped up to the old dragon rider, red-faced and looking like he may burst.

Meilene had to hold back a giggle at the sight of the usually stoic leader so out of sorts. He had several of his wing leads behind him. One tried holding him back, but the irate dragon lord broke free of his grasp and closed the gap between him and Namail.

"You arrogant fool!"

"Calm yourself, dragon lord. Whatever is the matter?" Namail turned to Meilene, putting on a face of feigned innocence as Tork sputtered nonsense. "Do you know what he is referring to, my Reina?"

"How dare you?" Pieces of spit flew out of the dragon lord's mouth. He was inches away from Namail and spraying her poor mentor. "I agreed to let you mentor the queen to keep her in check. Now I find out you have pulled this."

"It wasn't him." Meilene tried to get in between the two large men. "I'm the one who submitted the application, not Namail."

"And what do you hope to accomplish with this grand sort of pageantry?" Tork said, his eyes still trained on her mentor.

"Getting an imbecile like you out of the command center," she said firmly.

The dragon lord finally decided to acknowledge her presence. He looked flummoxed, but only for a second. "I know you are a vicious girl, but I didn't take you for a fool. I will not allow this."

Namail put his hand gently on her shoulder and pushed her behind him. "Maybe you should watch your tone, *dragon lord*."

"Do you even know what you are doing, you stupid little girl?"

A pair of riders attending to their blue dragons paused and watched the dragon lord with interest.

"I will not let you have control over who Aletzia mates with. I would rather take her to the edges of the planet before having her mate with your dragon or one of your old, crusty wing leads."

If they made it through this, she would make sure no queen was forced against their will again. Any queen would have the option to open her mating. No other man would choose who gets to mate with her.

"That is not up to you." Tork's eyes flashed dangerously. "As the dragon lord at this Fordde—"

"That is up to my dragon and her alone. I don't understand how you managed to bend the rules your way for so long. You can call me stupid, but I'm not the one running this Fordde into the ground. Because of you, the riders are a laughingstock across the lands, and we are ill-prepared against attacks from the Anvers. They're spreading across the lands, and you are doing nothing. When Aletzia mates, and we have a new dragon lord, that will change."

After having to hold her tongue and bide her time for years, Meilene would not back down. Not when they were so close. She had to put up with being talked down to for years by people to think she didn't care and was lazy.

Tork pushed past Namail and shoved his finger in front of her face. Meilene stayed rooted to her spot.

"I knew we were doomed from the minute she picked *you*. You know nothing about dragons or our people and shouldn't interfere in things that aren't yours. I've spent years leading our people, and you can't just take it away. You're no Reina."

A burly wing lead pulled Tork back. They started to draw a crowd.

"If I wasn't meant to be a ruler here, then why do I have a Reina? You were never chosen by the dragons for this role, Tork Streno, and soon, the dragons will have a new leader. A better leader."

"Stop it." Tork shoved off the hand holding him back. He seemed to collect himself in the presence of their onlookers. He straightened his beige riding jacket and sneered at her. "You think you're so smart, but I've been keeping track of your training. You're behind, refuse to take half of your flight lessons, and consistently shirk your classes. You'll never pass the trials. Even if you do, your queen is young, she may not rise to mate this season, and you only have weeks left. If she doesn't rise this season, you are finished."

Meilene stepped closer to the disgraceful dragon lord. "I will pass the tests, my lord. My Reina will rise to mate before the season is over, and you will be finished here forever."

Before the dragon lord could respond, Meilene turned on her heel and strode back into the Fordde, with Namail on her heels. Aletzia roared a challenge that was echoed by the dragons.

Soon, he would see what her dragon could do. They would all see.

Chapter Twelve

Namail circled her like a feline stalking its prey. His footsteps were quiet against the worn floors of her Maise. "Not good enough. Again!"

Meilene huffed and straightened up. She leaned against a nearby mantle and wiped a bead of sweat off her face. "That last one was perfect . . . and I need a break."

"If you're certain." He kicked up the overturned corner of a rug.

"I am. You're overthinking things and stressing us out. I want to take tonight to relax."

I am not worried.

Meilene relayed the dragon's message to her mentor, who merely laughed.

The pair had pushed aside the plush couches in her Maise, making enough room for her to go through Namail's exercises without breaking anything. The mess would have worried the old Meilene, but they'd put everything back perfectly when done, just as they always did.

Privacy was essential, so she told the guards at the entrance to make sure nobody disturbed her, not even the dragon lord himself. This set of riders appeared frightened enough by the Reina that they should heed her instructions.

She had no desire to see any visitors. Nobody cared about her before last week, and now, everyone wants to be in her ear. It didn't matter what they said, even if it was a loyalist telling her to go to Tork and beg for forgiveness or someone keen on new leadership and hoping to get in the future Reina's good graces.

Even if her plan failed, Aletzia would eventually choose a mate and become a full breeding queen, coming into her powers. That part would not change. All Meilene could do was try to give her a chance at a good mate and to give the dragon riders a better leader.

Everyone had an opinion on what she should do if their plan worked.

The only one that didn't have any advice to give her, besides checking in if she was prepared for the trials, was her instructor, Liam. So far, he was only concerned with ensuring she understood what would be required of her during the trials. He didn't want any surprises on the day of.

It was a nice thought but unnecessary. Meilene was confident in both her and Aletzia's abilities. They weren't any junior riders in their first year; they were a Reina queen and her partner, both ready for what lay ahead.

Not to mention the countless hours Namail made her practice for any of the contests that may come up during the trials. She wasn't going into this blind and unprepared, as the dragon lord thought.

Her favorite mousy-haired helper, Maeve, entered the Maise with two glasses of wine. She paused upon seeing the destruction in front of her. Her mouth hung open in terror.

"We'll put it back," Meilene said quietly.

"Finally." Namail grabbed the glasses and handed the larger one to Meilene. "Only one. You have a big day tomorrow."

Meilene sipped the red liquid. "Thank you, Maeve."

The worker shook her head and seemed to unfreeze herself. "Is there anything else I can do for you before tomorrow, Reina?" She eyed the red couches in the corner stacked haphazardly upon each other and dangerously close to the fireplace.

"No. I'm quite all right, thank you. Why don't you have an early night? Don't stress. I promise we'll clean up when we're done."

"If you're certain," Maeve said.

"Absolutely. We can handle this." Meilene nodded toward Namail, who already grabbed a pair of chairs and scraped them toward a small table.

"Just make sure you don't scratch the new upholsteries," Maeve said with a smirk. "The dragon lord ordered those especially for you."

Meilene rolled her eyes. Maeve knew how much she despised anything that came from that man.

When her friend left, Meilene took one of the chairs Namail set up and rested her feet on the table. "I'm ready."

"He's going to make it difficult," Namail said. "Keep a watch for anything out of place."

"I'd be insulted if he didn't try anything."

Why is he so concerned? Nobody can outfly me.

Meilene smiled as Aletzia curled up in her favorite spot at the edge of her outside den. Every day, she still marveled at the beauty of the golden dragon and her luck to be chosen as her rider.

"What is it?"

"Aletzia is feeling confident about tomorrow."

"She's a true Reina in all senses, especially the pride."

And why shouldn't I be proud? I'm the Reina.

Meilene passed on the message cheerfully.

"I'm not saying you aren't, Aletzia," Namail said. "Don't go into tomorrow too confident and get caught unaware."

Meilene scoffed. "I'm not as stupid as Tork thinks, and I know he isn't a fool, as much as he runs this Fordde like one."

"Good. Tomorrow you can show him."

"I'll be glad to have this over with."

Namail laughed. It was a hollow sound. "Don't be so certain. After tomorrow, the real work begins."

"I'm counting on it."

The first part of the trial was straightforward enough and meant to prove that the rider had a good handle on their own combat training. This was where Tork had probably thought she'd fail first, seeing as he hadn't allowed her to sign up for any of the combat training like archery or javelin throwing yet.

Like a fool, he underestimated her and that would be his downfall.

That night was a restless one, filled with incoherent dreams of scaly creatures and fiery heat all around her. She woke up several times drenched in sweat.

Eventually, she gave up on getting any more sleep and decided to get up. Wrapping herself in a thick blanket, she went outside to where her partner slept peacefully in the dim light of dawn.

She settled down at the base of her neck and snuggled close to her queen. Aletzia curled her body around her partner, and she was instantly warmed. Meilene drank in the moment of peace with her and her dragon.

How long before she would get another moment like this?

After sitting for a few hours with no company but the sounds of Aletzia's snores, her body started to ache. The sun hung fully in the sky, and she decided it was time to get ready for her day.

From her wardrobe were the riding pants and sweater she set out the night before. Once she was fully washed, with her hair tied back in the way that kept it out of her face, she pushed the double doors to the hosting area of her Maise.

Her mentor wasn't the only one waiting for her on the plush couches. The head trainer was there, along with one of the commanders she recognized from her visits to the command center.

Recognizable by the scar on his cheek and his long silver hair, Commander Yannet was always kind to her and never seemed to favor the current dragon leader. She wasn't surprised to see the old commander here.

"I see we have some visitors, Aletzia." She gestured at each of the men.

Maeve stood to the side, holding a piece of cloth. "I made you a new riding jacket, my Reina." She gave a small curtsey and handed it to her.

The jacket was stark black with gold bands on the arm to signify she was a queen. Just like the wing leads wore to identify their position. There was a small gold dragon embroidered on the front. It would be like Aletzia was always with her.

Not that it was hard to know she was. Right now, there was only one queen, a Reina, and everyone knew who she was around the Fordde. She was hard to miss.

"Instructor Liam and Commander Yannet have come to see you off before the trials," Namail said.

"That's lovely." Meilene put on her new jacket, and it fit perfectly. She felt more ready than she ever had. "Anything else?"

"There are fierce winds coming from the east corridor today, my Reina," the commander said. "If you fly above the peaks, you should be able to miss most of it."

"Thank you, Commander." She nodded. "I'll keep that in mind today."

I am not afraid of any winds.

"The rest of the skies are clear besides a small buildup near the village of Prael."

"Excellent."

"The tester for the flight portion is Instructor Enial, from the South River Fordde," Liam said. "He's a difficult one. He was brought in by the dragon lord himself for unknown reasons." He smiled. "Exceptionally known for his harsh criticisms, but I happen to know he favors those using the old forms versus the newer. If you happen to be proficient in both . . ." He trailed off with a wink.

Meilene could barely believe what she was hearing.

"Your instructor has also brought you a new saddle today," Namail added. "He commissioned it from Quartermaster Gaelen."

Liam motioned, and a second worker came forward with a fine-looking leather saddle. It was smaller than her old one. This would be perfect for the trials today.

"It's a fine craftsmanship," Namail said. "I checked it out myself."

Meilene understood the meaning behind her mentor's message. One could never be too careful when there was a vengeful dragon lord out for you.

"Thank you both for your kind words today and for the new riding saddle. I appreciate them."

For the first time, she allowed each of them to grasp her hands with their hand over their heart. It was the traditional greeting allowed only for a queen. There wasn't a lot of personal contact permitted between a queen and other riders, especially once she had risen with a mate.

Dragonfolk tended to be territorial at best, and mates were no exception, especially queen mates. It was best not to get close to a queen or else they'd risk their wrath.

Even though she'd grown accustomed to most of the riders' strange traditions, Meilene still felt this one was oddly peculiar.

"Will you be watching the proceedings today?" Meilene asked the pair.

"Yes," the commander said. "I believe the dragon lord will also be overseeing the trials with a keen interest."

"As expected," Meilene said. "Aletzia is eager to go. She will do well."

"Always a great sign when the dragon is eager," Liam said.

"I'll see you on the concourse, gentlemen." She dismissed the pair with a nod.

"I shall make a celebratory meal for your return," Maeve said with a smile. "Some of your favorites. Nothing too heavy, of course." She backed away to allow Meilene and her mentor time for last-minute tactic discussion.

By the time she made it to the small obstacle course set up in one of the old training rooms, a small audience had amassed. Namail explained how the dragon lord had to remove several riders from watching, including friends and family of the other participants, as he didn't want any *distractions* for Meilene.

They both rolled their eyes at the bold lie.

It seemed as though a few of the commanders closest to Tork remained to watch. Commander Yannet sent her a small smile while her instructor nodded encouragingly from his spot on a long bench. Namail joined them after wishing her good luck and happily sat next to the dragon lord, who ignored her mentor's presence.

Tork's eyes were nearly slits as he watched her pick through the dismal selection of half-broken arrowheads and bows with strings that were either much too loose, too tight, or fraying dangerously. A few of the testers huddled together in discussion with Commander Brawne. It was easy to know what their topic of conversation was as they kept stealing glances her way.

Meilene pretended not to notice and she grabbed a thick bow and set about tightening its string, taking great care to knot the ends just as Namail had shown her.

One of the testers, a sweaty man with a scraggly beard padded his way over to Meilene. "I know you haven't had much practice, my Reina. But the point is to try your best and no one will think any less of you. You can try a few practice shots first if you'd like to get a feel for your bow."

Meilene nearly snorted.

They do not think you can do it. Show them how wrong they are.

That was the plan.

Without waiting for the room to be cleared or for someone to offer her a spot, Meilene straightened up where she was, pulled back the least frayed arrow that she could find and let it fly. All noise in the room stopped as the metal head found its way to the middle of the furthest target they had set up.

She turned to the wide-eyed tester with a wide grin on her face. "I'd say that I'm ready."

Chapter Thirteen

A t the top of the hour, Meilene made her way down to
the grounds with Namail in tow, bolstered by her fine
showing in the first part of the trials. Aletzia escorted them from
the air above, with her scales glistening beautifully as she passed
overhead.

Her dragon growled at a pair of young green dragons on the
ground who scattered to make room for their queen. She settled
contentedly and folded her wings, enjoying the attention the
rest of the dragon riders paid to her.

While Aletzia was happy to have all the attention on her,
Meilene was less enthusiastic about her new admirers. Many
riders viewed her like a piece of meat, not that they didn't before.
She wasn't blind and knew the effect she had on men. She was
used to handling that.

These new looks were different. They were more calculating
and made her uneasy. That was one thing she didn't count
on since making her declaration for this season. Everything
changed after that.

One would think a queen's first mating selection would be
a normal event around the Fordde, but as there had been no

queen for over twenty years, everyone was on edge. Not to mention this queen was a Reina, which hadn't been around for nearly a century and had the potential to call on the blood bonds with all the dragons under her.

Dragon riders had strange traditions. Queens, especially Reina queens, were at the top of the command chain through the dragons' choice. As much as Meilene didn't feel like it, she had been chosen to lead the riders for the coming years.

Four years ago, she would have laughed at the prospect. Today, that was all she focused on.

By the time Meilene reached the judging panel, including those who had flown in specially for today, the murmurs had grown to a loud chatter. Everyone watched the newest rider attempting to pass the trials for independence today.

They watch because I am Reina.

"I know, love," she murmured. "You'll show them today."

The judging panel included several graying riders well beyond their prime. How these men were picked to be her jury today, she'll never know. Half of them looked days away from the grave, and the other half looked like they hadn't seen a good flight in years. The toughest instructor, Enial, had long silver hair, a thick neck, and dark eyes he used to watch her every move.

As infuriating as it was, it was fitting that these decrepit riders would be one of the final steps in her ascension to Reina. The last step would be the actual mating itself, but that was a problem for a different day.

Today, Meilene was focused, and Aletzia was ready.

"What a lovely bunch." Namail passed her a pair of leather gloves. "I think Tork was more than surprised earlier, so you can bet he's directed them to go even harder on you in the skies. Remember that there's nothing illegal they can do to stop you."

"I know. Doesn't mean they won't push the boundaries of what's allowed. He'll be desperate." Meilene nodded at her mentor, who took a seat with the other spectators. She approached the nearest tester.

"Where would you like us to set up?" she asked with a false bravado she hoped carried over in her demeanor. Now was not the time for any weakness. "Aletzia is all geared up."

The first tester looked flabbergasted to be approached by a queen and couldn't find his tongue. The one that was Enial came over to relieve him.

"Have you filled out all your papers appropriately?" He surveyed her over the bridge of his nose. "I would hate for anything to be missing."

"Yes," she said briskly. "I've finished submitting them yesterday, as you should be aware of."

"If you think you are ready, *my Reina*, you may take your place over there." He pointed to the lineup of riders to the side. "You will be told when to begin."

Meilene bit her tongue at the derision that came when stating her title. She had to remind herself he didn't matter in the long scheme of things.

I do not like that one.

"Me neither."

I could scare his dragon off. He watches me too closely.

"As fun as that would be, it will get us nowhere today."

Meilene took her place in between the vagabonds and other ruffians who wished to disassociate themselves from the Fordde.

A few shifted nervously, but most had the same look of deter-mination. They must have had their reasons for separation from the entity that had helped raise their dragons and provided for them from the moment they partnered. None of that mattered to those attempting the trials today.

Today was a day for new beginnings.

The one beside her was barely a few years her senior. He had dark-red hair and a beard to match. He eyed her curiously when she took her spot in the line.

"You ready for this?" the young rider asked with a tone of amusement. He focused his attention on the testers ahead of them.

Meilene scoffed and followed his gaze. The graying testers watched the group with guarded expressions.

"Are you?"

"Please," the rider said. "I've been ready to leave this awful place for years."

"Hmm."

Same here, in a sense.

At an unseen signal, the other riders approached their drag-ons. Meilene followed suit.

Aletzia had her saddle and gear ready to go, thanks to Na-mail. Meilene meticulously pulled the straps through the prop-er loops so that she would have a good grip during the flight. She made sure everything was tightened and that her new saddle sat securely atop her golden queen.

After what felt like hours, but was a few minutes in reality, the small group of misfits was deemed ready to begin.

It was time.

The frigid air whipped against her bare cheeks and dragged against Aletzia's wings. If it was any colder up here, Meilene's skin would start cracking. The blood pulsing through her veins kept her warm and focused. There was no way she was losing this.

I would never fail.

"I know you won't." She sent loving thoughts toward her dragon, keeping her focused as they climbed out of the Fordde's concourse and into the sky.

She sensed, rather than saw, the other dragons around her. Their wings thundered against the wind. Fourteen total riders took the trials besides herself and Aletzia.

Dozens of other dragons participated to stop them from completing the trials. She knew they would be focused on stopping one dragon in particular today and already felt the eyes of their riders on her dragon.

Even though she was the youngest by far, Aletzia was faster than the others and already bigger than several of them. She was built to outlast every other dragon.

None are as fast as I am. They are slow and weak.

Meilene wouldn't call dragons weak. None of them would hold up to a full-grown Reina once it was her time. She hadn't had her first mating yet but was a force to be reckoned with.

They flew high enough to see the towering circular shape of the Fordde nestled on the cliff that led into the rolling hills. She'd grown used to the sight of the circular stone behemoth over the years; it comforted her as a landmark of home.

To the east towered the smoky mountains, laying sharp against the grassy landscape in the distance.

A shudder ran through her as she remembered the last time they flew through there. No one ever found evidence of the Anver that attacked her. The dragon lord made sure of that. He also made certain they never returned to the mountains.

From far below, a drum filled the air, reverberating throughout the skies.

It has begun.

With a renewed fervor, Aletzia beat her wings against the tough air currents, taking a steep decline to miss another dragon. She moved in circular motions, back and forth, while trying to figure out a strategy.

To pass, Aletzia would have to find one of the lead dragons, which would be identified by its bright orange saddle flags. She had to get the flag before the others could grab hers and remove her from the trials.

If Namail was right, the dragon lord would have told the fliers to make sure she was the first one out. He may even have put a prize on taking out the Reina today. She didn't blame him, as she'd do the same. And he desperately needed her to lose.

Aletzia took them through an endless sea of light drafts and thin clouds. She sliced through them like a hot knife. Nothing could stop her. She was a relentless force against the winds.

Wham!

A spiky red dragon came out of nowhere and slammed into them. The force sent the gold spinning downward several feet while Meilene held on for her life.

Aletzia squawked but was able to fix her descent. She adjusted into a wild and unsteady climb, trying to lose the red dragon. She turned on her tail, sprinting as fast as she could, and diving in between a pair of other participants vying for independence.

The red dragon narrowly avoided crashing into the pair. By the time it adjusted, Aletzia was too far gone.

That was close. She had to be faster.

A current carried them near a row of tall trees. Aletzia raced past, sending leaves and twigs flying in all directions. Another rider on a green dragon dove at them from above with a dangerous recklessness. His claws were out and, for one horrible second, Meilene thought they meant to injure them.

Aletzia snarled and snapped her tail, barely skimming where the rider sat at the dragon's shoulder junction. It surprised the pair enough for the dragon to falter, so Aletzia turned on her side and rammed them, sending them careening away.

"That was a close one. Come on, let's go east."

To the mountains?

Yes. They would provide better cover and allow them to lose the dragons on her tail. There were enough dragons out that there should be no dangers from anything *else*.

The wind above the mountains was known to be tumultuous and erratic. It would be perfect to catch the orange dragon and lose those chasing her.

Two large dragons tried to cut her off before the Aogan pass. Aletzia hissed and dove at the closest green, challenging them with a deep bugle. Meilene smiled as they scattered out of the way.

Bonding with a Reina has its benefits some days.

A gust of wind tried to unseat her. Right. They needed to go higher to catch the updraft.

As Aletzia pumped her wings frantically, Meilene was thrashed about on her seat. Her new saddle kept her safely attached. It was a thankful addition to her flight today.

Meilene was built differently from these dragon riders, but that didn't mean she was less of a rider. She pulled herself closer to her dragon. She was small, light, and easy to carry. Her dragon was long and fast. The others didn't stand a chance at stopping her.

They never knew how fast she could go.

While they thought she was being lazy and skipping lessons, she was practicing with Namail. She studied up on the different formations, the best ways to fly against certain winds, the different markings of the lands, and the best attack strategies.

When Namail wasn't busy prepping her for the trials, he made her spend countless hours going through running the Fordde. She spent weeks learning about each of the positions and what they did, along with the workers and who they were loyal to.

Most of all, she researched the creature that attacked them and was responsible for several dragon deaths in recent years: the Anvers. It was hard to find any information on them without access to the past Reina journals and without tipping off Tork of what she was up to.

The dragon lord was weak and refused to acknowledge what was happening in the world. He was worried it would hurt the precious hold he had over the riders. Tork needed to go, and the Fordde had to prepare for another war.

Something wet hit her cheek. She wiped it off.

Rain.

Just her luck. Nothing ever came easy for her in this place.

I am not afraid of a little water.

"I'm more afraid of slipping off."

The trials wouldn't stop for anything, even if rain grounded most usual flights. This was the last hurdle in her way. She had already soared through the physical tests yesterday.

The memory of the dragon lord's stupefied face warmed her. He didn't expect her to make it past the first test. Namail made sure she practiced daily with a simple bow he fashioned for her and kept hidden from Tork's workers. Maeve once found one of the borrowed javelins, which he had her train on so she knew how they were balanced, but said nothing and quietly put it away.

When it came time to line up against the burliest of riders that Tork could pit her against, she matched his target hits arrow for arrow and could throw the javelin even further than him. This was all using the half-broken equipment she had been settled with. Her aim was true and her determination had been even stronger.

Clearly, the dragon lord listened to her professor's reports that she was skimming on their lessons. That was all on purpose. Part of Namail's plan was to keep her practices as discreet as possible. If Tork had ever found out what they were doing, he would have snuffed out their hopes for a change.

The one you seek is up ahead.

"Try to get closer."

Aletzia obliged. The sharp peaks drew near as she lowered herself to skim them. The blue dragon with an orange saddle flew lazily in a circular pattern near a cluster of wide ranges.

That was unusual.

Most riders tried to make it through the mountains as quickly as possible to avoid the lethal wind gusts. Something was off.

I can get close to him. Should I?

"Yes, but be careful."

Aletzia swept along the ridges of the white peak covered in layers of snow from the cold season. Meilene tightened her new jacket to protect herself from the wind. She was thankful Maeve lined it with fur again. Anything less would have been freezing after their journey through the rain.

It was too good to be true. Before they could get close to the blue dragon, two others whipped out from behind a dark-gray slope.

The dragon lord was a smart man.

"Move, Aletzia!"

The two dragons dove at them. Again, their claws were outstretched as if they planned to take her down by force. She never thought Tork would stoop this low, apparently she had underestimated his desperation to stop her.

Luckily, Aletzia was quick enough to just miss getting caught or hurt, and left them behind in a jumble of wings and curses.

She dodged and led them through a narrow pass, having to turn almost sideways to get through.

Once again, Meilene was glad her new saddle kept her from falling to her death.

They climbed until they could make it above the highest peak. Meilene had to take deep gulps to catch her breath in the thin air. She turned around to check if they still pursued them.

They are not strong like us.

The other dragons couldn't keep up against the turbulent winds pushing them back. They were turning around.

Eventually, the pair made it over the behemoth peak and dove into the thick clouds. Before long, they made their way out of the mountain pass.

She could hear the other dragons below trying to find them and the shouts of their riders, but Aletzia was stealthy. The clouds were so dense that Meilene couldn't see her dragon beneath her.

"Keep going toward the villages and stay out of sight. We should have coverage up until Prael."

I will stay in the clouds.

Feeling safe for the moment, Meilene allowed herself to relax, only a little. She hadn't realized how much tension she carried in her shoulders during their flight. As the cloud coverage broke, below them were empty skies. None of the hunting dragons could be seen.

Rolling hills and the outline of the nearby villages filled the view. The building domes and sharp rooftops were visible, even from this distance. Raindrops still drizzled down, adding a light haze to the scenery below.

Meilene hadn't been to visit any of them yet, as the dragon lord didn't think it was appropriate for an unmated Reina to go off on her own like that. She couldn't wait until she was free to do whatever she wanted.

"Keep looking, Aletzia."

Aletzia dove past a flock of avians, sending them screeching in all directions. She nipped at them playfully as Meilene dragged her hands through the air.

As they passed the second set of villages, with brightly colored windows, Meilene finally saw it.

Another red dragon carrying the bright flag. Exactly what she needed to finish this trial for good.

They needed cover. "Back into the clouds."

Aletzia kept to the thick clouds, hovering above the village as stealthily as possible. She circled the dragon below as if hunting her next meal. Focusing on the sounds to keep track of her target.

When it finally moved to head north toward the Fordde, they took their chance.

Aletzia dove from the safety of the scattered clouds, coming straight from the sunlight. The rider wouldn't be able to see her mixed in with the rays.

A large black dragon was quick on Aletzia's tail, seemingly protecting the flag dragon. It was fast, but Aletzia was faster and did not falter. She kept her focus on the dragon with the flag, even as the black dragon snapped at her tail.

The red dragon and its rider tried to veer away, but a third dragon intent on stopping Aletzia got in its way.

All it could do was yelp in surprise when Aletzia reached out and grabbed the flag with her talons, nearly frightening the poor red dragon and its rider to death. Before any of them could retaliate or strike back, they placed a good distance in between them.

Meilene pumped her fist in the air as Aletzia let out a loud, triumphant rumble that sent a group of birds scattering away. It was echoed by dragons down below.

Thankful for the first time that it was raining, Meilene wiped the hot tears mixed with rain and sweat from her face. All those years of hard work, and they were so close now.

Chapter Fourteen

"Will this never end?" Meilene shook off a stream of water that collected on her sleeve.

Namail laughed and squeezed out a dirty rag. "Having to properly care for your dragon? Never."

He gestured around the large wooden space filled with hay, buckets, and a cool stream of water running through it. The quiet and separation from the Fordde was calming.

The cleaning room was built for riders to attend to their dragons when it wasn't convenient to take them outside to the lake. Meilene hated going there, as Aletzia drew attention and unwanted visitors, especially since the trials and winning her independence for the mating selection. Whenever she had enough of the other riders, she had Namail book her a large cavern to bathe her gold in peace.

Today was one of those days.

"I wish I could get someone else to do this." She threw a woolen cloth into the murky puddle next to her. She must be quite a mess right now, if only those riders lining up to talk could see her. "Maybe a Fordde rider would like to court favor with the Reina."

Never.

"Count yourself lucky right now." He pointed at the scaly beast. "She is only going to keep growing. You'll be dreaming of the days you had this little of a dragon to bathe."

Little? Aletzia rose on her hind legs and spread her wings, spraying Meilene thoroughly. *Ask him if I look little now?*

"I meant no offense, Reina," Namail said when Meilene relayed her message. He gave a mock bow to the golden dragon, already larger than his green dragon, Mennon. She also ate more than his senior dragon now, too.

"I can't imagine her getting any bigger than this." She stepped back to admire the large torso and head of her Reina. She was quickly becoming one of the largest dragons at the Fordde and showed no signs of slowing down.

"She has a few more years of growth, then will slow down."

Meilene scoffed and kicked a bucket out of the way. "She better or else I'll have to source out her baths."

"As if your dragon would let anyone else touch her. She is a Reina."

"Yes, she is," she said fondly. She stepped back and reviewed the patch she just scrubbed. It gleamed perfectly, like the rest of her dragon. It was a nice reward for finishing the trials, a feat most thought impossible for the pair, and now the next step was finding a suitable partner during the mating to help take over from Tork.

Aletzia hummed. She was enjoying this far too much.

Meilene grabbed another bucket of water, a clean cloth, and a large pick. She took to the task of cleaning one of Aletzia's thick claws.

Namail surveyed the gold closely. "Maybe she'd let a mate attend to her. Then you could have help."

Meilene froze with a sharp talon wedged between her thighs. Not this again.

"Don't remind me." She renewed her scrubbing with increased vigor, getting out a large chunk of rock from the middle claw.

This was too much.

It feels nice against my claws.

"I didn't mean to upset you," he said. "I was merely making an observation, as most dragons are attuned to their partner's mates."

"Yes, I know," she snapped. "Trust me, *I know.*"

Namail understood her desire and dropped the subject. He dried off a patch of scales on Mennon's side. "Heard anything new from our favorite dragon lord?"

"Nothing besides the night after the trials when he came over to politely demand I stop this foolishness."

Namail's face lit up at this. "That one always had a way with words."

"Can't imagine what he'll do after Aletzia's mating when Vylor isn't selected."

The dragon lord would not go away quietly. He was furious after Meilene successfully passed the trials. He had gone around the Fordde confidently, telling his advisers and commanders that she'd be out at the first test. He threw a complete fit in front of everyone when she managed to hit all her targets perfectly.

After they passed the flight portion of the trials, she was certain the vein on his head would explode out of anger. Thankfully, there was a crowd, and he didn't dare say anything at the time.

"Let's not get ahead of ourselves yet," Namail said carefully. "Don't count the clutch before the queen's mating."

"I'm not getting ahead of myself. I want to be prepared." She plucked another piece of mud out of her back claw. It bounced off a bucket with a satisfying sound. "You're not the one he'll be coming after."

"We don't know he'll do anything for certain."

"At a minimum, he'll cause a scene."

"That's nothing. A scene we can handle. A scene would be easy."

"What about the others?" she asked in a low voice. Aletzia shook out one of her long wings, nearly scraping the wooden wall and knocking into a post.

"I think you'll be surprised by the amount of support you'll have. Most riders want a change, and they can't ignore dragon law."

"Most." She focused on the golden scales in front of her, getting lost in their color and shine.

"We can't expect full support but can hope for some, at least."

"Some," she repeated bitterly.

Nothing ever came easy for them.

The two continued attending to their dragons. They attacked old clumps of buildup the dragons could not reach themselves. Getting out dirt and grime picked up from the Fordde or through flight. Meilene took breaks from cleaning her dragon to massage the joints in between her wings that Aletzia favored.

About an hour went by, where Namail went to get another bucket and started to limp. His old injury must have been acting up. He refused to sit down.

Stubborn old man.

"I know you don't like to talk about it." She motioned at his leg. "But do you miss her?"

He paused in the middle of dumping a bucket of water on his dragon. He contemplated his answer for so long, she thought he didn't hear. "More than anything in this world."

Meilene nodded in understanding. "She must have been a lovely person. A great rider, too."

"She was, and she made me a better one. I miss who I used to be."

"I'm sorry." She picked up Aletzia's final claw and struggled to remove a chunk of rock. What was she digging around in lately?

Mountains. You took us through the mountains, remember?

How could she forget?

Namail resumed his ministrations on Mennon's injured hind leg. "We should never have gone out that day. The winds were fierce, especially along the shores." He scrubbed at a patch near the damaged ligaments with particular ferociousness. "I never saw what attacked us, but I remember the sounds."

Meilene nodded. They only spoke of this once before, but her old mentor had been through a lot in his years. He lost his life partner, and her dragon died as well.

We cannot continue without our riders. We should not. It is unnatural.

"And nobody believed you?"

He laughed bitterly. "You know firsthand that they didn't. People would rather keep living in their dream. No one wants to believe the monsters we came to fear are no longer just a fairytale we read about."

"They'll believe soon enough."

Chapter Fifteen

"How do I look?" Meilene twisted in front of the large mirror, admiring herself from every angle.

Fearsome. Your enemies would quiver at the sight of you.

Meilene frowned and ran her hand along the thin material of her green dress. The straps were beaded with a lovely lace pattern over the bodice. It would be perfect for tonight, even if it was something Tork would have never allowed her to wear. "Not quite what I was going for. I was hoping for something along the lines of beautiful or awe-inspiring."

"I would say you look like a dream," Maeve said. She entered the Reina's quarters with a bundle of fresh towels balanced in her arms.

"Thank you, Maeve," she said, with a pointed look to Aletzia's den. "Much closer to the compliment I was hoping for."

"I'm certain Aletzia thinks the same."

"In different words." Meilene turned around once more. "You have outdone yourself this time, Maeve."

"I thought you would appreciate the styling of this one." She tucked the towels into a small decorative cabinet and set about folding the sheets on her bed. "Do you need anything else for tonight?"

"Not unless you know of a way to skip this whole thing without losing the support of the lords and becoming a laughing stock across the Fordde."

"I'm afraid that's one thing I can't help with."

"I didn't think so. Feel free to enjoy the rest of your evening. No sense in both of us suffering tonight."

"Thank you, my Reina. Good luck with the mob tonight." With a curtsey, the mousy worker backed out of the Reina's quarters.

Meilene stepped outside so Aletzia could get a better view.

It felt like ages since she had a chance to dress up, and she wanted to make it count. Namail always wanted her to keep a low profile, and Tork never thought she was worth the effort to attend these things in the past. Now that she had a dragon who was ready to mate, it was time to be in the public's eye, looking like a queen.

Aletzia licked one of her large talons and stared at her through a jeweled eye.

But why would you not want to be fearsome tonight?

She smacked the side of her dragon's head and gave her a few scratches under the eye.

"It's not all about scaring your enemies away, silly. Sometimes, you have to outsmart them."

Why outsmart them when you are larger and stronger?

"Not everyone is the size of a small hill and has teeth as big as my head. Some of us have to find our own weapons." She tapped the side of her head.

I'd never let anything happen to you.

"I know you wouldn't." She sighed. It was almost time to leave.

Why can't you stay with me? We can fly and fight against the winds together.

"As lovely as that sounds. Tonight is important for us to make connections. They are important if we want to succeed in the future."

The dragon blew a gush of warm air on her. *I still think we should go off. The mountains call to me.*

"You and me both." She wrapped her hands around Aletzia's neck. "I'll see you in a bit."

For good measure, she gave one last spin, marveling at how the material made a green bubble. She was able to convince the quartermaster to order her some silks from the southern cities to make her dress. It wasn't quite the same as the lavish outfits she wore to parties in Valchar, but it would get the job done.

Once satisfied that she was more than presentable, she joined Namail to make their way to the grand room. She was surprised at how nicely the old rider had managed to clean up in his suit. He had even attempted to tame that usual mess of red hair on his head.

The Fordde hosted a large party to celebrate the start and end of every mating season, not that there were any mating queens around for there to be an actual season lately.

It was all a formality until then.

Aletzia was still young, and in some cases, queens wouldn't mature until they reached seven years. Meilene just hoped she was right to take the gamble this year. They only had two weeks left until the end of the season.

If only the historical books had some tips on how to make your queen rise to mate, not that Meilene wanted to force her Reina to do anything she wasn't ready for. Meilene wasn't even sure she was ready for this.

If Aletzia rose to find her mate this season, that would mean their plan succeeded. Meilene was equally terrified of what that meant, as much as what failing meant for them.

There was nothing she wanted more than to see Tork removed from power, but that meant another had to take his place. This meant taking his place as dragon lord on a much more personal level with the Reina, especially if Aletzia was enamored with their dragon.

"What is it?" Namail asked when she let out an involuntary shudder.

"Nothing." She wrapped her arms around herself. "It's a bit chilly here."

Her prickly mentor sighed. "You'd think three years would be enough to get you acclimated. I guess not."

"I got used to a lot of things, but I don't think I'll ever get used to this dreadful weather."

"A tradeoff of living in the Fordde."

This whole thing was a big risk. Hoping an unknown would be better than the current dragon lord. He had to be.

The dragons weren't wrong, usually.

There was a palpable shift in energy at the Fordde the last few weeks since Aletzia had passed the trials and declared it would be an open mating. New riders poured into the Fordde daily, and there was an energy that didn't exist when Tork was in charge.

Riders wanted to take that new power.

The entrance to the grand room had a few lingering guests outside. They were late— fashionably—and perfectly on time to make an entrance.

The first guests near the entryway paused to stare. Meilene couldn't stop the smug smile from filling her face, as it was easy enough to figure out what they stared at. She had picked the perfect dress for this.

The dragon lord would be furious when he saw her. This wasn't exactly the traditional rider attire and was more revealing than the conservative riders preferred. Not to mention the slit on the side went halfway up her side. She wanted to make a lasting impression that night.

A small group of visiting dignitaries clustered together below the entrance steps. Judging by the brightness of their attire, they must have been from the western islands. They stood out from the riders, who wore their plain beige formal suits.

Namail followed her gaze and slipped away into the crowds with a wink.

"Gentlemen." Meilene sidled up to the group with the most sickening smile she could muster. It was so fake it would have made her father proud. "Enjoying the evening's festivities so far?"

"Reina Meilene," the nearest dignitary stuttered. She saw his wandering eyes but pretended not to notice. "Such a pleasure seeing you out. We don't usually have the pleasure of seeing the Fordde's only queen at events such as these."

"It's a rare treat, indeed," a short man with a red sash added. "I'm Lord Nurel from Canit island."

"Things have been so busy for me with taking care of a growing queen," she drawled. "They can be quite demanding, even more so than a regular dragon hatchling. Not that I'd ever complain."

"Very busy, I expect," Lord Nurel said. "Especially if I'm to be correct and that we are expecting your Reina to pick a mate this season?"

"That is correct, Lord Nurel."

"That's quite soon, is it not?" the first lord asked. "Isn't the season almost over?"

"Dragon seasons tend to last for about six months of the year," she said. "With the last mating happening before the final moon."

A timeline she and Namail tracked with diligence.

A man with long hair and plain dress attire spoke up. "I heard it will be a, what's it called again, an open mating?"

"You are correct, my lord, ah—"

"Belesby," he supplied. "That's not traditional, is it?"

"Usually not," she said pleasantly, "but as we haven't had a Reina in many years, and this match will determine the next leader, we may as well open up the pool to all potential prospects. We want the best man available."

"Fascinating," Lord Belesby said. He didn't bother to hide his intentions as his eyes wandered. "Forgive me for asking, but that dress is exquisite. It reminds me of the fashions from Valchar in particular."

"Yes, that's where I'm from. You may know my father, Lord—"

"Eoibard Velum," Nurel finished excitedly. "I thought I recognized you, Meilene Velum. Your father and I had many trading deals in the past. Your family has quite the strongholds there."

"The best in all the lands," Meilene added.

"The most well-stocked and well-funded, too," Belesby added. Music started in the main hall. "I know this is unbecoming, but may I escort the Reina into the halls?"

He offered his arm for her.

In a move that would usually be unbecoming of a Reina, she took his offered arm and allowed herself to be escorted into the party, where a red-faced dragon lord looked ready to burst. Several other riders, including that disgusting wing lead, Simeon, ogled her inappropriately.

Under normal circumstances, queens would stay away from physical contact with others, as that could lead to jealousies with their mate. Meilene didn't have a mate . . . yet.

"Dragon lord," she said as pleasantly as possible when he approached the group, flanked by rider Simeon. "Such a pleasure to see you here."

Tork's wispy blond hair plastered against his head in a feeble attempt to look put-together. His formal attire was too small for his thick build and looked as if he was going to burst from it at any moment.

"I would say the same to you, *Reina*," Tork said in silky tones.

"You're looking well, my lady," Simeon said. The beefy wing lead was dressed similarly to the dragon lord and eyed her up in a way that made her skin curl. Meilene turned up her nose at the smell of the rider as he leaned in close to her. She took a step back.

"Thank you, dragon lord," she said through gritted teeth. She refused to acknowledge the repulsive wing lead directly.

"My lords." Tork bowed his head at each of them. "How were your travels in?"

"Quite pleasant. Thank you for the riders you sent," Lord Belesby said.

"Anything we can do to help the kingdoms." Tork raised his glass to the lord. "I see you have already made introductions with our Reina."

"We just discussed Aletzia's upcoming mating." Meilene edged around Simeon to grab a filled glass from a small table. "The lords are interested in hearing how the proceedings go, along with the change in leadership."

"We will surely be sad to see you go, dragon lord, but change is always good, and I'm sure our new Reina will do quite well in the coming years," Lord Nurel said.

"Well." Tork struggled with himself as the wing second scrunched up his face. "We don't want to get ahead of ourselves until the mating, my lords."

"Definitely not," Meilene said.

"Of course," Nurel said quickly. "Still, it's always good to prepare for all outcomes."

"Yes, it most certainly is." With a swift gulp, Meilene finished her drink. "If you'll excuse me, gentlemen, I have some riders I need to catch up with."

"Certainly, my Reina." Belesby backed away to allow her room to pass. "We look forward to catching up with you in the future."

"As do I, my lords."

Chapter Sixteen

The whispers followed as she stormed out of the head instructor's office. The thick door slammed behind her and dislodged a cobweb from the corner.

A pair of riders barely ten years old fell over each other as they scrambled to get out of the furious Reina's way. She was aware of the commotion she caused but didn't care.

Head Instructor Liam thought it was too dangerous for the Reina to run air drills with the other juniors today. He didn't think it was safe given the current *tensions* in the Fordde and not to mention the recent attack outside the village of Prael. No doubt he was grounding them based on instructions from the dragon lord.

"Move." She snapped at a guard blocking the doors to the dressing rooms. They scrambled out of her way. She was flying no matter what the instructor said.

What did he know, anyway?

The past few weeks were the first time she felt free from the dragon lord's control. After spending three years watching as life at the Fordde moved on without her, she was done. She was never able to participate, as she would have liked, or let Aletzia show her true strength as Reina.

None of that mattered anymore. She wanted to practice drills with the others, and no one could stop a Reina.

Within minutes, Meilene was ready to go with her dragon. She had spotted a wing of junior riders getting ready on the concourse and told the wing lead she was going to fly with them today. The poor wing lead didn't know how to say no to her, so he reluctantly agreed after a few words with his second.

Meilene painstakingly got her dragon ready, making sure all her straps and ties were done to absolute perfection; nothing would stop them today. She settled into her new seat, nestled on top of her dragon's neck, and grabbed the reins a rider offered her.

She did a double take as she recognized the cherub face of the rider. She hadn't seen the girl in ages.

The young rider was barely ten the last time they met and shook at the sight of the Reina's presence. Those three years served her well, as she held herself with more confidence than before.

"Oksana."

"My Reina." Her face lit up when she heard her name leave Meilene's lips. "I hope you have a pleasant ride today."

"Thank you, rider." Meilene nodded. "I trust you have been fitting in well and paying attention to your studies."

"Yes, my lady. My dragon, Bernal, has grown so much since then. Not as much as Aletzia, of course, but he's not a queen . . . Sorry, I mean a Reina."

"No need to apologize," Meilene said as she took the last strap from the girl. "Tell Bernal I'm glad he and his rider are doing well."

Oksana beamed. "I will. Good luck today." She bowed her head and walked away.

Her dragon outpaces many of the others his age. He will do well. Meilene smiled.

The riders around her mounted their dragons and organized into their formations. She recognized a few of this riding group from her previous lessons. None of them were particularly remarkable, and their names escaped her.

The blue one is Kien.

"Thanks, but what is his rider's name?" Meilene should know this, as there were so few women riders right at the Fordde. What was her name?

Once the riders had settled themselves, and the dragons had been deemed ready, the wing lead running the drill waited for Meilene. He was one of a pair of brothers, maybe the eldest? The other, she recognized from the hatchery the night Aletzia was born. She hadn't seen him around the Fordde in the past few years.

Both brothers had matching brown dragons with an impressive wingspan, if one considered that important. She nodded at the wing lead, and the group took off. Aletzia led from the front.

The rush of air that hit her face was welcomed. The Fordde's tall walls shrank below her as Aletzia climbed higher and higher, not caring about the dragon lord anymore. She opted to settle above a series of clouds as the riders below formed two neat lines. Meilene remembered it was an attack formation.

The second line struggled to keep in tandem, as several dragons vied for the front position. They must have been new at flying together and in need of more practice.

Aletzia flew around the group of dragons and decided to pass in between two dragons named Swali and Maleth, the brothers. The two moved to allow room to fly with them. Even the wing lead dragon had to adjust his position to allow Aletzia in.

No dragons would deny their Reina.

After boring of the formation practices, Meilene caught the eye of the leader and pointed behind them. He nodded in understanding and allowed Aletzia to glide to the outskirts of the group.

She dipped in and out of clouds, snapping at them as if she could catch them. Meilene loved the feeling of the wind against her face. It wasn't yet too cold where it would be unbearable, but warm enough to make it enjoyable. This was where she was completely free.

Aletzia hummed contentedly as they passed over the lake.

"What?"

I am happy to be with you. They are happy to be flying with us as well.

"Who?"

The dragons. They tell me how well I fly, how fierce I look against all my enemies, and how well of a rider I have.

The smile came unbidden.

"Thank them for me."

There is no need. They know they are privileged to escort the Reina. That is thanks in itself.

Oh, Aletzia. She reached down to pat her neck. "I hope you never change."

Why would I change?

"Never mind. It's a saying."

But who says it?

"People."

Any riders would be privileged to fly with the Reina, more now that she would have an open mating call soon. Dragons and their riders couldn't control that basic instinct at the prospect of a mating queen. Even if they were unsuccessful in the flight, it would still be an experience most didn't want to pass on.

How many dragons would attempt to partner with Aletzia when she finally did rise to mate? It didn't matter how many, since there could only be one successful mate in the end.

Aletzia hummed in response.

"Why are we heading back so soon?" Meilene asked as the dragons made a hard bank toward the Fordde. The wing lead brother signaled to the rest of the riders to follow.

The instructor says we are called back.

Meilene caught a hint of frustration in her dragon's voice. That was unusual.

I could tell them we stay. I do not wish to go back.

"That'll make things worse, as I know who called us back. Let's go home."

As soon as she dismounted her dragon, she found herself face-to-face with a red-faced Tork, the vein on his forehead pulsing dangerously. He was dressed in his casual uniform, wearing a light sweater instead of his riding jacket. He must have been in a hurry to get there if he didn't bother changing first.

"You may ride a Reina," he spat out, "but that doesn't mean you get to do whatever you want around here."

"Whatever are you talking about?" she asked innocently. The wing she had flown with were dismounting around her. A few edged close to the commotion.

"I gave specific instructions you are not to take to the skies this week," he barked.

"They must have gotten lost in the general confusion lately." Meilene removed her riding gloves slowly. She refused to look at him but focused on peeling off one leathered finger at a time. "Really, dragon lord, I think you might want to reconsider how you run this place."

The dragon lord raised his arms as if he was about to hit her. One of the rider brothers stepped in front of her, forcing a shocked Tork back. She knew that rider from somewhere but couldn't place it.

"Don't touch her," the rider said.

"Ryland, don't," another rider hissed, as he pulled him back.

The dragon lord ignored him and sputtered a few curse words at Meilene.

Aletzia crouched back on her hind legs and growled, baring her sharp teeth. It started as a low whir, then grew into a loud throttle that shook the ground underneath them. The nearest dragons cowered away.

Meilene had to bite back a smile. "Quiet, Aletzia. I can handle him." She walked around the rider to face Tork directly.

"I wouldn't be so snarky if I were you, my lady," Tork said menacingly. "You're on your own here and would be nothing if it weren't for your dragon. I've spent years running this place and have the fealty of all the commanders and lords. You're nothing but a spoiled girl who knows nothing about the riders."

"I know more than you think."

"You're a joke. A waste of a rider. I'm in charge here, and this season is about to end. If your dragon doesn't rise and pick a mate, then all your silly little scheming is for nothing."

"We'll see."

He gave her a cold, calculating look. "You made your point. It's not too late. Perhaps we can find a new arrangement where we both win. Enough with these games. There are thousands of riders across the lands whose livelihood is at stake. Think about it, Vylor is a strong beast and would make a perfect mate for Aletzia."

He speaks foolishness.

She mulled over his words for a moment. The only sounds punctuating the silence were Aletzia's guttural notes. A couple of the closest riders edged away.

"Dragon lord Tork, wait!" she yelled as he turned to leave.

He had a sickening smile on his face as if he thought he won. "Yes, *Reina?*"

"Take good care while running the Fordde these next days, for they will be your last." She brushed past a flabbergasted rider and didn't even pause to see the look on Tork's face.

Chapter Seventeen

M eilene's slumber was interrupted by a voice calling her
name in the dark.

"What?" She shot up in bed, shivering and drenched in sweat.
"Aletzia?"

Light pooled in stress across her bed from the windows. She
peered around the corner and saw her dragon asleep in her
stone den. Aletzia's ears flicked in her sleep, but otherwise, she
remained unmoving.

No one was around. Must have been the wind.

With a few grumblings, Meilene grabbed her blanket and hid
underneath her pillow. This was too early, and she had such a
nice dream before that rude interruption. She squeezed her eyes
and willed herself back to sleep.

After a few hours of fretful tossing, she finally gave up and decided to call down for Namail to join her for breakfast. Thankfully, Maeve had the sense to lay some clothing options out for
the tired Reina. She threw on a thick sweater and put her hair
up, not caring that she was a mess.

Looking like a disaster had its benefits while walking around
the Fordde.

No one recognized her and let her be on her way without any questions. Lately, riders would stop her to talk about something trivial or another. It annoyed her to no end, but Namail said that this was usual with open queens.

When she declared Aletzia would have an open mating, clearly everyone thought she wanted to be approached and wooed. As if it would increase their chances of getting their dragon to mate with Aletzia.

Meilene scoffed. Like she'd let them influence her partner's mating. The only scenario in which she may have interfered was if Tork's own Vylor was close to completing the bond. She'd do anything to keep that from happening.

"You look terrible." Namail slid a cup toward her. She took the seat across from him at their usual table overlooking the concourse. The morning patrols were just landing. "Bad sleep?"

Meilene stifled a yawn and nodded. "I feel like I've been hit on the head with a rock and then stomped on repeatedly by a large dragon."

"Aletzia still sleeps?" he asked curiously.

She gripped her cup and stared out into the concourse. She tried to focus on the wing that had just landed but couldn't concentrate. It was like she was in a daze. Probably from the lack of sleep.

"I told you what Tork said yesterday," she said.

"You did, yes."

"Do you think he was right? Did we make a mistake?"

That was her fear. It was finally voiced out loud.

She was terrified their plan wouldn't work, and she had failed the riders somehow. There was so much at stake. So much depended on who her dragon chose.

Namail surveyed her carefully. "You don't think that, do you?"

"I don't know what to think anymore."

"One way or another, Aletzia will mate."

"I'm not so certain."

"If not this season, then the next, or the one after." He leaned forward. "One day, she will be a full Reina and will start laying her own clutches with a new leader, a new mate. Whether that man is of Tork's choosing or your own."

"I mean, it could also be a female rider," Meilene said with a shrug.

"True, but that's rare and depends on the queen rider's preferences herself. So is whether or not you let your dragon's emotions overcome yourself and turn it physical. I don't recommend that for the first mating. Either way, I pray it's a strong rider. I want someone good for you, as they will be your companion after all."

"I'm less concerned with that." Meilene hoped her blush wasn't visible to her mentor. "If it's not someone we like, then Aletzia can choose a different dragon the next time."

A pair of dragons glided across the ground. They must have been headed toward the lake.

"It doesn't always work that way," Namail said. "Riders have spent thousands of years trying to figure out why some are chosen and others are not. If we had that figured out by now, then things would be simpler."

"Dragons know things we don't." Meilene repeated the line heard in her studies.

Whenever dragons did something riders couldn't understand, they'd play it off as "the dragon always knows" instead of considering that, maybe sometimes, the dragons just chose wrong.

"Ugh." Meilene pushed her empty plate away. "This is infuriating. I'm going for a walk."

"Let me come with you," Namail was quick to say. "I could stretch my legs."

"Whatever." She shoved away from her seat. "My head is pounding."

"Would you like to go to the infirmary?" He walked close beside her and kept moving his hand as if to help direct her. They passed a group of riders who eyed her curiously.

Meilene knew she was a sight to see. Their usually proper Reina must have been looking all-out of sorts today.

"No. I just need to move." The wind picked up with a terrible force. She brushed a strand of messy hair out of her face. "Can you find me a spare jacket? I'm getting a bit chilly."

"You there," he shouted at a nearby rider. The rider jumped at being addressed by the Reina's mentor-rider. "Please go to the quartermaster and grab a spare riding jacket for your Reina."

"Yes, sir," the rider squeaked out.

As terrible as she felt, she couldn't help the smile that came to her face at the sight. She'd never get over how easily startled some riders were.

"Why couldn't they have built this Fordde someplace tropical?" she asked. "Why are they all built in stony, cold lands?"

"Those were the easiest lands to get a hold of back then."

"And the cheapest to barter away from the lords."

"Plus, the mountain rocks were close to transport for building this place."

A wave of emotion and nausea overtook her. She pinched the bridge of her nose and focused on breathing through her mouth. A pack of birds flew overhead. Their squawks filled the sky as they passed.

Everything was annoying her with a particular intensity today.

A nervous commander approached. The tall man had beads of sweat dripping from his brow and shifted from foot to foot.

Namail stayed close by her shoulder. "Yes, Commander Elias?" he asked.

"Everything all right over here?" His eyes flickered over to Meilene.

Rays of the sun got in her eyes, and the chatting of the nearby riders irritated her. Her throat was dry, and her stomach growled, even though she ate minutes before.

"Quite alright." Namail spoke casually, as if talking about the cloud patterns that day. "Was that all?"

"I just—"

"Thanks for the update, Commander. The Reina appreciates it."

Namail grabbed her elbow and led Meilene away from the flabbergasted commander. Meilene didn't care. Her headache had grown, and she was feeling feverish. A ripple of illness coursed through her.

"Thank you for getting rid of him," she managed to choke out.

"Not a problem," he said lightly. "Here, let's sit." He directed her to one of the mantels at the edge of the grounds. She was uncomfortably aware that he watched her closely. "Those pesky commanders can be tiresome at times."

Meilene didn't respond. Her head was fuzzy, so she rested it in her hand. She allowed her hair to fall out of its bun and cover her face. Namail awkwardly pet her on her back.

Someone else came up to her mentor, but the voices sounded distant. She could rely on Namail to remove that irritation. After a few minutes, or was it hours, she watched the black boots disappear.

Finally.

"We should get you inside, my Reina. Aletzia is awake and at the grounds."

"What?" She whipped her head up and brushed her hair back. A small part of her knew that was important information. Why didn't she hear her dragon call to her?

Namail kneeled in front of her with a serious expression. "It's time for the mating."

Chapter Eighteen

There was a flurry of commotion as Meilene felt herself led by Namail through the stone passages. A woman came to help them who she recognized, but couldn't place the name. It was like she floated outside her body.

Eventually, she was helped into a seat in what she recognized as her own Maise. The warm drapes and tall ceilings comforted her. Aletzia was no longer sleeping outside. Namail had said something about her, but Meilene couldn't remember what it was.

All she could feel was an insurmountable rise of heat. Did someone turn on her fireplace? No, she didn't see any flames coming from it. An uncontrollable desire to get away from there filled her, but a gentle hand on her shoulder kept her from leaving her seat.

"Here, drink this."

She recognized the voice as her partner's favorite human. The one that brought her meals. No, wait. She shook her head. Those were not her thoughts.

Meilene took the cup and drank. It was crisp against her lips and cooled her parched throat.

Hundreds of voices spoke to her at once, calling out for attention. She felt the presence of every dragon within miles. In a sea of voices, a few stood out louder than the rest. Several she hadn't heard before, some she despised, and a few intrigued her.

Something brought her back into the stone walls. It felt like they were closing in on her.

"Don't touch her," a voice called out. "You're not supposed to touch her."

"Do you want to lie down, my lady?" a soft voice asked.

"What should we do?"

"Should we call someone?"

"Do not let the dragon lord anywhere near here or I'll stab you in the neck."

Panicked voices floated around her, and Namail answered an unheard question. He sounded stressed. He was never stressed.

The old ones annoyed her the most with their incessant pestering and calls, as if they stood a chance in the selection. Their blood had long since passed their time and would be a terrible match. She was hot and itching to get away from there, away from everyone else. She wanted to drift away.

Meilene knew Aletzia was in the air, flying fast above the lake and circling back to survey the grounds and the dragons there. Several of them crooned and a few took to the airs, circling her at a safe distance. She was an unstoppable force to be reckoned with.

Back in her room, the voices spoke and took over her attention.

Namail kneeled next to her. "What can I do for you?"

Aletzia sensed a few dragons attempting to get close, but she wouldn't allow them. The blue Vylor and brown Swali were persistent as they circled but she dipped low to lose them. She wanted to be free to survey all the potentials.

"Maybe give her some space."

"Yes, anybody who doesn't need to be here should leave."

Iliano gave a feeble attempt to rise to the air but was quickly winded and floated back to the ground. A feeble attempt. The old ones attempted to reach out again, preening in the skies: Selatiat, Macin, Elin, and Retten.

They were weak and would never be good mates.

Several dozen dragons now circled the skies with her, trying to catch her attention. Vylor was persistent. That one was used to ruling the dragons but he repulsed her.

Faster and faster she flew in the circles, her prey following her as a wave of heat rose up from within her belly, nearly consuming her. But it wasn't time yet.

Curious about the mountains, she turned toward the high peaks. She knew she should stay close but she always loved flying there with her human. Only the strongest could navigate the harsh winds there as she contemplated her options.

A few of their songs called out to her, nearly soothing her heated blood but not quite strong enough. The pull wasn't there yet. She was uncertain what she searched for but knew it wasn't them.

Aletzia glided against the heavy downdraft. It was nothing against her. She darted in between sharp peaks, not caring for anything else in the skies.

She raced around a particularly large peak, flanked by dual avalanches of water down its side. She enjoyed the feel of the cold against her scales. Her wings whirred at a furious rate as they pumped to keep her away from the others. They took her high above the peaks so she could watch the circling dragons, reaching out to each of them.

Searching.

One dragon made his way through the peaks opposite her, barely skimming them as he joined the circle of dragons below flying wingtip to wingtip in a canopy of colors. She remembered this new one. Maleth. He was fast thanks to his time at the races the humans looked down on.

Aletzia crooned, matched by calls from below. This time one stood out above the others. One called back.

The speed of the circling dragons sped up, blurring the colors together. A low hum started from within the group and spread to fill the valley below. Aletzia felt one of the hums echo within her, it brought the prior heat to a boiling rise. One that needed to be sated.

Without any warning, she dove into the circle of dragons.

That's the last thing Meilene remembered clearly. The rest was a jumbled mess of emotions and fluttering wings. Words from Namail rang in her head but her dragon's emotions were just too much to stop and she needed to satisfy that heat. There was a mess of tangled limbs, an overwhelming sense of comfort and satisfaction, and then a steady heartbeat that was not hers.

When she awoke, her nostrils filled with a lovely smell that she couldn't place. She cracked an eye open and traced the familiar pattern of her quilt. Judging by the light pooling in from the window, it was the next morning.

She didn't dare move to check if Aletzia was outside or she'd wake *him*. Whoever's chest she rested on was warm and quite comfortable. Even as her head felt heavy and muddled, she started to realize what she had allowed to happen. She reached out to her dragon for comfort.

We are both here.

What?

Meilene groaned and finally shifted her head to see the rider beside her. She faintly recognized his features and mop of brown hair, but her mind was too slow to piece it together. He was young, maybe a few years older than herself.

Meilene frowned.

The muscles in his tan body were clearly defined, probably from years of dragon riding. She stiffened as he moved. His eyes snapped open to reveal thick lashes and eyes that were a lovely shade of blue.

What was going on?

"And who are you?" she asked.

Chapter Nineteen

RYLAND

You need to get up.

But he was so warm and comfortable where he was. It was pleasantly warm and soft. Every inch of his body refused to move and begged to be pulled back into that sweet, sweet slumber he had been enjoying.

Ryland!

The seriousness in Maleth's voice hinted that something was off. As he slowly became conscious, he realized the reason why he was so comfortable before. This wasn't like his bed. He felt a movement beside him and cracked his eyes open.

Oh no.

Reina Meilene was next to him in the bed. Her mouth moved, but he couldn't hear a sound. The brightness of the room took a few minutes to adjust as he tried to pull his body out of its sleep.

A small hand smacked his shoulder, and his hearing came crashing back. "What is wrong with you? I said to get out of my bed!"

Ryland scrambled out of the bed as a fluffy pillow was thrown at him, bouncing off his chest. "I'm sorry. I'm sorry." He grabbed a crumpled-up shirt and pants and quickly threw them on. The Reina knelt on her bed with a hand on the sheet to keep herself covered.

"Who are you? How did this happen?"

He threw his hands up in defense. "I don't know. I don't know." He ran a hand through his hair and looked around the foreign Maise. "I'm Ryland. I'm Maleth's rider."

The Reina–Meilene–lifted a shaky hand and pointed outside. "Is that your dragon out there?"

In her stone den, the golden Aletzia lay curled up with his brown dragon Maleth. They looked so peaceful. "Yes," he breathed out.

Her eyes widened, and her mouth formed an O-shape as she slowly pieced everything together. Ryland still didn't fully understand what happened.

All that he knew was that she looked furious.

"Okay . . . okay." Ryland wasn't sure if she spoke to him or herself. She ran a hand across her face and through her hair. "This is fine. Everything is going to be fine."

"What—what are we supposed to do now?" he asked.

Her face hardened as she studied him for a moment. A little too long for his comfort.

"*Namail*!"

How did this happen to him?

Ryland huddled to the side of the long table, seated between Reina Meilene and his brother, Alistair. He made sure to leave plenty of space between himself and the sour-faced Reina from the moment they entered the command center.

The too-small riding shirt his brother brought him this morning was constricting, and the heavy lights shone on him like a spotlight. The curved table they sat at overlooked the Fordde concourse, giving him a view of all the dragons coming and going. What he would give to be one of them.

The only time he was in this room before was to be reprimanded by The dragon lord. This felt strange.

To say that morning was awkward was a huge understatement.

The thought of Maleth participating in the mating never occurred to him. Everyone was eager to give their dragons the experience, and he didn't want to be the only one left behind, so they entered at the last minute. It seemed like a solid idea at the time. He had barely returned to the Fordde after Tork's banishment and then *this*.

This was the last thing he expected. What had he done?

What you did? his dragon, Maleth, asked. *I don't recall seeing you above the smoky mountains yesterday.*

The amusement in the dragon's voice annoyed him. He didn't bother giving him a response.

"And Commander Brawne and wing lead Simeon?" the Reina's right-hand man asked. Namail splayed out the two commanders' folders in front of her.

The crusty rider was known for his acidity and cunning. He had to be since he managed to guide her to successfully take over from Tork.

A feat most thought impossible.

"Ew, no," the Reina said dismissively. Her dark hair was tied back in a tight bun, highlighting her sharp features. "Get rid of them."

"Any issues with that, Reinaleader Lewes?" he asked, as if Ryland's opinion mattered at this point.

After waking up in the strange Maise by a less-than-impressed Reina, the day passed by in a blur.

As soon as she understood what had happened, she called for her aide. He and the others entered the queen's Maise to harass the pair. Ryland was never as grateful for his overbearing brother as he was today. As intrusive and controlling as he was, Alistair knew a lot about the inner workings at the Fordde and was there to help his younger brother through this upheaval.

The entire morning had been generally confusing for Ryland.

The Reina and her mentor were prepared for the transition of power. As soon as Namail came in, he and the Reina went to work as if Ryland wasn't there.

As much as he tried, Ryland couldn't get a private word in with the Reina.

The pair only consulted Ryland on a few matters. Besides that, they whispered away hurriedly while Alistair kept trying to pull him aside to talk. Both the Reina and her mentor blew up when he tried to ask a few questions, so he decided to keep to himself most of the morning.

The old dragon lord, Tork, was already removed from the command center before they came in. At least that was a problem for later.

With everything that happened that day, he was glad he didn't have to deal with the ousted leader, who always had something against him. He was probably brewing in his failures and trying to plot a way to get out of this entire arrangement. As if he could overthrow centuries of dragon law and tradition.

Ryland had no love for Tork and his leadership style. He was a terrible man who somehow thought he was doing what was best for the Fordde. There were many others who felt the same way and were excited for the prospect of new leadership that would come with Aletzia's mating.

There were several wing leads and a few commanders who everyone thought would be successful yesterday, his brother included among them.

Was this the outcome they had hoped for?

"I'm fine with that decision," Ryland said quietly in response to the mentor's question.

"Simeon will not go easily," Alistair said. "You should send extra guards to help."

The Reina nodded vehemently, obviously not a fan of the former wing lead. Ryland always got a bad vibe from him the few times they interacted.

The wing lead was overconfident going into the mating. He clearly thought his prior interactions with the Reina would have ensured his dragon's success. Too bad for him.

In that moment, Rylan felt like nothing more than an accessory they needed to nod and confirm their decisions, which he did without question. This was all so overwhelming and the last thing he thought he'd be doing.

Why did this happen to him?

And why not you? If not you, who else would be better? Who else could have matched with Aletzia during the mating?

Practically anyone else but him.

"And Garett, Calenth, and Yannet?" Namail asked.

"Yannet is a yes, obviously." The brunette swiveled her chair in annoyance. "Calenth . . . he can stay, for now. Garett, I guess, stays if he changes his attitude."

Rider Namail turned expectantly to him. "Reinaleader?"

"I'm good," he said. He hated the title that signified someone whose dragon mated with the Reina queen. "I'd keep an eye on Garett, though."

Meilene and her mentor ignored him. He got used to that in his years at the Fordde.

The crusty rider pushed away the remaining files on Fordde personnel. They must have gone through at least half of the leadership by then. He was nothing if not thorough.

With each passing rider they reviewed, he sensed it. That all-consuming disappointment coming from the others, especially her. There'd been so much talk of the Reina's new mate taking over and whispers of hope for a change.

Now this.

"I think we can break on this until tomorrow," Namail said. "I'll make arrangements to remove those you've requested . . . What about the previous dragon lord? He's currently sequestered in his quarters. Commander Yannet had the good sense to arrange so before your arrival."

Ryland glanced back toward the Reina. It was a delicate matter and should have been her call. She was the one who had worked so hard to get him out.

"I want him gone," she said without hesitation. "Out of the Fordde, any of the Forddes forever."

Ryland nodded.

Smart.

It would do no good to keep the vindictive dragon lord around. He had firsthand experience of what damage he could cause if left unchecked.

"If I may suggest," Alistair added. "You should take care of him delicately, so he can't cause any issues on his way out."

The Reina looked like she could care less how quietly the previous dragon lord left. She turned to Namail, and something unspoken passed between them.

"I agree with him," the rider said. "As much as it pains me to say . . . I think we should offer a nice retirement arrangement on one of the warmer islands, which needs dragon riders for light activities. Far away from any of the Fordde settlements and far away from you, my Reina."

As if Tork would accept anything less than dragon lord.

The Reina, Meilene, took a deep breath and seemed to combat some inner turmoil. "Whatever." She crossed her arms. "As long as he is far away from here, and I never have to hear about him again."

"Absolutely, my Reina." The old rider clasped his hands together and brandished a new file. "Now, onto you, our new Reinaleader." He opened the folder, which had Ryland's name on it.

Oh no.

In the back of his mind, he heard Maleth's laugh and ignored him. His brother shifted uneasily in his chair.

"Quite an interesting—ah, *history,* you have, Reinaleader Lewes—"

"You can call me Ryland." The title felt too foreign for him at that moment. Acknowledging it meant this whole thing was real, and he wasn't ready for that.

"Whatever you want, *sir*." Namail opened the file and flipped through the pages. "As I was saying, it's quite the colorful background we have here."

Alistair crossed his arms and sent him a scathing look. Ryland had to stifle a laugh. Now was not the time.

"Bonded with your dragon early. Maleth, that is."

"Obviously."

Ryland would never forget that day. He was not even eight at the time he heard Maleth's call in the middle of the night. Everything changed the day they bonded.

I waited a long time for you.

"Your family comes from an extensive line of riders; that's one good point," Namail said with a small nod. "One. But I do see here the dragon lord sent you on probation twice, that your files from early lessons indicated you are resistant in your lessons, and that you have yet to match with any wing besides your brother's here, which you were placed on temporarily. There is also a mention that you and your dragon were seen at several of the underground races, though never implicated as a participant, which is *acceptable* for now. At twenty and five years of age, you haven't been able to keep down a position with any stability."

Alistair groaned and hid his face in his hands.

When read out loud like that, it didn't sound as bad as he originally thought. So, he didn't like to follow the rules. Was that a crime?

He chanced a glance at Meilene, who remained quiet throughout the exchange. Thus far, she was difficult to read, but he thought he detected a hint of a smile on her face. She watched her dragon do loops around the concourse with Maleth. It was weird to see.

"It all sounds about right, rider," Ryland said. "Was there a question in there that I missed?"

The Fordde life was never one he had dreamed of. If he had his choice, he would have gone to a smaller Fordde outpost where fewer rules and surly riders told him what to do. He should have taken that last position when he had a chance.

Participating in some of the dragon races as a way to expend energy when he was younger was not the smartest decision he ever made. Thankfully, they were never caught participating, or else Tork would have had him thrown out.

The weathered rider glared at him for a moment. "No question. Just wanted to make sure I had a correct understanding of our new Reinaleader."

There it is. That tone.

He'd had hints of it all day from any of the commanders he was introduced to and from any of the workers who came up to meet him. The tone that indicated they were less than impressed with the new Reinaleader.

Ever since Aletzia hatched over three years prior, there was that unspoken division throughout the Fordde for those who wanted change and those loyal to Tork. Everyone had high hopes for the new Reinaleader, especially when Meilene managed to get an open mating for herself.

An open mating call meant endless possibilities. Hundreds, if not thousands, of dragons and their riders to choose from. So many options for a new, strong leadership to help them through these worrisome times.

All that hope . . . and they got him.

"Oh." Ryland was surprised by the amusement in Namail's voice. "You'll both need to think about who you want assigned to your wings. Neither of you have anyone, given that you," he nodded at the Reina, "still can't find anyone to work with and you," he nodded at Ryland, "haven't been able to hold down with any riders either. Not to mention you have yet to complete your final tests."

The heat that crept to his cheeks couldn't be stopped. He wished he took the time to finally go through those last year. It didn't seem important at the time, given where he was sent.

"We'll have to progress him through quietly," Alistair said. "Nobody needs to know."

Namail nodded. "Any thoughts on wing riders so far?"

"I'd like Alistair as my second." His brother had served as a wing lead for years and was on track to become a commander at the Fordde before all this. He would be an excellent second in command.

Alistair straightened up in his seat. "I have some ideas for the others, which I can discuss with the Reinaleader after."

"My Reina?" Namail asked. "Any thoughts for yours yet?"

The brunette didn't take her eyes off the window, through which she still watched Aletzia and Maleth. She sighed heavily. "Let's leave it for now. I've survived this long without and can do it for a little longer."

"It's not traditional—" Namail said.

"I'd rather wait for—"

"We've talked about this before, and—"

"No! Not today, please." She silenced the room with a deadly look. The old rider didn't even flinch.

Ryland felt himself flinch at her harsh words, and even his brother winced. They must both be thinking the same. These next few months were going to be interesting.

How was he going to get through it all?

I am with you.

At least he had his dragon on his side; it seemed like no one else was.

Chapter Twenty

MEILENE

Meilene threw her jacket onto the couch and kicked at its wooden leg. She glared at the offending article of clothing, as it insulted her.

Stupid couch. Stupid jacket. Stupid Maise.

This bedroom felt smaller than usual, more like a prison than it ever did before. She held back the scream she wanted to let go, so she didn't scare *him* off.

What's wrong?

"I've had an excruciating day?"

"What was that?" a voice piped up.

The rider hovered by the doorway. He ran his hand through his brown hair and shifted his weight from foot to foot. Why did he just stand there?

You are upset. He is wary of you.

As he should be. She was not in the mood.

You should talk to him.

About what? It wasn't her job to babysit the new Reinaleader.

After dinner, he and his brother went off, talking for nearly an hour. Not that Meilene complained, as it gave her and Namail some alone time to discuss this new *Reinaleader*. So far, Meilene was unimpressed, but Namail told her to give it time for things to settle in.

Did she do something wrong in the mating? Besides allowing Aletzia to fully take over, that was.

"You can come in." Meilene waved around to her room—their room now. She had grown to love her ample quarters, down to the ornate chests that she kept her clothes in and the delicate white couches that reminded her of her. "Are you waiting for an invitation?"

A worker had brought his clothes and a few of his belongings in, probably Maeve, judging by the delicate care by how neat the items were placed. Those forever empty shelves were now full, and the room that had once been her reprieve would have a stranger living in it. They were always so focused on getting Tork out, Meilene never stopped to think about this part of the deal.

Namail never prepared her for this part.

If she wasn't so upset about this entire arrangement, the sight of him standing awkwardly by the door would have made her laugh.

Was she that bad this morning?

The way he looked around the room reminded her of a child seeing a new toy for the first time. It must have looked strange to him, as she preferred to outfit her Maise in lighter, warm colors, whereas the riders here preferred the darker tones the Fordde was famous for.

"It's your Maise, too, now." She failed to keep the bitterness out of her voice.

This was the one piece all her practices and studies hadn't prepared her for: how to suddenly live with and share a life with a total stranger. She should have taken Aletzia back to Valchar when they first bonded.

She pulled her bun out and let it fall across her back. The relief felt nice. She leaned against a chest and watched her new roommate absorb his new surroundings. Everything this morning went by in a blur of yelling and confusing questions. He must not have had a chance to take it all in.

As he examined the second drawer filled with his belongings, Meilene did feel some pity for the poor rider. He looked about as happy with this arrangement as she was. *At least he is good to look at*, she thought.

No. Stop that, she told herself.

Those thoughts would get her nowhere. Most likely, he wouldn't make it past the next mating, and Meilene would have to prepare for yet another dragonmate and Reinaleader.

Another stranger.

That was one thing the books didn't go into detail on. Some queens mated with the same dragon for years, and some changed their partners every mating.

There was no way to determine what a queen would do.

Judging by the greenness of this rider and how out of place he seemed, he wouldn't last longer than one mating. He allowed his wing lead brother to make all the decisions and do all the talking that day, as if he was afraid to speak up.

Why was he chosen for this one?

The dragons always know. That old saying repeated in her head. She'd never doubted that saying as much as she did in that moment.

Namail had mentioned that his dragon was from one of the ancient hatches. Maybe it was good for breeding the next Reina? Riders around here always bragged when their dragons came from a good line.

That and whoever had the largest dragon.

There was also some mention about the races that could have factored in. She'd heard mention about that illegal sport from Namail.

Leave it up to her to pick a Reinaleader with no experience and one who most likely engaged in prior unsavory activities.

Either way, his days as Reinaleader were numbered.

Maybe. Maybe not. Time will tell.

Aletzia was right. This rider was meant to lead beside her until the time Aletzia chose a new mate. She shouldn't discredit him so quickly, especially seeing as the next season wouldn't start for half a year at least.

They were stuck together for the time being.

From the nearest ornate drawer, she grabbed her nightclothes and set about getting ready for bed. She was exhausted from the past days' events.

After changing in private in the washing room and taking more time than she should, she finally slipped into the bed she would share with her dragonmate. She pulled the blanket up to her chin and watched as he prepared for the night.

She sighed. This was not what she expected. Well, to be fair, she never thought this part through. Having a dragonmate. A partner. Someone who would share every aspect of her life and leadership, including those parts in that moment.

The room went dark for a moment as a dragon swooped over the outside den, followed by another. Aletzia and Maleth settled in. The two dragons curled around each other, with Aletzia resting her head upon Maleth's.

It was nice to see her dragon so content.

The bed shifted as Ryland gently settled himself under the covers. She had to bite back a smile when she realized he was flush against the edge of his side like she was on her own.

As terrible as this pairing felt, at least he wasn't a handsy rider looking to collect his payment as dragonmate.

The idea of these pairings had always been so foreign to her. They were wrong about the bond. She didn't feel any pull of emotion toward this stranger coming from her dragon bond. Nothing besides a twinge of guilt for the poor rider.

Meilene tried to loosen up as she realized how tense her body felt. No wonder she was developing a headache. She forced herself to take a few deep breaths before pulling the covers tighter.

Her eyelids grew heavy as she stared up at the reams on her ceiling. She traced their outline in her mind until she couldn't focus anymore. She fell into a deep sleep, only waking up when the sun started to trickle across her face.

When Meilene woke, she was spread across the bed, like usual. She felt dazed, cold, and alone. It took her a moment to realize something was off.

"Aletzia?"

Yes?

She threw off the covers and ran outside. "Are you okay?"

Why wouldn't I be?

The sight in front of her made her stop dead in her tracks. *He* was outside with the dragons.

With *her* dragon.

Most riders gave the Reina dragon a wide berth whenever they were on the grounds. Not him. In a sight she'd never seen before, Ryland reached out his hand and Aletzia pressed her large head against it. He stroked under her jaw, and she nudged his shoulder.

I like him.

Meilene scoffed. "Don't get too attached," she said quietly.

"I'm sorry." He pulled his hand back and moved several steps to the side toward his brown dragon. Meilene held back a laugh. As if his dragon could protect him against anything here, no matter his size. "I didn't know you were awake. I was up early, couldn't sleep, and Maleth needed attention, and then . . ."

She approached Aletzia's head and scratched at the same spot he just attended. "It's fine. I just woke up."

He looked down. "I was trying to be quiet, sorry."

"You don't have to apologize." Meilene focused on a soft patch next to the ear. "It's your Maise, too, now, I guess."

"I guess." He stepped back to his prior spot to attend to the golden head. He mirrored her movement and attacked the opposite ear. Aletzia practically purred with pleasure.

Do not stop.

While he focused on the dragon, Meilene took the time to admire his features. He had dark brown hair and blue eyes she'd seen around before. He wore a cut-off shirt instead of the usual rider attire.

Not too bad for a rider with absolutely zero experience running a Fordde.

"Did you sleep well?" she asked.

"I did. Thanks."

Meilene would be surprised if he did. After he huddled up on his side of the bed, he barely moved an inch. He was probably afraid to jostle his bedmate.

An uncomfortable silence filled the void again, stretching out for an eternity.

Meilene focused on giving her dragon the attention she deserved after such a wonderful first mating.

Did you expect anything less?

"Reina." Namail ran into the queen's concourse. They both withdrew their hands as if touching a hot coal. Ryland stepped several feet away from her.

"What is it?"

"You should come down to the command center. Both of you," he said, with a dismissive glance in Ryland's direction. "The former dragon lord is making a scene."

Chapter Twenty-One

RYLAND

Whatever he expected to be waiting for him at the command center, this was not it. This place always felt foreign and off-limits, today was no different. He adjusted the collar of the riding jacket Namail made him change into before coming.

Yesterday wasn't his first day here. He'd been called down several times when the old dragon lord placed him on probation.

The first time wasn't even his fault, but the second time definitely was. He had only refused to follow Commander Garett's orders. To be fair, those orders would have put several rider wings in danger, so he had no regrets for that punishment.

The command center was a giant circular room with large windows that had a great view of the courtyards and surrounding lands. One could usually watch dozens of dragons patrolling throughout the skies. It was the perfect location to spot enemies approaching for miles.

The inside was built to best survey the lands and make any key decisions. Several large tables stretched across the room, with offices set aside for key commanders and leaders. There's a large station for monitoring flights and weather across the countryside, helpful to find any unpredictability in upcoming patterns.

Opposite the bright windows, one wall of slanted rock stood tall, as if cut directly from a mountainside. The dragon lord's offices took up most of that side and were in the process of being emptied . . . as much as it could be while Tork stood in the middle, throwing items and screaming at the nearest workers.

Commander Yannet was already on the scene with several guards, attempting to smoothly pack up Tork's possessions in between the commotion and flying objects. The man looked as if he didn't get a minute of sleep and wore an old, wrinkled jacket, as if he hadn't changed for days.

As soon as the old dragon lord saw them enter, he pushed the commander aside. "I will not be cast aside like this. Do you know what I have done for this place?"

Ryland opened his mouth to answer but was too slow.

"What you've done for this place?" Reina Meilene scrunched up her face. She'd also been made to wear her official riding gear, but at least hers were a darker color and a perfect fit. "All you've done is drag this place through the mud. You've done nothing but slowly destroy the reputation of the riders."

"I have only elevated our riders." Tork's face was red as amber, and there was a particular vein on his forehead that threatened to explode. "I've given up much for the past twenty years to keep this place running."

"Please," the Reina said disdainfully. "You're lucky we don't have you arrested right now. You're an absolute disgrace. A complete joke. I'm sorry we couldn't get rid of you sooner."

"You." He pointed his finger at Meilene. "You absolute deranged, deluded, idiotic simpleton."

Tork closed the gap between him and the Reina as if he wanted to hit her. Without thinking, Ryland stepped in the middle, blocking his path to the Reina. Namail stood by her side, his stance one of complete alertness.

Streno may have had quite a few years on him, but Ryland wasn't intimidated. The man hadn't been in the field in years, let alone had any combat flights in just as long. Tork stopped inches away from him. Ryland kept his stance and refused to move for the disgraced dragon lord.

"You should watch yourself while talking to your new Reina," Ryland said.

To his surprise, Reina Meilene didn't even flinch at the sight of the large man trying to get to her. She tried pushing Ryland aside.

"I am the dragon lord!" His face turned purple, and he splattered drops of spit. "And this is what you've chosen as my replacement? *This* rider? I should have sent you both away for good when I had the chance. You will both bring us into ruin."

"What you think doesn't matter anymore," she said.

"I will not be removed like this. If you think this girl can do half of what I've done for this Fordde—"

The fiery brunette kept trying to go around Ryland and spoke from behind his elbow. "If you mean burdening us under a crippling debt and losing the patronage of several large kingdoms in the past three years alone, then you're correct, and I won't be doing any of that."

"I will make sure you regret this."

"Let's have calm Tork," Namail said. "This is unbecoming of a former dragon lord."

The ex-dragon lord tried to reach for her again. White-hot anger filled him, and Ryland pushed him back several feet, not caring about the squawk of surprise from Meilene.

Something seemed to register on Tork's face as he surveyed Ryland. He swung his fist, aiming for Ryland's face, but Tork was old and sloppy. He ducked easily.

The ex-dragon lord lost his balance and nearly toppled over.

Before Ryland could think about retaliating, one of the commanders had the common sense to intervene and forcibly pulled Tork to the side.

Rage from Maleth's thoughts filled him, but he kept that pushed away.

"Let's not do anything rash," Commander Jian said in a calming voice as several dragon roars could be heard. "You'll rile up all the dragons if you continue like this. I'll have someone finish packing your things and bring them to you, Tork."

"I will not be handled like this." Tork swung his arm wildly. It was unclear who his target was this time, as he was close to neither Ryland nor Meilene.

A guard intervened and pulled Tork's arm behind his back. Ryland stepped forward to help, but a gentle squeeze on his arm stopped him. Meilene stood beside him, looking as fierce as he'd ever seen her.

"You forget where you are and who you are now," she said. "I wouldn't want to have you sent to the dungeons for your hysterics."

This set Tork off even worse. He struggled against his hold as a string of curse words spewed from his mouth.

"Calm yourself, sir," the guard holding him said to Tork. "Or else we'll have to detain you."

"Listen to the guards," Commander Garett said. Where did he come from? "This won't help you today, Tork." The commander gently grabbed Tork's upper arm from the guard. "I'll make sure he's escorted back."

"I cannot, will not—" the dragon lord spat out as another guard came over to help.

"We don't want to have a scene, now do we?" Commander Garett allowed the guard to help him direct the ex-dragon lord out. This new guard did not handle the old leader as gently as the commander did.

Tork Streno was escorted out unceremoniously. That was not a way for a dragon lord to leave, but Tork was a special breed.

Hopefully, he'll be far away from the Fordde and their lives by the end of the week.

"Are you all right, Reina?" Namail asked as the small crowd dissipated.

The small brunette still stood inches away from him with her hands on her hips. Her face turned into a lovely scowl that was surprisingly directed at him. "I didn't need your help," she bit out at Ryland.

"I was only trying to—"

"I can handle him on my own."

"Next time, I'll leave you to fist fight him by yourself, then."

"Whatever. You're useless anyway." She turned away and grabbed a stack of papers a nearby rider was waiting to give to her. "We're supposed to meet with the commanders so we can be sworn in officially. Think you can handle that?"

Meilene didn't bother to wait for his reply before storming off to talk with Namail.

He groaned.

There was no winning with this one.

Left alone with the rest of the commanders and other elite officials staring at him, he started to wonder how he would make it through the next few months. He never wanted to lead a wing, let alone every single rider in the Fordde. He only wanted to take care of Maleth and find some place they could do whatever they wanted.

The dragons made a mistake when choosing. He was out of place and underqualified for this position he somehow found himself in . . . and they all knew it.

Chapter Twenty-Two

MEILENE

What a waste of time.

I do not think so. It is necessary.

Meilene tapped her foot against the side of the curved table, which always reminded her of the spine of a dragon. She didn't see the point of all this pomp and frill for introducing the Reinaleader's official wing. Most likely, he'll have left running by the next mating, and they would be going through this all over again.

Aletzia grumbled.

Meilene winced. She should try to keep those feelings in check, for her dragon's sake.

Namail nudged her leg under the table and shook his head ever so slightly. She sighed and sat up, pretending to listen with interest to the introduction of the red-haired woman with a horrible crop haircut, Lora Vanne.

Strange choice, naming a woman to his wing. It wasn't very traditional. Not like Meilene could say much against it, as she still had no riders named to her own.

The usually barren meeting room was now filled with riders wishing to impress their new leadership. Most of the commanders wore their formal gear. A bit over the top, in her opinion, but at least they wanted to get on her good side.

As for the Reinaleader's wing, she still hadn't made her mind up about them yet.

Meilene had already met his older brother, the wing lead, with years of exceptional service and several loyal riders under him. He was more comfortable in the command center than his self-conscious brother. Once again, Meilene wondered what she did wrong to end up with *him*.

After the redhead, she met a pair of bearded twin riders, whose names she couldn't remember, a blond rider who had many years in the dragon militia forces, and then several others who were easily forgettable.

"Reina?" Namail's sharp voice brought her attention back to the conversation at hand. All heads turned to face her again.

"Sorry, I missed that. Aletzia needed my attention." She flashed her most brilliant smile.

"Have you made any progress on choosing your wing members?" Namail asked with a hint of amusement in his tone.

The new Reinaleader chanced a glance in her direction but quickly turned away when she caught his eye.

"I haven't made any final decisions yet," she said casually.

"You'll need to do that soon," Namail said. He didn't buy her lie. "A queen can't fly on her own. It's not traditional."

"I've managed this far," she said dismissively.

One of the new wing riders stifled a laugh at this. She glared across the table at him and recognized the redhead. He was one of the riders with her at her trials, which felt like ages ago. He seemed less than enthused to be here.

But it was not the time to argue with Namail, especially in front of this green Reinaleader and his brand new wing, half of whom may pass out from nerves at any moment. Namail wanted her to settle in as smoothly and quickly as possible, but it had to be on her terms.

"It's unorthodox for a ruling queen," Commander Garett pressed. "She needs to make a decision."

"She will," Namail said irritably. "Reina, I know you met with several candidates the other day. Surely, there was at least one of those that will work out?"

She sent him a disparaging look. Those last five riders were dreadful. How could he possibly have thought any of them were a good match? They were almost up there with the type of aides Tork tried to pair her with ages ago. Almost.

"Nope," she said with a smile. "Aletzia did not like their dragons. I guess you'll have to keep searching."

Namail's eyes flashed a warning, but he looked bemused. The commander did not seem pleased with her response.

The commanders were an aged group, still stuck in the old ways.

Namail was on her side, mostly. In this case, he thought she should make a decision to appease the commanders. They thought she should settle on a few senior riders to help her.

Meilene refused to give in to anyone who wasn't a perfect fit for her wing. She was the one who would be stuck with them for years, after all. Not to mention, she didn't think any of their dragons would be able to keep up with the Reina dragon.

Aletzia was quite particular.

I did not mind those dragons we met. There are worse ones that could have been chosen.

A few of the Reinaleader's new wing looked shocked at her exchange with Namail, and the new second in command was not thrilled at her response. What was the brother's name again?

Out of the corner of her eye, she caught the Reinaleader stifling a smile behind his hand. Ryland. She should probably call him by his name.

This entire situation still irked her. A queen dragon should be able to rule by herself. Who made these rules anyway?

That is how it has always been done.

"Either way, you're not a junior anymore. You'll need riders to fly with," Namail reminded her.

"I'll find a wing to come with the next time we—"

"You can't do that," Commander Garett said with pursed lips.

"It wouldn't be proper," the brother added smoothly. "She'll have to make some sort of arrangement."

Meilene scoffed. "I can do whatever I want."

"He's right," Namail said carefully. "You can't fly with just anyone. You're not a junior queen anymore. You are a mated Reina. There are certain expectations of you now, both of you."

Meilene was happy that he, Ryland, was as uncomfortable with this conversation as she was. He shifted in his seat uneasily.

Jian, the senior commander she always liked and who doubled as the Fordde's resident historian, leaned forward. "Traditionally, if the queen doesn't have her full wing decided upon yet, the next best option is to fly with the queen's mate." He nodded in Ryland's direction.

"I'd rather fly alone, Commander Jian." He winced at her words, but she didn't care. She's done being told what to do.

"That's a great idea." Namail turned to Commander Jian. "A perfect alternative while the Reina takes her time to find the *right fit* for her wing. If that's all right with you, Reinaleader Ryland?"

The rider looked startled at being asked for his opinion. "That's fine with us. If she wants to, that is."

"There's no other option," Commander Garett said dismissively.

"I think that's a satisfactory solution for now," Namail said pointedly. "What do you think, Reina?"

Meilene stared at him for several moments before turning her head to glare at the Reinaleader. They talked about this before, and she knows there aren't other options. It doesn't mean she has to like it. "Great. Well, that's great."

Namail nodded. He and the commanders went through other items required to set up the new Reinaleader's wing. This all seemed to be happening so fast and felt like they didn't care that she was in the room. Luckily, Namail was by her side, even if they didn't always agree.

As much as Meilene tried to understand the Fordde, she didn't grow up here like the rest of them. It took time to understand what they wanted from her.

There was no choice but to fly with this new wing of the Reinaleader's. She supposed she should get to know them, since they were being forced together.

Not only would these riders help her, and the Reinaleader with the daily running of the Fordde, but they would also move into the Reina's Maise. Those dozens of empty rooms would soon be filled with complete strangers.

How did queens get through this in the past?

After the group settled on their next steps, they broke for a brief interlude. Namail and the wing second brother went off with the war commander, Calenth.

Before she could excuse herself, the Reinaleader, Ryland, pulled her to the side. "I'm sorry if you felt ambushed back there." He shifted from foot to foot. "You don't have to fly with my wing if you don't want to. We can find something else for you—"

She put up her hand to stop him. "Just don't."

"I don't want you doing anything you aren't comfortable with," he said.

She stared up into his blue eyes and saw the sincerity in them. That incensed her more. "It doesn't matter what I'm comfortable with, so I'll deal with it. Either way, your new wing riders are going to have to learn to keep up with Aletzia, or she'll be the one leaving you behind."

Annoyance filled her when he smiled at her threat.

"I don't know. Maleth is pretty—"

Whatever his dragon was, she didn't hear. A rider came running into the room and went straight up to Commanders Jian and Garett. He was out of breath, and his eyes bulged.

"What happened?" Meilene asked.

"There was an incident, my Reina," Commander Garett said. "Something happened to a wing out past the eastern mountains."

"Several dragons have injuries, and we lost four," the small rider said.

"What?" Meilene said. "What happened?"

An attack!

"I can handle this, Reina," Garett said. "We've had a few similar incidents in the past weeks, which the previous dragon lord determined were weather-related—"

"This doesn't sound like something small." Meilene clenched her jaw. Why did no one take her seriously in these matters? "I'd like to know what happened. Was it an attack? Aletzia thinks so."

"We're not sure," the rider said.

Commander Garett waved him off. "I can give you the full report after—"

"I believe she asked to know the details now." Ryland cut across. She forgot he still stood next to her, as he had thus far remained silent throughout the exchange. "Let's go to a briefing room."

The force coming from the new Reinaleader shocked Meilene. The gruff commander considered him for a moment before conceding. "Of course, sir. Right this way."

This was beyond annoying.

It was going to be tougher than she thought to get the old riders to change their ways. She can't imagine how difficult those loyal to Tork would be if she had kept them around.

After settling in the small room with the bald commander and his young rider, Meilene and Ryland listened to his story intently.

"And after they found the dead patches of trees, what happened?" Ryland pressed. It was hard to read his facial expressions.

"It was hard to see because of the cloud coverage, but something was there. Maybe more than one, I'm not sure. All I know is whatever it was spooked the dragons. It was quick and attacked from above. They didn't even have a chance."

"Did anyone get a good look at it?" Meilene asked.

The weight in her stomach increased the more the rider described the incident. Aletzia tried asking the rider's dragon, but it was young and too frightened to make much sense.

"Yes." The rider's voice was hesitant. "But I'm not sure how accurate it could be given the duress the dragon and rider were under."

"What was it?" Ryland asked.

The timid rider looked back toward his commander, who nodded encouragingly.

"A creature of sorts. It had black scales with dark wings and—"

"Red claws," Meilene finished. Ryland did a double take.

Everyone knew about Meilene's *incident* during her and Aletzia's first ride together. Nobody believed her back then, thanks to the old dragon lord. She'd never been more glad he was gone than right then. The problem would be getting people to believe her.

"Yes. The dragons said it was their enemy."

"There's only one thing that spooks them like that," Meilene said darkly. "And I don't think those creatures being out here is a good sign."

Chapter Twenty-Three

RYLAND

W ould the Reina's quarters ever feel like home?

This new home was larger than the entire Maise he last shared with ten other riders, and the section was meant for merely the two of them. He'd never been in anything so fancy and felt out of place every second in this place. Half of the ornaments on the shelves felt as if they'd break if he even looked at them wrong.

A mousy worker plopped another tattered journal in front of the Reina. He remembered this one, as the Reina seemed to favor her, which was rare. Reina Meilene didn't seem to like many things or people here.

Ryland counted himself on the top of that list.

"I made sure to scour the reserves to find all of these, my Reina," Maeve said. "I almost had to fight with the archivist to let me remove them. He was uncooperative at first."

Meilene smiled. "I hope he didn't give you too much trouble."

"I was able to persuade him," the worker said with a wink. "This one is from Reina Alianne's rider, Torianne. She had details until the last year of her death, although, again, sections were missing, like everything during that time. There were mentions of the Anvers during her first twenty years as a dragon rider . . . then nothing after that."

"Anything useful?" Meilene asked. She pulled her long hair behind her ears and leaned back against the white couch.

"Nothing of note that I could tell," Maeve said. "The journals from her Reinaleader had a bit more information about some of the twisted magic they came from. Something about a fight and a queen's death. Then more about separation of lands and continuation of blood. It's pretty vague and a bit confusing. Should I find those?"

"That would be helpful."

"I'll be back as soon as I can." Maeve backed away with a curtsy, leaving the pair alone.

Reina Meilene had spent the better part of the night tucked away in her quarters and pouring through volumes from the past Reinas and Reinaleaders. Namail mentioned how she couldn't get the journals before, as Tork kept them restricted.

Usually, they were given to the current Reina from the moment the dragon hatched. Tork didn't think it was appropriate to share those journals with Meilene, as she was too junior and didn't understand the workings of the Fordde.

Ryland never understood how that man managed to stay in power for so long. His uncle flew the last queen before she died twenty years prior, and somehow, Tork managed to take over after. Nobody dared to stand up to him before.

"You find anything good in yours?" Meilene nodded at Ryland, acknowledging him for the first time in a while.

At first, she said she wanted to work alone and kicked him out. It took a lot of convincing before she accepted his help. Only after Namail came in to talk to her did she agree and give him an old text to him to review.

Alistair was not happy with this turn of events.

His brother preferred that he stay outside and help the rest of his new wing riders to settle into their Maise. Ryland felt his time would be better spent helping Meilene. He had plenty of time to get to know his new riders. This Reina was more of a mystery, and he needed to figure her out if he wanted to survive this whole thing.

Last he checked on them, everyone in his wing was settling in pleasantly. Lora's brother, Blaise, was one he had to keep an eye on. Ryland knew he passed his independence trials before then and had problems finding a commission outside of the Fordde. He agreed to take Blaise on, only as a favor to his old friend, until he could find something else.

"There was a bit from Reinaleader Baele about some of the best air combat tactics against them. I've marked them over here." He pointed at the leather journal he was reviewing. "It's a little vague but may be helpful to find weaknesses. This one here mentioned some of their origins."

"Oh?" She walked around the small table to his spot. "All of the others are vague on that point." She brushed her hair out of her face and read over his shoulder. "From the east, yes, we know that already, but how far?" she mumbled.

"This part here," he pointed at a diagram, "is how far they made it five hundred years ago. They even managed to take over several of the western islands completely."

"I can't believe they made it so far. Why are they here again?" she mused, flipping through his pages.

"It could be the weather?" Ryland supplied. "We're entering a warm season, and they could be attracted to that? I know it makes for stronger wind currents, which they could be using to travel."

"Hmm, maybe. It wasn't warm out there today based on the reports."

The Reina's eyes focused on the fireplace next to them. It had burned all the way down to its embers. The hour must be late.

On the table underneath their volumes lay the leftover tiles from the Callavan game the Reina and Namail were playing prior. She seemed to enjoy it, at least against her mentor or her aide. Ryland never liked the game himself, as he lacked the patience needed.

"Aletzia was attacked by one. An Anver," she said with forced casualness. Her eyes watched him closely.

As Reina, she was always so confident and certain about everything she did. Even in the days before, where everything seemed a mess, she was steady throughout. This was the first moment he saw cracks in her shield.

"I remember. Everyone heard about it." How could he forget the incident during her first flight with Aletzia? His brother was one of the dragons escorting her at the time, but Ryland was sent away as a punishment from Tork around that time.

The dragon lord thought the attack was nothing, and his brother brushed it off as first flight nerves for someone who didn't grow up in a Fordde.

"And?" She rested her head on her elbow. He could make out the worry lines on her face in the dim light.

"I believe you. If they were in hiding or scouting, and a queen flew by virtually unprotected, they wouldn't pass up that chance."

She nodded.

"My brother," he hesitated. Should he tell her? He didn't want to lie to his new dragonmate already but was unsure how she'd take it. "Alistair flew that day with you. He said he didn't see anything."

"I think I remember him."

"I'm sorry."

"You don't have to be. No one else stood up for me." She flipped through a few pages. The light from the fire cast shadows across her face. "I'm sorry for getting mad today."

"It's fine."

"Thank you for today with Commander Garett. You didn't have to."

"I wanted to make sure you were heard."

Her expression closed off again. Did he say something wrong?

"Your brother seems to prefer the rules," she said with tight lips. "He and Namail will get along great."

He sighed and leaned back in his chair. "Alistair was always one for following the rules and those that make them. He's been a great wing leader for years because of it."

"Your family are all riders. How was that?"

"My father and his brothers all bonded with dragons, as well as their father before." He ran his hand through his hair. "It puts a lot of pressure on you."

"I know the feeling. Parents want your life to be a certain way. When something doesn't go according to their plan . . ." She shrugged.

Ryland nodded. Coming from a royal line in Valchar, naturally she'd gone through a similar experience growing up. He couldn't imagine the pressures that came from her demanding father.

Riders' parents tended to be tough and distant, and his were no different, but there was always love there. He was certain Meilene had it worse in her household.

Even Tork used to drone on about the importance of good family bloodlines. He always liked to brag about his own lineage whenever he got the chance.

"Even though he's older than me," he said. "I bonded with Maleth before my brother did with his dragon, Swali. It made for a lot of unpleasant months."

"I bet." She smiled. She must have been reliving her own bonding time with her dragon.

"Once Alistair had Swali, everything was fine. We even went through some of our first years training together. He was a little older compared to some of the beginners but made it through fine."

"I don't see the difference. I bonded with Aletzia when I was seventeen. Everyone's time is different. The—"

"Dragons always know." He finished bitterly. Unless he was mistaken, she smiled at this. "What about your family? Your father never had any other children. What's he doing about the kingdom with you gone?"

For the second time that night, she closed off to him. Her face hardened, and her lips formed a thin line.

"We're getting nowhere with these. I'm going to bed," she said with a slam of her book. "You should, too."

"Whatever you want, Reina." He grabbed at the books littering the small table. "I'll clean this up. You go on ahead."

Mental note: do not ask about her family in the future. He should make a list somewhere about what could set off the Reina. The one he had so far was quite extensive.

Chapter Twenty-Four

MEILENE

Meilene was in the middle of a pleasant dream when the door to her quarters bounced off the wall with a resounding thud. Before she could register what was happening, Ryland already shot up in bed as the footsteps approached.

Judging by how dark it was, morning had yet to arrive. Meilene groaned.

They are worried. What is it? Aletzia's voice was laced with tiredness.

"I don't know," Meilene said. She pulled the cover up to her chin and glared at the newcomer who dared barge into her Maise like this.

This had better be good.

Her body protested being woken up so early. It took her a while to fall asleep last night, with *him* sleeping on the opposite side of the bed again. When would the uncomfortableness stop?

"What is the meaning of this?" Ryland asked. His voice was hoarse from waking up.

Meilene blushed when she noticed he didn't wear a shirt to bed.

"You should come down to the command center," a rosy-cheeked wing lead said. She remembered this one's name: Kevan. "There's been an attack."

"What?" Meilene threw off her blankets. "Another one?"

"Yes, we can update you at the command center. This one hit some of the villages."

"We'll be right out. Please make sure to prepare Namail. I want him there."

"Yes, ma'am." The rider backed out of the room.

In a flurry of movement, Meilene jumped out of bed, followed closely by Ryland. The two rushed to grab clothes and dress. Both were too busy to care who else was in the room.

There was no time for embarrassment.

"What do you think it is?" she asked as she dug through a chest in search of a warm jacket. The past few days have been absolutely freezing in the mornings. With the sun not slated to rise for at least another hour, she wanted to stay toasty.

You would be warmer if you had a thick hide like me.

Meilene paused. A mass of shadows was barely visible in the dim light outside, but the two dragons wouldn't bother moving for hours still.

"I don't know," Ryland said. "There were similar wind patterns near the Yalian villages this week."

"So many people live there."

Ryland threw on a thick sweater. He decided to opt-out of the formal attire he had dressed in the days prior. "You ready?"

With a nod, Meilene led them out of the room. They weren't the only ones woken up at this early hour. A few of Ryland's new wing riders were also there, bleary-eyed and as if they, too, had just rolled out of bed.

Maeve walked around, making sure everyone had a cup of tea to help with the weariness.

The wing second brother sat in the corner by the fireplace, talking to a commander with their heads bent together. His head popped up when he saw the two emerge from their quarters.

The Maise was alive with noise. Meilene rubbed her arm uncomfortably.

Seeing those strangers reminded her of how awkward it was the night before. Her once quiet Maise was now full of riders she didn't choose.

"Ryland. My Reina." Alistair marched up to his brother and barely paid her a second glance. Lora and her brother, Blaise, huddled around a chart with another worker. "I was catching up with Jian. Some of his wings are located nearby."

"What did you hear?" Ryland asked.

"It was one of the villages," he said briskly. "They're not sure which one yet."

"Have Calenth meet us at the command center," Meilene added. The gruff war commander would be needed.

"I'll send someone once we get there," Alistair said. "I'd rather listen in myself."

"I can catch you up. You should go wake him. Now, please," Ryland said crisply. The wing second nodded and gestured to one of the guards to go with him.

Meilene clenched her fist at her side. Why did no one here listen to her still?

"Are you all right?" Ryland asked. He had a worry in his eyes that made things worse.

"Let's go," she said through gritted teeth. She counted to ten in her head to calm herself. It wasn't his fault, but it was hard to separate that from her emotions.

❦

The command center was buzzing in the early hour. Half of the Fordde must have been stuffed in the offices.

Maleth and I will try to talk to the dragons. I will let you know what we find out.

"Thank you."

A hint of sunlight could be seen out the large windows overlooking the concourse. Outlines of sleeping dragons were visible as bumps throughout the grounds and Meilene could just make out the sight of several flying in the air above.

At least someone had the sense to send out extra patrols, given the circumstances.

Several riders huddled around a large map near the far slab rock wall. Namail was talking with a hook-nosed military leader. As soon as he saw the Reina and Reinaleader, he waved them over.

"Just outside the Yalian villages," Namail said as Meilene rested her hands on the edge of the table. The map splayed out in front of her held no answers. "We have dozens of reports coming in about a creature of some sort."

Meilene and Ryland exchanged a dark look at this. Her blood ran cold, and she felt a prickle on the back of her neck.

"Any injuries?" she asked.

"A few of the locals," a hook-nosed rider said. "Nothing fatal from what's coming in. We checked, and they already have medics assigned on location to help out."

None of the dragons were hurt.

"Aletzia says there are no dragon injuries."

"Good. Good. Show us the nearby maps, Lieutenant Trat," Ryland said. He approached the map beside Meilene and surveyed the lands closely. "Is there anything else close?"

"No, sir." A worker pointed at a smaller series of buildings near the outskirts of the villages. "Their stores also reported damages after the attack. A rot of some sort."

"What caused that?" Meilene asked. She reviewed the section he pointed out. There were close to three thousand households in that village. They had to stop whatever it was from spreading.

"We should send out scouts to see the damage," a wing lead suggested.

"Agreed," Commander Calenth said. He and the brother joined the group by the map. He moved the map to point to a small hillside. "This is where the first reports came from. There have been fires in the area lately, killing the crops."

"We tried to get more information from the wing lead in the area. He was unhelpful." Namail scratched the birthmark on his neck uncomfortably.

"Why's that?" Meilene asked quickly.

Namail cast his eyes downward.

"He's unhappy with some of the new leadership," Ryland supplied. "Some of the older riders have been uncooperative lately, right?"

Her mentor nodded. He refused to meet her eyes. How many more were there like that?

"I'm sure, with time, more of the riders will see how well the Fordde is being run and will come around," Ryland's brother, Alistair, said. "Maybe Maleth can talk to his dragon, Pelal, and reinforce the chain of command to see what information he can get."

He will answer Maleth.

"He's asking," Ryland said.

"Either way," Alistair said. "We have to find out what happened and if it's going to happen again."

Commander Calenth waved his hand back to the map. "Which is exactly why I think we should send two scouts to confirm—"

"Where there was an attack barely hours ago, are you insane?" Meilene scoffed divisively. "I'm not sending them out on a suicide mission. We know what's there, and you've already seen the report. Send at least two full wings."

"We don't want to cause a panic," the brother said delicately. He pushed his sleeves up. "That's the last thing this leadership needs right now—"

"And I'm not leaving an entire village unprotected. Send them all."

"I'm not sure we have the forces to spare, Reina," Calenth said. "We have several wings out on assignment."

"I'm sure we have some to spare."

"But—" Alistair started.

"Alistair," Ryland said impatiently. "Just do it."

The wing second looked ruffled for a minute but quickly regained his composure. "Right away, Reinaleader."

The red-haired siblings exchanged exasperated glances at this.

"Keep us updated if you hear anything else," Ryland said to the group as they dispersed.

"Will do," Lora said.

Meilene turned around and noticed she was left alone with Ryland and Namail. She could hear the blood pounding against her skull, and her mouth was dry.

"Are you all right?" the young rider asked hesitantly.

Namail stayed back cautiously.

"Don't think you're doing me any favors." She kept her voice low and clenched her hands into fists at her side. "I can handle those commanders on my own."

"I know how difficult they can be," Ryland said. "I've worked under them for years."

"And that makes you better than me?"

Ryland threw his hands up. "I thought I would—"

"Well, don't." She shoved past him toward her own offices with only the sound of blood pounding against her skull to fill the silence.

A break from everyone was needed, and no one dared interrupt her there. It was one of the last places she had of her own.

"Let me come with you." Namail jogged up beside her.

"Can't I be left alone for two minutes?" Meilene slammed the door behind them and threw herself into a chair.

The Reinaleader is trying to help you.

"I don't want his help!" She winced. "Sorry, Aletzia."

Namail carefully sat in the seat next to her and crossed his legs. He waited expectantly, looking about the room, as if her new drapes were the most interesting item he'd ever seen.

The Reina's offices were slowly being decorated according to her desires. She had them change out the coloring for something light and added several plants and paintings that reminded her of home, Valchar.

"Stop it," she said to Namail.

"I'm not doing anything," he said pleasantly. "You're the one making a scene."

Meilene shook her head. "I don't like this. Why didn't you say it would be like this?"

"You always knew it would be difficult. With time and stability, it will get better. Keep patient."

Meilene got up and paced around the small room. Namail's eyes followed her path. "I have been patient. For over three years. Everyone keeps saying to give it time, and it doesn't mean I have to like it."

"If you had the backing of the Reinaleader and worked as a united team, that would help. Even if he's gone after the next mating, you don't need an enemy like that in your leadership."

"He's helping a little too much. You don't know what it's like to have someone come in and try to take over."

Namail smiled. "That's how some of the commanders are seeing it. You have to put yourself in their position."

"But this is the Reinaleader!"

Namail leaned forward and clasped his hands together, his expression one of grave seriousness. "It won't change. Never. If it's not him, then there will be others in the role. You must figure out how to work with newcomers . . . and so do the commanders. We have to figure it out together."

"It's unfair." She sank into her seat and pressed her fingers against her temple. "My Maise is full of strangers. I don't see you having to live with them."

Namail cocked his head to the side. "As much as I'd like to help you in that area, I'm not the Reina. It'd be odd if I casually walked into your Maise and crawled into bed with the rider."

Meilene cracked a smile. "As pleasant as it is to visualize that scenario, unfortunately, you can't. It has to be me."

"This new Reinaleader is not an invalid, has no prior loyalties to Tork, and doesn't seem to be ill-tempered. He's very inexperienced, but it could have been much worse."

"I don't even know what I was expecting." She ran her hands through her hair. "We never really talked about this part."

"It's difficult to prepare anyone for. I don't envy you, but I do have faith in you."

"That's one person at least."

"More than one, I'm certain." Namail slapped his leg and jumped up. "Now that that's settled, you should keep busy. Why don't we go down to oversee the newest class's drills on the concourse? It will be good for you to be seen throughout campus."

"I love that idea." The young riders were always easier to deal with, especially compared to some of the cynical, tenured ones at the Fordde.

"It should be a weekly occurrence. I'll make sure we invite the new Reinaleader as well," he said with a smirk. "Helps to show that united front."

Meilene made a strangled noise, but he silenced her with a stern look. That man knew how to push her buttons.

He is always kind and helps scratch behind my ears.

"Hush you," she said dryly. They both know they'd be nothing without him.

❧❧❧❧❧❧ ❧❧❧❧❧❧

Say what some will about Namail's methods, but going to visit the new class was a brilliant idea.

Days later, Meilene found herself and the new Reinaleader walking among the group of jittery youngsters. They reminded her of the early months with Aletzia. Meilene was once that anxious girl, afraid to puncture a hole in her dragon's wing by handling her too roughly.

You'd never. My wings are strong and unbending. Unbreakable like a mountain.

Meilene had since learned that.

The sun cascaded streams of gold as they walked around the group of riders, and their young dragons, far from perfect in their formation on the concourse ground. Her only decent instructor, Liam Mal, helped get the youngsters all together when he spotted the pair approaching.

"Now, everyone, line up, line up. Just like we practiced." The sandy-haired instructor waved his arms in an attempt at producing a semblance of order in the group. "Everybody! This is your Reina and Reinaleader. Please show some measure of decorum."

Meilene smiled as the youngsters tripped over themselves to get in line, twittering at the sight of the newcomers. At least they were quick about it.

Ryland also looked amused by the nervousness of this group. He wasn't used to this. Meilene was.

"How is the class doing?" Meilene asked as Liam escorted them through the rows of dragons and their riders. She nodded at several as they passed.

"They are progressing right on track, my Reina."

A small, dark-haired boy stood next to a towering black dragon. Meilene paused by the pair.

That one is Speni, sired by the prior Reina, Alianne.

She addressed the boy directly. "Your dragon grows quite large. How much is Speni eating?"

The boy squawked at being addressed by the Reina. Liam nodded encouragingly at the youngster. "He's already moving on to large bucks now, my Reina. Twice a week already."

"He's got quite an appetite, like Aletzia. She never seems to stop eating."

"Yes, ma'am."

Aletzia was eating almost daily now. She, alone, could bankrupt the Fordde based on the number of bucks and hares she went through.

I am Reina, and as such, need to be well fed.

"How old is he?" she asked.

"I've had Speni for fifteen months now." He turned back to his dragon with a loving look. "He's bigger than some of the two-year-old dragons."

"He should still double in size by the time he is fully mature," Instructor Liam added. "Mash's dragon will be one of the larger dragons."

"A large dragon is a sign of a well-taken-care-of dragon," Meilene said. "And a sign that he and his rider will do remarkable things to come."

"Thank the Reina for such a compliment," the instructor said.

"There's no need." Meilene waved her hand. "I look forward to seeing your dragon out in the field one day, Mash."

"I'm sure he'll be a fearsome dragon out there," Ryland added. He caught Meilene's eye and smiled, perhaps reliving one of his memories with Maleth, like Meilene was. One day, she'd like to hear him recount his own experiences growing up in the Fordde in detail.

"Thank you," the boy squeaked out.

"Now, if you come this way," the instructor led them toward the end of the row, "we can have our new class take to the air in a demonstration of *everything proper they have learned for you*." He finished with a glare around the group.

"That would be great," Ryland said.

"Tell them not to be nervous," Meilene added. "They are new, and we understand it will not be perfect. We just want to see them try."

"Of course, Reina." The instructor nodded to himself before setting off around the group, ensuring the young group was prepared to begin.

"Go ahead." Ryland stepped back and gestured for her to lead the way.

Meilene smiled as she remembered trying to bumble her way through their beginning flights, when they weren't too busy fighting for their lives.

I never bumbled. My wings were untried, but once used, I was a glorious flier.

They'd come such a long way since those junior riders that she was excited to see what the future held for he and her dragon.

Chapter Twenty-Five

RYLAND

"What do you want to do about Lottle's wing? They're still hesitant to fully conform to the new leadership?" Alistair asked from his spot at the curved table.

Ryland covered his face in his hands. They had been at this for hours without a break, and he was beyond exhausted.

The walls of the command center felt like they were getting closer. He focused on the far slab wall and studied its smooth lines. "What do you think, Raphael? You've flown with him before. Think he'll come around, or should we release him?"

Ryland.

"One minute, Maleth."

A wing of dragons landed unsteadily out in the concourse. They must have been that wing of juniors assigned under Commander Calenth. He remembered overseeing their assignment ceremonies with the Reina two weeks ago. The group was excited to have the Reina oversee their assignments, but when she showed up, the group turned into a jumbled mess of nerves.

It was the Reina. Meilene had such a powerful presence whenever they went down to oversee the classes that it overwhelmed the green riders, no matter how nice she was. At least the younger riders weren't afraid of her yet, as it wasn't drilled into them at their stage. It was clear why she preferred visiting with them.

Either way, Namail and his brother insisted they continue doing it, so their presence was known throughout the Fordde. It made sense.

Ryland almost laughed when one of the riders slipped out of his saddle and nearly face-planted in the mud while an instructor ran around, trying to get them all ready.

Whoever designed the command center understood this place. The room was perfect for keeping an eye on all the comings and goings within the Fordde. There wasn't much that could get by from this viewpoint, and there wasn't much missed in the command center from his spot right now.

"Lottle is a tough one but was always more of a talker." Raphael shrugged. "Once he sees Tork isn't coming back, he'll want his commissions from the new Reina. He'll have no choice."

"That one tends to jump to whoever will benefit him the most," Blaise said. "I've worked with him before, and he's insufferable."

"That doesn't matter. I doubt he's adventurous enough to declare independence," the youngest commander, Dynial, added. "He'll fall in line."

"He can be made to," Garett said pointedly. "There *are* methods the old dragon lord used."

The room filled with a heavy silence.

Ryland scratched along his jaw and thought for a moment. He was aware of how much everyone in the room studied him. He'd rather not use Maleth or Aletzia to force dragons and their riders into anything. Starting things off that way would set a dangerous precedent for the Fordde.

Leaders in the past used the dragon law to bend riders to their will, but it never seemed to be the good ones who resorted to that measure. Ryland would prefer to not use Maleth to force anyone against their will. They'd never make any allies that way.

"I'd rather not resort to that," he said. "Let's send a notice for him to come back to the Fordde within a fortnight. Meilene and I can meet with him and see what will make him happy."

"Good idea." Raphael nodded approvingly. "He'll be much more malleable in person."

"Thanks, Raphael."

Even though he had never met him before the mating, Ryland liked his new rider. Raphael was one of his brother's best additions to his wing so far. He was level-headed, extremely smart, and impartial when it came to big decisions. Not to mention the fact he worked a lot with the smaller Forddes and knew many of the riders personally.

The last three weeks had been the most chaotic of his life. Ever since Maleth mated with Aletzia, he barely had a moment to himself. Just when he thought he was starting to figure things out at the Fordde, some new issue came up that sent him into a tailspin. It was good to have smart people on his side.

At least he had his new wing to help him through most of it. Even if they were as lost as he was half the time, at least he wasn't the only one. The one who struggled to fit in was Lora's brother,

Blaise. As if he blamed Lora for him being stuck at the Fordde, Blaise tended to lash out whenever the new wing struggled with their flight practices.

If it wasn't for the promise he made to Lora, he would have kicked Blaise off already. Alistair would be more than happy if he removed him, but Ryland was determined to give him another chance, and it was his decision that mattered.

For the time being.

While dragon bonds were law around here, that didn't mean every rider was pleased with their new Reina being in power or the young, inexperienced rider chosen as Reinaleader. Not that it would change anytime soon.

Meilene would always be Reina. There was no changing that. Her mate was a different story.

It varied across the queens of old. The new Reinaleader could change as often as every new mating, or Aletzia could choose to stick with one mate her entire life.

Ryland knew which choice everyone was hoping for.

Ryland.

"Great," Alistair said. "I've noted it and will make the arrangements to bring Lottle's wing back on assignment."

One of the elder commanders, with a scar on his cheek, opened his mouth, as if he had an objection. Calenth thought better and closed it.

The bald Commander Garett didn't like their plan, either. He leaned forward in his seat with a shrewd look. "The old dragon lord would have never shown such weakness. He would have swiftly dealt with any mutiny. They need to be made an example of."

"That's not going to get us anywhere," Ryland said. "If we punish every rider who worked with Tork, we'd be left with less than half, yourself included, Commander."

The commander's face screwed into a grimace, but he kept the rest of his comments to himself.

Garett was one of those few Meilene kept after taking over from Tork. His knowledge of the running of the Fordde, along with his relationships with some of the lords, would hopefully prove useful, even if he had a sour attitude most days.

Ryland.

"I reviewed the accounts from the last eighteen months, and it's not as terrible as we first thought," Lora said with a nod toward Ryland. When his oldest friend was excited at the prospect of joining the Reinaleader's new wing, she was less than thrilled when he assigned her the task of righting all the accounts from the past few years. "Eventually, a trip can be arranged to gather the books from some of the smaller Forddes, but the old commander there said it'll have to wait."

"To see if there's a new mate next season, you mean?" Ryland finished with a wry smile. A few riders shifted uncomfortably, but nobody responded. Blaise bit back a smile. At least Lora had the decency to look guilty about it. "Just start the preparations for now, at least."

"Already on it." The redhead pursed her lips. She'd been having problems getting details from the older riders. A lot of them didn't like having to answer to a young female rider, no matter if she was a part of the Reinaleader's wing.

"I'm certain we'll be able to get the numbers back in shape remotely for now," Commander Jian said. "Historically, the old

Reinaleaders didn't visit the smaller Forddes until later years in their leadership."

As hurtful as it was, the commanders at those smaller Forddes had a point. There was hesitation throughout the Fordde to make any major changes or concessions until they knew what the next mating brought them.

It didn't make sense to change processes if a new Reinaleader was coming in every few months. That would create complete chaos.

No, it was better to keep most things as-is. Meilene could make changes later on. Things would be easier.

A part of him hoped Maleth wouldn't fly next season, but he kept those thoughts far away from his friends and even farther away from his dragon. He felt terrible for what it would mean for Meilene, who already seemed to struggle with her current dragonmate as it was.

Surely, there was somebody else better suited for this than him?

Ryland!

"What?" Did Maleth hear that?

The Reina needs you.

"Problems with Maleth?" Raphael asked with concern etched on his face. He turned to the window, as if he could pick out the dragon among the hundreds sunbathing on the grounds or the few dozen gliding through the sky.

"No," Ryland said slowly as he tried to decipher Maleth's incoherent message. "It's Meilene."

"Is there something wrong?"

"No." He shook his head. "He doesn't sound worried. I don't know what he is."

"Is she still on her morning flight?" Alistair said. "It's late, and I haven't seen her come into the command center yet."

Reina Meilene spent every morning flying around the grounds with Aletzia. She said it helped clear her head before starting her day. Ryland thought she preferred having the solitude from the crowd of riders thrust into her life.

"I don't think so," he said. When he thought of it, he hadn't seen her go out for her flight that morning, either. Aletzia was easy to pick out from the command center. "Maleth says she requires my presence."

"You should go find her," Raphael said. "Don't want to keep the Reina waiting."

Alistair pursed his lips. "We're in the middle of this. You should stay and help us with all the new militia assignments."

"That can wait," Ryland said dismissively. "Why don't you guys finish up here, and I can review in the evening."

"But we need to—fine. Go ahead."

The last thing he wanted was to keep her waiting on him. Anything could set off the temperamental Reina, and they'd finally managed to settle into a somewhat familiar pattern, at least.

"Alistair, when you're done, why don't you check in on the patrols that just came in?"

His brother pursed his lips and nodded. Good. That'll keep him occupied and out of his hair for a while.

Since the attack near Yalian, the entire Fordde was on edge, especially the dragons. Even though none were old enough to have faced them the last time that the Anvers had come this far into human lands, they still put fear into the most seasoned riders and dragons.

I am not afraid.

"There's not a lot that scares you."

Why should there be?

"It would do you good to have some humility sometimes. Now, where am I going?"

Maleth flooded him with a series of discombobulated thoughts and images. Eventually, Ryland understood where he wanted him to go.

Within minutes, he was outside the doors of the hatchery in search of his Reina. The dragon emblem on the door brought back memories of when he used to be placed on guard duties there. Back when all his problems started. That felt like a lifetime ago.

A guard approached him before he could enter. "She won't let anyone in, sir." He must still be in his early teens. He forgot how young they would start.

"Who won't?"

"Aletzia," the rider said plainly. "We tried to help, and she did not like that, so we're back here." He nodded at the other guard.

"I think she should be fine with you." The second guard opened the double doors and gestured for him to go through.

Ryland entered cautiously, not knowing what to expect. Why would she be fine with him and not the others?

"Let us know when we can come in," the young rider called from the door before firmly closing it.

The room was as bright as he remembered it and even larger than he recalled. Hundreds of eggs ranging from twenty to hundreds of years old remained from previous clutches.

They wait for their riders.

Ryland wished he took the time to soak it all in when he worked here before. He sighed. How much he missed those days when his only problem was getting off in time to make it to the parlors for a drink or figuring out how to sneak out of the Fordde for his other activities.

The floor was covered in hay to keep the room warmer than the rest of the Fordde. It was good for the eggs but would get all over your clothes and stuck on your shoes. It used to take him forever to clean his uniform after a shift in the hatchery.

On a raised platform in the middle of the giant room lay the golden dragon. What was she doing here? Aletzia raised her head at the new intrusion and made a humming sound, but it wasn't an upset noise.

The guard was scared for no reason. The Reina dragon didn't pose a threat.

He walked by a large egg that he remembered was from an old Reina's clutch and another small one that had come from the last queen the Fordde had. The dragons inside would be safe in their shells for years to come.

When he passed a blue egg that reached just below his waist, he stopped.

This one was different.

It had a fresh membrane attached, and its shell was thinner than the rest. This wasn't from a prior clutch. He reached out, and it radiated heat.

It was the first time he'd seen a fresh egg before. All the eggs he used to watch over had already been here for years.

"Not that one!"

He must have jumped at least several feet in the air.

"What?" He whipped around to see the small brunette standing on the dais beside him. She still had her riding jacket on, and her hair hung in a jumbled mess as if she didn't have time to comb it this morning.

"That one stays. Aletzia says it'll bond along with others soon." Meilene pointed to a cluster of six fresh eggs next to the dragon. "The other one." She pointed to a large green egg. "Should be moved up on the back dais. It won't hatch for a while."

"For a while?" he repeated in a hollow voice.

"Sixty, maybe seventy years. Hard to tell."

"How do you know all this?" He stumbled over a chunk of hay as he moved beside her. Several fresh eggs lay on the dais beside her.

Meilene's chest heaved, as if she was out of breath. Had she moved all the eggs on her own?

"I don't. Aletzia knows." She wrung her hands together, and her eyes pivoted around the room. "Nobody is coming in, silly."

"The guards said they'll wait," Ryland said. It was unclear if the dragon or her rider heard him as Meilene focused on the eggs in front of her.

"You sure about this one?" Meilene grabbed the green egg and gently rolled it toward the edge of the dais. "Sounds like an impressive rider."

To someone not familiar with riders and their bond, Meilene may have seemed like she'd gone insane. Ryland knew
better. Aletzia must be giving her some interesting instructions for each egg.

"Here." He jumped forward. "Let me."

Together, they pushed the heavy egg toward the platform
that Aletzia thought it needed to go on. She wouldn't allow
any other place.

They settled it on the dais and pushed a nest of hay around
it. This set of eggs had sat around for over two hundred
years. Their riders still had plenty of time before showing if
Aletzia was correct.

We wait as long as we have to.

Maleth was in his egg for over five hundred years. He
always wondered how the dragons chose their partner and
why Maleth picked him out of so many riders.

"Thanks." Meilene wiped the sweat from her forehead.
"Aletzia has done nothing but shout orders at me for the past
hour."

"You should have called me sooner."

"I meant to. I kept getting distracted." She reached out to
another smaller egg. "She's a bit demanding right now."

Meilene's eyes glazed over as she listened to something
Aletzia said. Most likely a retort back, as a gentle smile filled
the Reina's face.

*Aletzia wants you to know that she is only as demanding as
she should be.*

"Please tell her that there's no judgment here."

Aletzia grunted and moved to find a better position to lay, and Ryland finally saw it. That must be why she was so concerned with having any riders here.

"Is that?" he asked.

"Yeah." Meilene wiped the sweat off her face.

The new Reina egg glowed brightly. It was easily larger than the others and already gleamed in gold and bronze colors. A warmth of feelings and tenderness radiated from Maleth.

Ryland tucked a stray hair behind her ear. He was surprised she didn't stop him, but she must have felt a similar pull from her dragon.

Meilene turned to gaze at the golden egg with him. "She won't let me touch it yet. I'm sure she'll settle in a few hours and then we can let the others help."

"It's . . . big." Was that the best he could come up with?

"I know."

"It's amazing."

"It's crazy to think of," she said. "I've known since she was hatched that this day would come, but it all seems surreal."

"It's crazy to think that they come from something so small." Ryland ran his hand over the bumpy surface of the closest brown egg. It reminded him of the one Maleth came from seventeen years prior.

"It's a lot of hassle coming from one tiny egg." Meilene smiled and jerked her head at Aletzia. "But worth it."

"Definitely worth it." He gestured at the golden egg. "She'll be a great Reina one day."

Yes, she will.

That was new. He did a double take and looked around for the source of the voice. "Was that Aletzia?"

"Yes." Meilene had a brilliant smile on her face. This time, it was for him.

No matter what happens during the next mating, this would never change. This next Reina would hatch years from now, sired by his dragon and Aletzia.

Nothing would ever change that.

In a movement that may have been too bold, he put his hand on Meilene's shoulder. She jerked at the sudden contact but, for once, didn't seem to mind the Reinaleader's presence.

For a moment, they stood frozen. Meilene leaned her head back and rested against his shoulder. In a moment he'd remember forever, he felt both Maleth and Aletzia's pleasure flood his emotions together.

The bloodlines will go on. The bloodlines will remain strong.

He wasn't even sure which voice said that. At that moment, he didn't care.

Chapter Twenty-Six

MEILENE

W ho let all these people in?

Would you like me to get rid of them? I can raise an alarm to call them away.

"No need to resort to those measures . . . yet." Meilene rubbed her temple. She was feeling ill from all the noise.

If only it wasn't improper to kick everyone out so soon. It was essential the riders and commanders at this Fordde liked her, no matter how much she wished for the quiet of her own quarters.

This was the safest spot she could be in. She sat on a plush sofa, tucked away from the crowd of riders. Someone, somehow, decided that a gathering in the Reina's Maise as a celebration for Aletzia's first clutch was a fitting celebration. The once empty Maise was packed more than Meilene was used to, even given her new *roommates*.

A long table was brought in, and food was set out for the guests. Perfect. They would never leave now. She pinched the bridge of her nose and squeezed her eyes shut.

When they arrived at the packed Maise, Namail was smart. He immediately took her to the side and muttered a few harsh threats to ensure she'd stay.

How had he known she was planning an escape route within the first five seconds?

Several of the commanders wanted to make toasts, which annoyed her to no end. Maeve made sure she had more than enough wine to keep herself sane during it all. That poor girl was running around, checking that all the plates were replenished. She'd have to give her a day off afterward.

Jian drawled on for too long for his toast, while Garett managed to make his speech about himself. No one called upon herself or Ryland to say anything.

After saying some personal words to each of the commanders, she managed to slip to the outskirts of the commotion. It was nice to finally be alone with her thoughts.

It still didn't seem real. All those eggs came from her Aletzia.

Where else would they come from? I am Reina.

"I know you are."

The den Aletzia slept in was empty. It was strange to not be greeted by the sight of her dragon resting on her favorite stone.

I am not far.

The Reina dragon wouldn't leave her new clutch for a while. She'd stay until their shells hardened, and she could be certain of their safety.

Meilene thought that was a bit overdramatic, but what did she know?

Aletzia grumbled a response.

Maleth was also absent from their den. Ryland told her the brown dragon kept guard near the hatchery. At least it wasn't only her dragon hovering over the new clutch and pitching a fit with any newcomers.

Aletzia still hadn't let anyone else in besides herself, Ryland, and Namail. The latter was only allowed because he had forced his way in and scolded the dragon when she tried to snap at him. He was the only person either of them would tolerate that from.

Since the Fordde riders weren't allowed into the hatchery still, they decided on throwing a small party in her Maise . . . to her great displeasure.

Namail was being his usual quiet self after his initial bout of schmoozing dried up. She noticed her mentor took up a similar position in solitude against the far wall. She should have talked with him but feared someone would pull her aside for more congratulations before she could make it there.

Quartermaster Gaelen already told her twice how excited he was to outfit the new riders and their dragons when they hatched, while Commander Yannet droned on for twenty minutes about the large clutch size and how it meant fruitful seasons ahead. There was an endless stream of those offering their congratulations and advice to the Reina and Reinaleader.

Thirty-seven new eggs were cause for celebration, no matter where loyalties lay. At least that was one thing she managed to do right since taking over from Tork.

There were a few others who seemed out of place, including the Reinaleader's wing riders. Only one of them spoke to her that night, the white Kono's rider, Raphael. He was nice and seemed incredibly sharp from the limited interactions they'd had so far. The rest of his wing, she was still unsure of.

The Reinaleader's wing will do well.

"How do you know?"

Aletzia didn't answer. She must have returned her attention to her clutch.

Ryland kept busy most of the night, chatting with his new wing and some of the commanders. He made sure to check in on Meilene a few times during the night but gave her space. She didn't feel up to entertaining anyone—even him— today.

The wing second was enjoying himself, entertaining the masses. Ryland's brother was more comfortable in this setting. She noticed he kept a close eye on the Reinaleader throughout the night, as he did on most days.

The wing second liked to be in the know for every key decision, as if he thought he was Reinaleader himself. She didn't like the way he looked at her; it reminded her of the way Tork used to. She'd have to keep an eye on him.

Those negative thoughts would get her nowhere. She pushed them back or else Aletzia would hear.

It was a stressful day for the Reina dragon, and anything that caused Aletzia stress gave grief to Meilene, too.

"It's been a long day."

"What?" She jumped. Somehow, Ryland managed to sneak up on her.

"Here." He handed her a glass of herbal tea and leaned against her armrest.

Just what she needed. She took the cup in both hands and clutched it for warmth. "Thanks," she muttered.

Ryland sighed as he surveyed the small crowd. "There are so many people here."

Meilene nodded and blew on her cup.

"I hate these pompous events. Never did understand the point of them. Not that I was invited to them before." He shrugged. "Wasn't the right kind of rider, apparently."

"I was." Meilene stared at the table in front of her. "They're not worth it, even though the food is usually delicious."

"The pastries were amazing. I stuffed myself with several."

"Mm-huh."

"I was thinking of calling it a night," he said, stuffing his hand in his pockets.

"What?" That was strange, as he didn't seem tired when she had last checked on him.

"Want to join me in sneaking out?"

"So much." She grabbed the arm he offered up and let him lead her back to their private quarters. She caught Namail's eye so he would know where she went off to. He nodded encouragingly.

The party would continue without them. That was enough socializing for her, and hopefully, her old friend could sneak out, too.

As soon as the doors shut behind them, Meilene leaned against the wall and let out a sigh of relief.

"You doing all right?" Ryland folded back the top blanket on their bed. He kicked off his shoes and settled on the bed, still fully dressed. "Maleth has been driving me insane all day with his constant fretting. I assume Aletzia is the same?"

Meilene grabbed her dressing gown and threw it over her arm. "You have no idea. Well . . . I guess you do," she added as an afterthought.

She disappeared behind a screen to change into her night-clothes.

Tiredness seeped into every muscle of her body. She didn't realize how exhausted she was until that point. She heaved her body into bed and laid on her stomach.

Climbing under the covers seemed like an impossible task.

"Do you think they care that we are gone?" she asked, kicking her legs and picking at a piece of fluff on her pillow.

"I doubt it . . . for me, I mean," he said quickly. "I'm sure your absence is missed."

"Not by the commanders. They never cared much before."

"At least everyone is happy with the new batch of eggs," he said. "Even grumpy, old Calenth."

Meilene lifted her head. His brows were furrowed, and his eyes glazed over.

Was he that worried about Aletzia's clutch before?

What is there to worry about? I am a dragon and I lay my eggs.

Sounds simple enough, the way the dragons looked at it. Things were easier for them. She understood his worries, as she used to have them.

"It'll be a strong batch of riders," she said determinedly.

Aletzia echoed her statement and sent loving thoughts her way. The rush of emotions nearly overwhelmed her.

"Tonight was a lot," he said. "But at least everyone is in a good mood."

"Who knows how long that'll last." Her eyelids started drooping and she struggled to force them open. "I wonder how long Aletzia will keep herself cooped up there."

"I'm sure she'll be back within a week or two and roaring to go. At least, that's what Jian said, and he knows more than anybody."

"Uh-huh." Meilene lifted her head to check the empty den again. She forgot how comforting the presence of her dragon was, especially at night.

I am still with you.

Laughter filtered in through the wall. The party showed no signs of dying down anytime soon.

At least everyone had the decency to know to never enter a Reina's private quarters unless it was a dire emergency. They wouldn't be disturbed.

"I know you haven't picked wing riders yet," Ryland said, "but you don't have to hide in here all day. You should eat with us tomorrow night if you want. It'll be better than staying cooped up by yourself. It's your Maise, and you don't have to hide."

Meilene stuffed her face into the fluffy pillow and inhaled scents of lavender. Was she that obvious?

"I know it's uncomfortable with people you barely know. Some of them, I didn't even know four weeks ago."

She lifted her head up and studied his face closely. "Why'd you pick them?"

It didn't make sense. Why let his brother practically pick his entire wing when he could have anyone he wanted?

Anyone with a good sense would have stacked their wing with riders loyal to them, no matter their skills. All the leaders of the past knew to do that.

His lips parted slightly as a sigh escaped. "I didn't have many people who would be good for something like this. I didn't exactly hang around with the best crowds, as you'd know from Namail's report. Alistair worked with a lot of great riders. Plus, I wanted what was best for the Fordde."

"That sounds oddly altruistic for a repeat rule-breaker taking part in illegal races." He laughed, and it was a lovely sound. She wanted to sleep, but curiosity overcame her. "Why'd you do it?"

"Just didn't seem to find anything I was good at. Felt nice to be good at something for once."

"Hmm."

"What?"

"Nothing." She curled up on her side so he couldn't see her face. She couldn't keep her eyelids open any longer. "I'll think about your offer for dinner."

He snorted. "It's not a formal invitation or anything. It's just eating with the rest of us."

This was foreign to her, as Meilene never had a wing of her own to spend time with. She didn't know how things like this went at the Fordde.

"I'll consider it. Have a good sleep."

His voice was low when he spoke, "Goodnight, Meilene."

Sleep well. I will guard the eggs.

"I know you will."

Exhaustion overtook her, and within minutes, she fell into a deep sleep, not caring that she wasn't flush against her side of the bed as she should be. She could feel his body just inches away from hers, radiating heat.

It was comforting to know she wasn't in all of this alone.

When Meilene woke, something felt off. She didn't bother opening her eyes, as it was still hours away from morning. She was warm and toasty and was still groggy from the night before.

An awful smell filled her nostrils. It was putrid and disgusting but somehow familiar.

What was that?

She flipped around and cracked an eye open. Her heart stopped.

A figure towered over top of her.

Chapter Twenty-Seven

RYLAND

The sound of Meilene's shriek woke him with a jolt. Adrenaline pumped into his heart, and all he registered was that something was wrong. Very wrong.

Someone standing next to their bed. A flash of metal caught his eye in the moonlight. He grabbed at Meilene and pulled her toward him as the blade sliced through the air.

Meilene cried out in pain, and the two of them fell in a crumble onto the floor. After untangling himself from the blankets, he pulled them both up and pushed her behind him. There was no time to check if she was all right.

It was hard to see in this light, and their attacker was dressed in all black, with his face hidden. The attacker moved quickly and with purpose toward the Reina again. Ryland threw her to the side as the blade missed him by inches. He couldn't let anything happen to her.

"You," the man bellowed, his voice laced with venom.

Ryland!

Maleth's thoughts screamed at him as the man charged again. He blocked out the sounds of his dragon and Meilene screaming at him and tried to stop the deranged man. All he could hear was the blood pumping against his ears.

The blade swiped at him and caught his chest. It felt white-hot where the steel made contact, but it wasn't deep. He'd had worse.

The man drew his arm back to strike again, this time with lethal force. Ryland caught the man's wrist and pushed back with all his strength.

All that ran through his mind was that he couldn't let him get to Meilene.

"Ryland!"

The man forced the blade closer to him, and the two fell to the floor heap. A hand scratched at his face while the one with the blade inched toward his chest. Ryland reached out to grab the knife but missed and grabbed at the blade directly. The pain that burst from his hand was unbearable as it cut through skin. He couldn't let go and pushed back with everything he had.

Ryland aimed a kick at the man. He managed to catch him in his chest and got only a second of reprieve. The man lunged at him again.

A scream reverberated across the room, and new voices thundered into the room.

Rough hands grabbed at him and separated the two. He struck out at the intruders and recognized one of the voices.

"Ryland, stop!"

He froze before making contact with a newcomer.

Someone helped him to his feet. Not just someone, it was one of their guards. The shouting must have got his attention.

Pain burst from his side as he struggled to catch his breath. He struggled to keep his eyes focused as he searched for Meilene.

"Are you okay?" She rushed up to him with bulging eyes. She grabbed his arm and checked over him, as if searching for additional wounds.

"Get Royce in here and call the medics." That was his brother's voice. Smart of him to call for his wing rider, as Royce was medically trained and could help Meilene.

Spots filled his eyes as a commotion sounded across the room to where a pair of guards subdued the attacker. There were several grunts and scraping of furniture against the hard floors.

"How did he get in here?" Alistair asked harshly. "Where were the guards before?"

"The ones outside must have left." Raphael pointed at the group holding down the attacker. "They just started their shift."

The short medic ran into the bedroom. Royce pointed at the blood on Ryland's shirt. "Let's get you looked at."

"No. Help her first." Ryland's head stopped spinning, and he pointed at the trail of blood down Meilene's arm. Her hands shook, and her skin was oddly pale.

Ryland helped Meilene to a plush couch, holding around her shoulders.

Royce knelt in front of her and examined her cut. "At least those aren't too deep." He grabbed strips of cloth from a bag.

Ryland's chest sagged with relief.

The medic produced a bottle and poured a clear liquid on her lacerations. Meilene hissed when he wiped at them.

"It's fine," she said. "Just stings a little."

"I don't think it'll leave a scar." Royce's voice was smooth and calming. Meilene seemed to relax under his ministration. "It could have been much worse."

"Here." Alistair pressed a piece of cloth into Ryland's hands. His face was wrinkled in worry as he stared at Ryland's wounds. "Put some pressure on your wounds for now."

Ryland took the cloth absentmindedly and dabbed at his bloodied hands. When he had a moment to process what had happened, the pain from the puncture on his chest and the gashes on his hands came in full force. He allowed his brother to help him with the bleeding.

Raphael came running up to the pair, looking out of breath. He gestured for them to move away from where Meilene was sitting. "Remember that disgruntled ex-wing lead, Simeon Aone?"

"That was him?" Ryland exclaimed.

"Why?" Alistair asked.

"Some grudge against the Reina," Raphael whispered. "He was pretty close with the old dragon lord and was let go in the cuts after the mating."

That would explain why the man was focused on hurting Meilene. Ryland felt his blood boil at the mere thought. Maleth echoed his anger.

Tell them to bring him to me. I will make sure he never harms you or the Reina again.

It was difficult to separate his dragon's thoughts from his own, and he had to keep a level head. He pushed those thoughts away as much as he wanted to comfort Maleth.

"Do you think he knew the guards?" Alistair asked. "We can't find the ones that should have been here. Why did they leave their post?"

If they had issues with the guards, that meant there are bigger problems throughout the Fordde to think of. They had to get to the bottom of this right away.

"It's possible," Raphael said quietly. "He must have had other help, as he was removed from command weeks ago. I'll have everyone checked again."

"Thanks. Work with Namail on that tomorrow. If there's someone else still around who isn't trustworthy, we have to know." Ryland patted his arm with his good hand. "We should tell Meilene."

"I wouldn't want to worry the Reina with—"

Ryland didn't wait for his brother's reasoning and strode over to Meilene. She was getting nicely patched up as he filled her in on what had happened. She wasn't as surprised when she heard the ex-wing lead's name.

Royce was more concerned with his terrible bandaging job and kept sending him disparaging looks. His hand twitched, as if itching to fix up the gauze Ryland and Alistair applied.

"I always got a bad feeling from that man." Meilene stared into the newly lit fire that some worker had the good sense to start. "Ever since I bonded with Aletzia, he was always hanging around. Maybe he thought he'd have placement after Aletzia mated."

"Good that you axed him when you did," Alistair said. "Who knows what he would have done if you kept him around."

"Make sure you question him thoroughly," Ryland said. "We have to know who he was working with."

"Why now, though?" Meilene mused. She surveyed her bandaged arm in the firelight. "Why wouldn't he have tried something before?"

Alistair and Raphael shifted uneasily and exchanged a look.

"What is?" Ryland demanded.

"Simeon was crazed, but he was a loyalist through and through," Alistair said. "He was adamant on following the old ways. If he was intent on hurting the Reina, this would be the perfect time. The bloodlines need to continue on, and Aletzia—"

"Just laid the next Reina egg," Ryland finished darkly.

As much as it incensed him, Simeon's timing made perfect sense. Killing the Reina and her dragon before her first hatching would all but ensure the extinction of the dragon race.

The riders, as they knew, it would die out.

Meilene looked shocked at this but didn't question anything. She pushed a strand of her tangled hair out of her face. "Whatever his reasons are, at least he'll be taken care of now."

"I'll make sure of it," Alistair said.

Another rider entered the Maise. Meilene frowned. "We should all try to get some rest. You especially." She grimaced when she saw Ryland's poor excuse for a bandage he and his brother put together. "Who did that?"

"It's fine. I'm fine."

Royce scoffed.

Ryland waved him off. "I'm sure that Aletzia is having a fit. Do you need to go calm her down?"

"She'll be fine," Meilene assured. "I told her she can stay where she is to keep an eye on the eggs. Maleth has come back and will stay the night."

She gestured out the window to where the outline of his dragon was visible. How did he not notice him before?

You weren't answering me before. I wanted to make sure you were not hurt.

"I'm fine, you meddlesome dragon."

The Reina's rider was frightened. She called for me to come.

Did she, now?

Meilene wouldn't meet his eyes, and Ryland understood. He had half a sense to be offended.

She gave a half shrug, which was meant to be an apology. Some riders could be finicky about their dragons. Not him. Especially not when it came to her.

It took another hour for everyone to clear out. News of the attack spread to the rest of Ryland's wing riders and to others in the Fordde, who insisted on coming to ensure the Reina and Reinaleader were safe with their own eyes.

It was annoying at first, even if they had the best intentions. The night's activities, along with everything that had happened with Aletzia's first clutch, had finally caught up to him, and he was beyond exhausted. Meilene finally had enough and yelled when Commander Garett tried coming into the Maise to check in. She forced him out and told everyone else to leave.

Maleth assisted with a loud bellow, and the rest quickly followed.

Namail insisted on leaving two guards right outside their door. It was annoying to have them so close; he could practically hear them breathing.

After the last straggler left, Meilene released an audible sigh.

"Are you sure you don't want an elixir to help you sleep? Royce can add it into some tea for you," Ryland asked for the third time that night.

She shook her head and snuck under the covers. "I have terrible dreams with those, which I'd rather not have tonight."

"Fair." He crawled in next to her and stared up at the ceiling beams.

"Thank you," she breathed. "You saved my life today."

"Let's hope Simeon was the last of those old loyalists. I never understood why Tork kept some of those guys around for so long."

"He's not the last. They all hate me because I'm not from here—Tork made certain of it."

He turned on his side so he could make out the outline of her face in the pale light. "No, they don't. Riders are a rough bunch. We don't adjust well to change."

She laughed a bitter laugh. "You're telling me."

"We are also a people who fall in line behind leadership by nature."

"Something to do with dragon law, right?"

"Something like that. It doesn't seem like it, but people are changing—and for the better, all because of you."

"Ryland." She turned on her side to face him. "You sure you're okay?"

"I think so." He lifted his head to look around the large Maise. "Are you?"

"My heart is still racing." Her eyes kept darting around their room. He could sense the tension rolling off her in droves. He felt the same.

Outside, his dragon kept watch. Still agitated from the night's events.

"Want to sleep with Maleth tonight?"

Meilene released an audible sigh. "Yes," she breathed. She tossed the blanket to the side and picked up her pillow while Ryland grabbed a few of their blankets.

Maleth hopped down from his perch and laid on his side in the middle of the den. The brown dragon lifted a wing so that the pair could fit in along his belly. The stone floor wouldn't be the most comfortable, but he'd slept in worse spots.

"Here." Ryland laid down a few blankets, hoping to soften the bite of the floor. He laid flush against Maleth and motioned for Meilene to join him. Without hesitation, she curled up tightly against his side, moving around to find a comfortable spot. Brown hair got in his face as she rested her head in the crook of his arm.

"Is this okay?" She froze, her voice full of hesitation and worry.

He brushed her hair out of his nostrils so that he wouldn't be smothered in the night. "Absolutely."

At his words, her body relaxed and melted against him. He tossed the blanket over them, making sure she was fully covered. The heat radiating from Maleth would keep them warm throughout the night, and his presence would hopefully ease Meilene's worries.

"We won't let anyone hurt you," he said.

Maleth echoed his sentiments.

"I know." Her voice was thick and heavy with sleep. "Can you distract me? I don't want to think about tonight anymore."

"What do you want me to talk about?"

The blinking lights of the sky disappeared as a dragon wing enveloped them in a brown haze. It was as if everything else faded away, and it was only the two of them and Maleth in this hidden world. The worries of the Fordde felt far away.

"Anything." She looked up, and her lips formed a small smile. "Tell me about the first time you flew with Maleth."

"Well." He wrapped his arms around her as Maleth sent him comforting thoughts. She melted into him. "That's a lovely tale. We weren't exactly cleared to fly by my instructor at the time, but Lora and I were both eager to test out our dragon's wings. We had that young overconfidence and decided to sneak out one night during the rain, thinking it would provide the necessary cover for us. We didn't know that Tork had night drills planned with Commander Brawne at the time and nearly flew into an entire wing within the first fifteen seconds."

As he continued recounting his story, her breathing slowed into a steady pattern. All of his pains disappeared as he listened to her steady heartbeat.

Tonight was the most worried he'd ever been. He was frightened he was going to lose her for good. He tucked her in closer and took a deep breath, inhaling her sweet scent. His eyes felt heavy, and he feared closing them again.

You are safe. I watch over you.

Chapter Twenty-Eight

MEILENE

It took a moment for Meilene to fully register where she was. The soft mattress felt more comfortable than usual, even though it wasn't fully underneath her. Ryland's arms held her tight against his chest, and not for the first time this week.

No complaints from her. It was nice to feel safe for once.

The comfort disappeared as the events of the last week all came back to her. Aletzia and her hatch. The new Reina eggs. Simeon. Traces of pain shot up on her arm from where the rider's knife caught her, the scars nearly faded.

Meilene groaned.

"Sorry, I tried not to wake you."

Meilene was met with the gaze of her dragonmate and rubbed her temple. "Have you been up for long?"

"Maleth woke me early."

The brown dragon no longer lay outside in his den. Did something happen?

Since Simeon's attack a week before, the dragon stayed close to his partner and his Reina dragonmate. Aletzia still hadn't left her eggs yet, but having the brown dragon close settled her worries for her own rider.

The night before, Meilene woke in a panic, drenched in sweat from another nightmare. Ryland had comforted her, and they fell asleep together, just like they had the night after the attack.

"Where is he?" she asked.

"He's been famished for the past week but didn't want to go far from us or Aletzia. I finally grew tired of his grumblings and told him to go eat before he wastes away and won't be able to keep up with the Reina in flight today. That got him moving quickly."

Meilene chuckled. Dragons were such a funny breed.

Ryland rumbled underneath her, and she remembered where she was and who she was cuddled up with.

"It's late." She pushed herself away from him. "Namail wants to meet up after our flight, as he has updates on Tork's whereabouts."

"Do you think they got something out of Simeon?" Ryland rolled out of bed and grabbed a change of clothes. He looked upset about something. "They haven't got anywhere yet, and it's been days. Sounds like he's tough to crack."

Meilene furrowed her brow as she listened to Aletzia's message from Mennon. "Sounds like it. He was traveling with Tork to Rokawi. Apparently, he has loyal riders near there."

"There's a lot of underground riders he may find more sympathy with. I'll ask some of my old contacts." He shoved his tunic on. "Just what we need right now."

"It never stops, does it?" she asked dryly.

"Apparently not." He adjusted his face into a bright smile. "At least we managed to neutralize one problem this week."

"Two problems." Meilene held up her fingers to him. "Simeon *and* settling the commanders with the laying of the new Reina egg. They've been in a much better mood since then."

"True. That last one's all thanks to Aletzia. I won't take any credit for it." He scrunched up his face at some unheard words.

"Maleth would like some credit for it, I'm guessing?" Meilene laughed. "Tell him we'll give him a small portion of the credit."

"That's more than generous." His eyes focused on the door. "We should probably get going before anyone changes their minds about us leaving."

"No, we don't." Meilene smiled. She allowed him to lead her down to the concourse to prepare for their flight.

Where are you? I have been waiting.

"Please be patient, darling." Meilene rolled her eyes and continued attacking her riding boots. Why were these laces so difficult?

She leaned against the wall for balance and peered outside the changing stall they occupied. The golden dragon had already landed on the concourse by herself. Maleth must be finishing his meal.

It was a nice spot Namail arranged to get ready for her flights in quiet. She hated how busy the main dressing rooms were.

This one was nice and private. It had plenty of natural light, comfortable benches to use, had multiple heating vents, which were helpful on those chilly days, and tons of storage for Aletzia and Maleth's gear.

I have been inside for a week now and am eager to stretch my wings.

Ryland paused and cocked his head to the side. He had a rider's jacket in each of his arms. "Aletzia?"

"Yes." She snatched the smaller jacket out of his arms. "Someone is a little antsy."

"Give her some slack." He threw his beige jacket on. A terrible color, like all the rider jackets. She'd have to talk to Maeve about getting him something new made. "She's been cooped up, guarding eggs for over a week, not counting everything that happened with Simeon after the laying. She's stressed, and I'm sure she's excited to get out."

"Either way." She pulled on her braid and tucked it into a neat bun. That was the best way to keep it from tangling in flight, as she learned through many trials. "She can learn a bit of patience."

Raphael poked his head into their riding room, pushing the double doors aside effortlessly. "Are you two almost ready?"

"Just about," Ryland said pleasantly. "Are the dragons on the concourse?"

"Yes, except Maleth, but he's coming. They're waiting for you." He pointed. "Just like the rest of us." He didn't sound angry but merely as if stating the facts. At least this rider managed to keep his emotions in check, unlike others in Ryland's wing.

"We'll be out in two minutes." Ryland finished his bootstraps and straightened up. He set about inspecting Maleth's gear to keep himself busy.

The dragon rider backed out of the Reina's riding room to give them some privacy.

After tying her leather boots and fastening the final strap, Meilene sighed. This was as ready as she was going to be.

Morning rides around the Fordde were supposed to be her alone time. It was when she could gather her thoughts and prepare for the day ahead.

Not today.

Since Simeone's attack, Ryland had been hesitant to let her go out on her own, and Namail hovered incessantly. Even Maleth was more protective of the Reina dragon lately.

Ryland insisted that they fly with her that day. It made him so happy when she finally relented that she had a tough time staying mad at him for interrupting her alone time with Aletzia.

I am glad they come with us.

Naturally, she would be happy to fly with her dragonmate. As much as Meilene refused to admit it, she was loath to go up alone after everything that happened. As much as it pained her to admit it, it comforted her to have Ryland close.

The bond with Aletzia was surely to blame for those new-found feelings, as they were definitely not hers.

When Ryland put on his gloves, he turned to hide his wince. Royce said that his injuries had healed up nicely over the week and even helped Ryland rebandage them this morning, so he was good to fly.

"You sure you're still up for this?" She grabbed a gloved hand and turned it over, as if she could see the scars beneath the leather.

"Absolutely." He squeezed her hand as if to show they were perfectly working. Rays of sunlight streamed across his face, highlighting his sharp features. He lifted her hand and planted a kiss on the back of it. The skin underneath felt like it could explode from the contact.

They stood inches away from each other. Almost as close as last night when he held her as she fell back asleep.

Were his eyes always such a lovely shade of blue?

"If you're still hurt, then you can stay behind, and I can find another escort," she said. "I won't be mad."

"Maleth didn't want you flying alone today. It's not safe for someone so important to him."

The fluttering in her stomach was new. She ignored it, even though she felt Aletzia pipe up upon feeling it. "Maleth didn't want that, did he now?"

He was unfazed as ever as he flipped her hand over and traced a pattern onto her palm. "Correct. You know how much he worries."

"Such a worrier. Someone should tell him that the Reina can handle herself."

"He knows that." He closed her palm and squeezed. It was as if the rest of the room melted away. "But you still haven't named anyone to your wing, and you need safe riders to fly with."

"Are you sure you guys can keep up with Aletzia?"

"We've had tons of experience with fast fliers. Maleth used to win so many of the races we—"

"I thought you guys never participated in the races?" she said slyly. "At least, that's what you said about Namail's report."

"Absolutely." He remained cool and unflustered, his expression unwavering. "I'm just saying that *if* Maleth had been in the races, he would have won every single one he entered."

The brown dragon circled the concourse, landing neatly beside Aletzia and sending a group of carrier birds squawking away. The sight brought a smile to Meilene's face.

"As impressive as that sounds, none of those dragons he beat were as fast as a Reina."

"No, they weren't. Still, you haven't seen Maleth in action . . ." A wicked smile crossed his face. "I mean, I guess you have."

Before Meilene could formulate an appropriate response, a rider had rudely interrupted them. She pulled her hand out of his and threw it behind her back.

Alistair strode into the room, dressed in his riding gear and looking as agitated as ever. "Let's go, guys. You're dressed. What are we waiting for?"

"We just finished up," Ryland said without taking his eyes off her. She stepped away to grab her riding jacket.

"We should hurry this up." Alistair held the door open for them. "We have tons to do today, and I still think we should have sent a scout ahead of time to check the route for any weather patterns."

Ryland broke their eye contact and reluctantly nodded. "We're riding out near Prael, then back. No need to waste any resources."

"Still." His brother's head twitched. "Whatever you want, I guess."

The Reinaleader's wing were all geared up outside, along with each of their dragons. They looked nervous, with the prospect of their first flight with Aletzia. Hopefully, the rest could keep up.

Ryland's Maleth waited next to her Aletzia. It was a comforting sight.

Both unfurled and stretched as their riders approached. Someone had the good sense to get their saddles ready, at least.

You are finally ready?

"Yes, yes. It wasn't even that long, you impatient beast," she said lovingly. She grabbed the pile of straps next to her dragon and sighed.

"Here." Ryland stopped on the way to his dragon and took Aletzia's straps from her. "I can do that for you."

"Thanks." Meilene grinned when he stopped to scratch Aletzia's chin first. The dragon's head was already taller than the rider.

Ryland effortlessly prepared Aletzia. The way he took the time to meticulously check the tightness on every strap sent her stomach into somersaults again.

Once satisfied both dragons were adequately prepared, Ryland helped Meilene climb onto Aletzia, holding her hand for two seconds too long.

After a quick check to make sure the rest of the wing was ready, he gave the signal to take off. Meilene knew he was still uncomfortable taking the role of leader but was growing into it well.

Aletzia spread her golden wings and beat against the air. In three full swoops, they were airborne. Maleth flew close behind with the other riders.

A queen always leads first. Meilene remembered that from her lessons.

The air was crisp, and the temperatures deceptively cool. It was a good thing Ryland told her to use the lined jacket.

Today's flight was strange. She was used to flying solo or with an escort that stayed far away. She never flew with riders of her own before.

Well, they were the Reinaleader's riders. It was still the closest she'd had to a wing of her own.

If they can keep up with me.

"He did it once before," Meilene replied smartly. "But agreed. No sense in taking it easy on them."

They wanted to fly with me. They must keep pace.

With several heavy beats of her wings, they cleared the skies above the Fordde and passed over the lake. The other dragons struggled to follow at first and nearly lost them as they passed a dark forest. There was some confusion with their own positions.

They struggled to find their formations with Blaise's blue dragon, Terak, nearly bumping into Raphael's white, Kono.

Maleth had no problem matching pace and stayed right behind them.

He is a fine dragon.

"Don't go too far, dear. We are only to go to the village. Nothing further."

Aletzia grumbled at this. Meilene pet her neck reassuringly.

"Be happy we are allowed out without an escort or Tork trailing our every move."

Because we ride with our wing.

"It's not our wing."

Maleth glided up along her left side. He cut through the air and zipped up and down with the drafts. He was enjoying himself as much as Aletzia.

Aletzia hummed a response. She banked a hard left and cut the Reinaleader off.

Maleth squawked and chased after them. Aletzia whipped through the air high above the rolling hills with the brown dragon right on her tail the whole time. The tall peaks were still a few miles out, but Aletzia knew she was not allowed there today.

Eventually, she slowed into a lofty glide and descended to align with the brown dragon. Their wingtips nearly touched as they flew close together, like a dance. They flew in a large loop around the village.

Are you happy?

Meilene tried to hide her shock at the question. "Why wouldn't I be? I have the best dragon ever."

We can do this again?

"We shall have to see."

Aletzia's pleasure seeped into her own feelings. Her dragon enjoyed having other dragons to fly with, especially her dragonmate. It was a bond difficult to describe, and Meilene tried to keep her dragon's emotions from overtaking her own.

It was hard to do some days: separate what her feelings were and that of her dragon.

The pair continued cutting patterns through the air for some time. When it got chilly, Meilene looked down to see their location. They had passed the village and moved closer to the mountains.

The wing second would not be happy they went so far.

I'll tell the others we should turn back.

"Thank you. Let's go home."

Before the dragon could respond, Aletzia let out a strange cry.

Both she and Maleth turned so quickly, Meilene almost fell off. She grabbed her reins tightly and pulled herself closer to the Reina. Aletzia pumped her wings with renewed fervor.

Something was wrong.

"What is it?"

Danger.

Meilene whipped around to see what had spooked the dragons. The clouds were thick and hard to see through, but there was a sound she'd only heard once before. The same sound from the creature that attacked them three years prior.

She caught Ryland's eye, and he looked frightened. He knew what it was, too.

The sinking feeling filled her once more. How did one of them manage to sneak up on them?

Chapter Twenty-Nine

RYLAND

"Watch out," a voice shouted. He could hear the panic in it from here.

Maleth swooped down low to avoid the sharp claws that came out of nowhere. He kept the Reina in sight as he searched for the origin of the attack.

Ryland's view was blocked by a wall of white clouds. He was thankful Maleth knew where he was, as he could only see whiteness.

"Meilene," he cried. He wasn't sure if she could hear him over the howl of wind and dragon growls.

There was another swoosh of wings, and a dragon cried out in pain.

We must protect the Reina.

"I know. We have to get out of these clouds. I can't see anything."

Maleth must have signaled Aletzia, for at the next moment, they both dove. Ryland hoped the rest of his wing would know to follow. The density of these clouds was too dangerous.

They will follow.

They burst out of the cloud cover, and a black creature came their way. It must have followed them.

This was the first one he'd seen. He'd only heard reports from others. It moved like a dragon but was twisted and dark. This one was less than half the size of Maleth and had a black, scaly head with dark eyes focused on his dragon.

A flash of white blurred by as Raphael and Kono dove to intercept the Anver. They collided against it with a thud, blasting it off path and tumbling down several dragon-lengths.

The Anver caught itself and diverged back on its path. A larger creature came charging from above. Ryland caught a glimpse of narrow eyes and sharp claws that seemed focused on the golden dragon.

"No!"

The creature snarled when Maleth flew in between them. Ryland had to duck as a red claw almost took off his head. These things moved quickly, similar to their dragons.

Lora's blue Kien was there in a rush of air, with her brother's Terak close behind to block the Anver. The next thing, the ground came closer with a sickening speed. Maleth kicked off the creature and turned around. His wings flapped frantically, and he was able to stop them before they hit the rocky ledges. Kien helped keep it away while Maleth adjusted himself.

As soon as he was back up, the large Anver dove into pursuit. Maleth turned on his wing and banked to the side.

"What are you—"

Ryland couldn't finish his sentence, as within the next second, Aletzia dove at them with her claws outstretched. Ryland ducked, thinking she meant to attack them.

The golden dragon narrowly missed the top of Maleth's head, but her true target became clear. She practically crashed into the Anver that pursued them.

There was a howl as she collided with the beast. Ryland turned his head in time to see the black creature stuck within the Reina's claws. One of its wings was secure in her jaw.

With a sickening rip, black liquid splashed across the two dragons and their riders. The Anver made a languished sound as the Reina dropped it, letting it plummet through the skies.

Ryland whipped his head around in a frenzy. Where was the other creature?

It is gone.

Maleth's voice was strained, and he flapped his wings laboriously.

"Are you all right?" He tried checking for any injuries, but the brown scales were covered in black liquid. It was hard to see anything beyond the creature's blood.

I am all right.

"Is anyone else injured?"

Swali received small injuries but is able to fly. Everyone else is fine ... Aletzia is pleased with herself. The dragon finished with pride in his voice.

"Tell everyone to get back now."

He caught eyes with Raphael, who nodded, having received the message from his own Kono. After making sure the Reina was right behind him, he raised his arm to return. The dragons followed behind him and Aletzia in tight formation.

Meilene was covered in the black goo but looked otherwise unharmed. His assurances from Maleth helped him not check in on her every thirty seconds.

The flight back seemed to take forever, and his heart was racing the entire time. He kept checking over his shoulder, expecting a creature to fly out at them. An escort of two wings met them when they were still ten minutes out from the Fordde.

I called for them. They were worried.

Good thinking. He rubbed his shoulder, still sore from being jarred so unceremoniously. If that was the extent of his injuries, then he was lucky.

Alistair's Swali flew behind him. He had several shallow scratches that would hopefully heal in no time. His brother looked fine as well.

The moment they touched down, Ryland jumped off. He checked over Maleth to ensure his dragon had no injuries.

I told you I was not injured.

"I had to see for myself." As soon as he was done, he went to check on Meilene and Aletzia, who landed with a thud.

"Are you guys all right?" He helped her off the large gold and settled her on her feet at arm's length. She was a little unsteady and still had drops of that creature's blood caked on her face.

"Yes, we didn't get hit. Is Maleth all right?"

"He's fine. Everyone else as well."

"What do you think—"

"What in the skies happened?" Namail stormed up to the battered group. His face was red, and his birthmark was an impeccable shade of purple. He was with Commander Calenth and a newly assigned one that Meilene helped pick, Commander Effront.

Ryland reluctantly let go of Meilene and turned to face the newcomers. "We must have gone a bit too far and were attacked."

"I told you that the Reina shouldn't go out," Commander Calenth said. His finger was inches away from Ryland's chest. "You put us all at risk."

"It wasn't his fault," Meilene said. "Aletzia and I were the ones who took us past the village. She was having such a good time, I didn't even notice—"

"I knew this was a bad idea," Alistair said. He had a spattering of black blood mixed with sweat dripping down his face. "Swali could have been killed today because of your incompetence."

Meilene sent him a look that would have peeled the skin off Ryland's body. Alistair looked unfazed.

"This was not the Reina's fault," Namail said with a glare at Ryland. "We should have sent scouts out ahead, as your wing second suggested. It would have been safer, given the activities of the past week."

The bald Commander Garett stood to the side with an odd look on his face. "I can't believe they attacked out in the open like this. They would have never attempted this before."

"They have," Meilene said. "Several times under him."

"If the old dragon lord were still in charge here—"

"He's not," Namail cut across Garett. "The Reina is in charge, and she is allowed to make any decisions she sees fit."

"It's not just her in charge," Alistair said.

"Don't talk about me like I'm not here!"

Commander Garett put up his hand as if to shush her. Meilene's face froze.

"Don't do that to her," Ryland ordered.

The commanders ignored him. "You should know better to protect your Reina," Effront said scornfully.

"This could have been completely avoided if you listened to my advice," Calenth said.

"Next time, the Reina should—"

"No." Ryland was surprised at the authority in his voice. "Stop it. We're fine. Everyone is fine, and we know to prepare better for next time. I'll discuss with my wing and let you know what to do from here."

Commander Garett did not look pleased with this.

Alistair nodded slowly. "We'll have better preparations next time."

"Thank you," he said. "Alistair, Blaise, please help Commander Calenth put together a few wings to hunt down the last one. Make sure it's out of our territories and check on the surrounding villages to make sure there are no damages."

"Right away, Reinaleader." Alistair led the commanders away. He had faith his brother could handle this, and Blaise was always raring to get into the middle of a fight. Their energies would be well spent helping the villages.

All around the concourse, new riders showed up to help the wing and assess the injured dragons. That was one rule drilled into them since they were young: help your dragon first, then yourself.

It was simple and made sense. He'd never forgive himself if he let something happen to Maleth.

If you let something happen?

"Now's not the time."

Namail still glared at him with an intense heat while helping Meilene get out from her ruined jacket. Surely, he didn't blame him for the attack.

"I'll go check on the others," Ryland said.

Meilene blocked his path. "I have to talk to you," she said stiffly. "In private." She shooed Namail away.

What now? He followed her until they stood a distance away from the group of riders. He needed to check on the others.

As soon as they were out of earshot Meilene rounded on him. Her eyes were bulging, and she still had remnants of blood that started to cake and crack. "What was that?" she demanded.

"What was what?" he stuttered. He racked his brain trying to figure out what he did wrong.

"I told you I don't need your help," she snapped. "You're undermining me in front of all the commanders when you do that."

"I didn't mean to."

"I'm trying to fight battles on two fronts now. Don't tell me I have to deal with you now."

"I wanted to make sure you are heard—"

"It's not up to you." She clenched her fists at her side. "They have to learn to listen to me! I've been working at this for years on end and can't have anyone working against me."

"I haven't been against you." He looked around as if hoping someone would come to his aid. "You know that I've been on your side this entire time and just wanted to get them to listen to us."

"It doesn't matter. I'm the one who'll actually be around after next season." As soon as the words were out, she clapped her hand over her mouth.

Ryland recoiled, as if she slapped him in the face. At least Meilene had the decency to look like she regretted her comments.

Ryland.

He ignored Maleth.

"All I'm doing," he said in a dangerously low voice. It was calm and steady. Surprising, considering how he felt inside. "Is trying to make sure we don't get everybody killed when the next attack comes. Sorry for overstepping your boundaries, your highness. Clearly, you know best, and I'll try to remember my place in the future."

Before she could utter another word or apologize, he stormed off. If he stayed there, he'd say something he would regret.

Chapter Thirty

MEILENE

A blue dragon spun in lazy circles above the grounds while a group of riders watched below. Meilene would have given anything to be in the air at that moment, flying above the circular building that felt like a prison.

I want to fly with you, too.

If only. Yet somehow she was stuck in the stupid command center again.

After her blowout with Ryland, it was as if the other commanders sensed the tension among them. They took advantage and constantly questioned all her decisions and calls. Commander Calenth went to the flight controller to ensure Meilene couldn't go off flying on her own.

Ryland didn't even try coming to her defense, and she had to rely on Namail to help the commander see why that was inappropriate. He may not have even known what was going on with her giving him the silent treatment and all, but still . . .

"We've had reports of four more attacks by Pumille," the graying Commander Yannet said. His uniform was faded as if it had seen better days. She'd have to check into that with the quartermaster. Everything seemed to be falling apart here.

"Is that from the same ones that ambushed the riders outside of Swom?" *he* asked. "We haven't tracked them down yet."

"We think so, Reinaleader. The patterns were similar and there were four of them. Same as Pumille."

"I suggest we send out three wings along that coast to help out," a senior wing lead, Nitan, said.

The brother sifted through a list of the current wing locations. "I don't know if we have three wings to spare with the contingents we sent north," he said.

This wasn't news to her, as Alistair reviewed the situation with both Meilene and Ryland before this. That was an icy meeting, to say the least. At least it was over quick.

"If we pull back a few of the scouts, we'll be fine," Ryland said. "We need to find that group of Anvers, so send them out."

With a nod, he dismissed the wing lead Nitan, who ran out to fulfill the Reinaleader's orders.

"I hope that's all right with the Reina?" Ryland's voice was cold and distant. It hadn't changed since they arrived back from their flight together, and she blew up at him.

Meilene reluctantly tore her eyes away from the outside concourse to face the group at the long table.

"Yes," she said stiffly. She tapped her toe against the leg of the table and refused to meet his eye.

The rider infuriated her to no end. She shouldn't have been mad at him still, but she refused to make the first attempt at reconciliation. She was a Reina and shouldn't have to explain herself to anyone.

Why should you?

Meilene didn't bother to respond. Dragons sometimes struggled to grasp complicated human emotions.

What's so complicated with them?

Aletzia saw things differently. She had a purpose, knew what she wanted, and was able to get it.

Meilene wished things were that simple for her.

". . . and it's an all-out war," Kono's rider, Raphael said. "I've never heard of anything like this."

"It's happened before," Commander Jian added. As the resident historian, he would be the one to know. "Never this quickly and on this scale."

"And we've never been down to these few dragons against them." Yannet glanced at Meilene.

"We're in a bad spot," Garett said with another pointed glance her way.

Her mouth dropped open, and she was too stunned to speak.

"What do you want her to do about it?" Namail demanded. He leaned forward with his fingertips on the table. "Aletzia's had her first mating and laid the first hatch—early, too. The next season isn't for months. We can't do anything to speed it along."

Again, she sensed *him* watching her. She studied the fine grains on the curved table instead of meeting his gaze.

"Of course," Commander Garett quickly corrected. "I wasn't trying to insinuate anything, merely making an observation."

"I'm sure the future matings will be as fruitful," another wing lead added. "The Reina dragon is young and vigorous in her matings."

Meilene sensed several eyes on her and felt her face heat up. Didn't they have anything better to talk about?

With the distraction, she chanced a glance at Ryland. His head was down. At least there was someone else who hated the direction of this conversation as much as she did.

"I think that's everything we have for today," Namail said jovially. "Let's break and regroup on our strategy in the east tomorrow."

"Excellent idea." Commander Jian clapped him on the back. "Let's get a spot to eat, old chap."

Namail looked back as if checking permission. She forced a smile.

It was good for him to catch up with some of the older riders he had once flown with. He'd spent so much time with her these past three years that he should get away on his own. Plus, maybe he could help soften up the disgruntled commanders.

"I have some plans tonight I must attend to. Don't bother waiting up for me," she said to Ryland. He looked shocked at being directly addressed by her. "I'll be up late."

"My Reina." He nodded and followed his brother out. Something heavy formed in the pit of her stomach as she watched him leave.

That was a problem for later.

⁘⁘⁘⁘⁘ ⁘⁘⁘⁘⁘

Hours later, Namail unceremoniously plopped another book in front of her.

It was falling apart at the seams. She was afraid to touch it or else she may ruin it.

"Don't even ask what I had to do to get my hands on that one."

The label said this one was the first Reina's personal diary. Mara, rider of Anarillia. It must have been close to two thousand years old, judging by the smell of it.

It was a miracle it was still around, even if half of it was missing. How did this manage to make it past Tork's rampages?

Meilene blinked and rubbed her eyes. How long had she been at it?

After their meeting with the commanders, she ventured to an old reading room where she knew she'd not be disturbed. It was dark, cozy, and quiet. She loved it.

Namail surveyed her curiously. "The guards said you requested no visitors, so I'm here." He shrugged with his palms out.

"I'll have to have words with the one who let you in," she said with a wry smile.

"Please do. He'll let just anyone in, apparently." He picked through the pages of the delicate book. His eyes squinted in the dim candlelight. "Interesting hiding place you chose."

"I'm not hiding. I'm reading. Is there a law against that now?"

"The Reinaleader was asking after you."

"Oh, he was, now?" she snapped.

"Is it him? Is that why you're so moody? Because we can get rid of him easily. There will be many more matings, several a season, in fact."

Meilene knew that. She was aware she'd have to go through that same experience with leery riders many times a season for the rest of her life.

"It's not that. I feel like you couldn't understand. No one can."

Namail was unperturbed. "I've spoken with the commanders, and they'll keep you apprised of any future decisions they make. That won't happen again. I'll make sure of it."

"Glad they'll listen to you." She scowled. "They should have done that all along."

"I know. They should have, but it's taking more time than I thought, and I'm sorry." He looked down. "Read anything good?"

"All about the glory of our prior Reinas. Saving lives. Leading armies. Discovering and killing the first Anvers. All that stuff."

"Reina—"

"Look at Mara and everything she accomplished." She pointed at the page he flipped to. A pair of intimidating gold dragons on the battlefield took up half the page, the other half was torn off. "I want to be a fraction as good as her, but no one will give me a chance. They never have. I'm a disgrace of a Reina."

"How can you say that? Look at where you are now. If it weren't for you, Tork would be leading us into our deaths. You did that, and no one else."

"I can't do this!" She looked down. "Everything is falling apart, and they all think I'm a joke."

"You're trying, and I know that they see that." Namail pushed the candle closer to Meilene. "These are unprecedented times. We've never had the Anvers move so quickly in our recorded history. Why do you think the Anvers have come out so brazen against us?"

"I don't know. They're hungry?"

She shoved the book away. Its presence mocked her.

"Because they needed to attack quickly and before our Reina reaches her full strength. A swift movement to take out the bloodlines." He swiped at the flame, almost extinguishing it. "They are afraid of what you'll become. They know it. I know it. Most of the riders here do as well." He leaned forward in his seat. "Aletzia is strong, and her rider is even stronger. Maybe strong enough that we can finish this for good."

Meilene huffed, and the flame danced again. "Now I know you're lying."

You are strong. You are Reina.

"Thanks, Aletzia."

"I also know you can't do it alone."

"That's why I have you."

"You need the commanders on your side, too. The wing leads and the lords, too."

"Is the disgraced ex-dragon lord still running around the southern villages?"

"Yes, he is," Namail said delicately. "Trying to find any new backers. He seems to be on the move lately."

"Any news on finding the rest of his loyalists in the Fordde?"

Namail shook his head. "Nothing yet. I think we'll find more success once we find some of his old finances. There seem to be a lot of leakages there."

"I'm not surprised." Meilene pinched the bridge of her nose. "It feels like I can never truly be rid of that man."

"He's trying to find any weaknesses . . . instabilities."

"There's so many to choose from." She waved her arms wide. "He'll have a tough time focusing on merely one."

"He's nothing but a slight obstacle along our path. We know him, and we know how to deal with him. The real issue is more difficult to wrap our hands around."

"Their flight patterns are off." She pointed at the pile of journals. "Nothing like what was previously tracked. Have they learned from before?"

"Who would have thought they were smart animals?"

"Smart enough to change their patterns. Smart enough to know to go after a Reina. What else are they hiding?"

"A lot." Namail pushed Mara's tattered journal toward her. "There's much missing from the first Reina's accounts. We have to know why."

"You think the first queens were hiding something?"

"I'm not sure if it was them or if the accounts were destroyed in the fires a few hundred years later. There's a lot we don't know."

"Why would those riders hide what they know about the Anvers? This doesn't make sense."

"Why indeed?"

Chapter Thirty-One

RYLAND

"Here you go." Raphael plopped a plate of food in front of him. The long table had half-eaten plates leftover from Damon and Royce's earlier meal. "I don't think she's coming any time soon, and you need to eat."

They were the last two left in the Reina's Maise, as most of the wing had retired to their private quarters by now. Lora was trying to find her wayward brother, and Meilene was still avoiding this place at all costs.

"Did you find out where she is?"

Ryland asked Raphael to keep an eye on Meilene, especially since she was determined to ignore him. His brother was getting on his nerves and thought he should write her off completely. He'd been off ever since Aletzia's mating, probably from the stress. So, Ryland had to go to another source for help.

Of all the riders he and Alistair had picked for his wing, Raphael was turning out to be the most reliable. He didn't come from the best of backgrounds, but was an invaluable asset when trying to run the Fordde, a thing that was a scary enough thought on its own.

"She was going through some of the old journals in one of the lesser-used wings. I made sure to assign several guards who won't let anyone in." He quickly added upon seeing Ryland's face, "I picked riders who I personally know. She's fine."

"Thanks." He pulled the plate toward him. He hadn't eaten anything all day and didn't realize how hungry he was until then.

The Reina's favorite worker, Maeve, walked past to prepare their quarters for the evening. She glared at Ryland as she passed and didn't return the wave from Raphael.

Ryland felt his stomach drop. He wasn't the least bit tired and had no desire to retire to the Reina's quarters by himself.

"What's got you so moody?" The blond rider tapped the table and watched him closely.

Ryland scowled.

Raphael knew. His brother knew. Everyone in this Fordde knew.

"I'm sure things will turn around," Raphael said cheerfully. "I mean. It can't get much worse than it already is."

"Really? Alistair is constantly mad at me, and I feel like the commanders barely listen to me or any of us. They tolerate me at best and only when I'm doing what they want. It's a complete disaster. Not to mention, I'm sure that Meilene most definitely hates me."

"Don't think you're special." He patted his arm. "She hates everybody."

"She's a bit mercurial, that's all."

Raphael snorted. "That's putting it lightly. At least I'm not the one living with her."

"She isn't that bad, you know . . . once you get to know her."

"I'll have to take your word for it. I'm sure she'll come around."

"Do you think?" he asked hopefully.

It seemed like she'd never speak to him again. He wasn't sure how to fix this but knew he had to. He just wasn't so sure where it all went wrong.

It just felt like something was missing when she gave him the cold shoulder. Things weren't perfect before, but this was different, and he didn't know how to fix it.

Raphael surveyed him carefully. "Oh no. Don't get attached. I know there's some weird pull when your dragons are mates . . . Ryland, please do not."

"Please, Raph. Don't make me laugh."

"I'm keeping my eye on you, both of them. You don't know the kinds of emotions that can be involved in these things. Make sure you can separate your thoughts from Maleth's."

"I know how to do that. I'm not stupid. Maleth and I have been together for seventeen years."

"I know."

"I've been with him longer than I've been on my own. I'm not some junior."

"Thank the skies you aren't, but still. We all know the trouble you got yourself into at the races . . . and here you are, getting yourself into more trouble."

"To be fair, I feel like Maleth and I have done a splendid job at keeping straight lately." Raphael didn't look convinced. "Even before all of this mess, we barely got in trouble the last few months that Tork was in charge."

Raphael shrugged. "It's not hard to do when your measuring rope was at rock bottom before."

"Thanks." Ryland pushed the food around his plate. "Did I tell you I was there? When Aletzia hatched, that is."

"I may have heard about it from your brother." The rider scratched his chin. "Several times, in fact."

Ryland rested his head on his hand. "I was on rotation that night. I was supposed to keep an eye on the hatchery grounds and make sure no one went in without the dragon lord's approval. You know how he was."

"A narcissistic control freak running this place into the ground? Still, he had strange rules." Raphael shrugged. "Given that not even a dragon lord can control the bonding process or stop it. Tork loved keeping everything under his control."

"There was no stopping her that day."

"I heard."

"He was livid when he found out," Ryland said. "Her father . . . and the dragon lord. I don't think I've ever seen Tork so furious."

"I also remember hearing that Tork pulled you from your wing at the time and assigned you to quartermaster duties because of that. Then, he sent you off to one of the smaller Forddes for months on probation doing clean-up duty before you were allowed to return to your flight patrols."

"That wasn't my fault, either."

"It was because you got too close to the Reina again. He told you to stay away after the hatching, and you didn't."

"I did stay away and was working for the quartermaster, like he assigned me to. I was doing my job when she came in for a saddle."

Raphael smirked. "Not a good enough excuse to save you from near banishment to the Red Bay Fordde."

I missed our flying together during that time, Maleth said grumpily from his perch outside the Maise. Both he and Aletzia had just returned from flying around the Fordde together. *No one could beat us.*

"Don't remind me," he said darkly. He used to dream of claiming independence and finding commissions in the smaller villages.

The Fordde life never suited him, not like it had his brother. He had even saved up enough money from the races to help get him started. He was hoping to make it into the next independence trials and finally getting out of here.

That was before returning to visit his brother and getting talked into participating in the mating.

Ryland didn't know where he belonged anymore. He liked Meilene, but why was he chosen? Surely, there was someone—anyone—better suited to run the Fordde.

"You should be reminded daily. Don't forget the trouble you got into because of her and what other trouble you could get into now. Not even your brother can help you talk your way out of this one."

"None of it was Meilene's fault." The anger that bubbled up at the thought of the insult against her was unwarranted, but he couldn't help it.

"Not directly, no. Yet, here you are again, and here she is. And you're not just helping her pick out a saddle anymore."

"What's your point, Raph?"

"I'm only saying to tread carefully."

"I'll keep that in mind while I'm trying to not let this place burn to the ground."

"So far, it's still standing." Raphael crossed his legs and stared at him, as if trying to determine what to do with the Reinaleader.

"Back to my dilemma and why Meilene is mad at me."

"Because you undermined her?"

"I didn't mean to."

"But you still did," he said with a dismissive nod.

"I'm just trying to help her."

"I'm sure that's totally how she sees it. Definitely not as another rider trying to overrule her and take control of the Fordde. All that fun stuff. She needs a partner, not another one of them trying to control her."

Ryland cast his eyes down. "I don't want to control her. Maleth and I are merely here to elevate her. She is the weapon and we are merely the sheath to help protect her. But I guess I never thought about it from her point of view."

"That was your first mistake. I don't think that girl wants any protection." Raphael went to an ornate cabinet and pulled out a bottle of bitters and two crystal glasses. "Your second mistake." He handed Ryland an overflowing glass and poured himself one. "Was listening to the ministrations of your brother too much."

Ryland took the glass and examined the dark liquid in it. At least there were some perks to this new role. "I would like to make it out of this in one piece." He downed his glass in one gulp. "This isn't exactly easy."

"Be careful. I don't want anything to happen to you after, after—"

"After Aletzia chooses a new mate?" he finished for him. The cold pit in his stomach was back. "You, too?"

"I didn't mean it like that." Raphael's eyes pleaded with him. "You know what I meant."

"But still . . ."

"You're doing all right so far. As good as can be expected. I want us to be prepared for anything and try to get through this all right on the other end." Raphael refilled their cups.

"It seems like a lot of people want to be prepared for anything these days. Anything except the problems we actually have in front of us."

"Give it time, and they'll come around . . . all of them. I'm sure it's hard for the commanders to take orders from a rider who didn't pass his tests and has never been a wing lead in his life before, not even a wing second, for that matter. Let's not forget all the other fun activities you used to do that are very frowned upon."

Ryland's mouth hung open. "Thank you . . . I think."

Raphael gave his arm another consoling pat and refilled their drinks. "On the bright side, things are slowly getting better, and you even have the backing of some old commanders I'd never thought would turn on Tork before. Plus, this means I won a bet with your brother, who didn't think you'd last this long."

"I can't believe you guys."

"If you make it to the next mating, then Royce owes me a full month of patrol scheduling. If you make it to a third one... let's just say I'll have a lot to cash in."

"Lovely. Glad that my current misery is working out in your favor." He cast his eyes down at his plate. "Any bets on when she'll talk to me again?"

Raphael grimaced. "Now, that is a hard one to predict. I'd rather not ruin my winning streak."

"I guess we'll have to wait to find out."

"I do know this," Raphael said with an all-knowing smile on his face. "I know it's never good to bet against a dragon choice. Somehow, they always know."

Chapter Thirty-Two

MEILENE

"I'm sorry. I didn't realize anyone else was up at this hour."

Meilene paused in the middle of the Maise, package in hand, feeling like she was caught sneaking sweets after bed. How had she become so uncomfortable in her Maise?

The red-haired Lora was sitting at the long table with a cup of tea in her hand. Her brother sat at the end of the long table, staring off in his own world.

The fires were down to their embers, and most of the lights were out. They must not have expected any newcomers. Both looked just as surprised to see the Reina and Lora stood up awkwardly.

"It's fine." She gestured for the rider to sit down. Her eyes searched the large room, expecting another rider to pop up at any minute. The Maise was always full of people ever since the mating. "I assume everyone else is in bed?"

"Ryland and Raph finished off an entire bottle of bitters together." She gestured at an empty bottle and a pair of glasses at the end of the table.

"They should both be in a deep sleep by now," Blaise added. "If they're not dead."

"Blaise!" The rider didn't look the least bit chastised by his sister's ministrations.

Perfect. No need for any uncomfortable encounters. She'd been stressing herself and Aletzia with trying to figure out how to make everything right.

"Cup of tea?" Lora tapped the side of her cup. "I can make more hot water."

Meilene hesitated. She was never alone with either of the siblings before, let alone having to carry a conversation with them. The thought of going to her room with him was too much at the moment, so she didn't have much choice.

She nodded and sat in a chair across from Lora. Judging by her stiff posture, she was as uncomfortable as Meilene was. Blaise didn't shift from his prior position, resting with his head in his hand.

"Did you get something from the quartermaster?" Lora pointed at the package. She had a low, raspy voice, which Meilene always figured was from a previous illness. She'd never had the chance to ask the rider about it.

"Yes," she said stiffly. It had seemed like a great idea at the time she commissioned it. Then she had doubts about everything. "Just something I requested."

That was all she was willing to share, and the rider didn't press.

Lora grabbed a kettle and poured out a cup for her. She slid it across the table in silence.

By the smell of it, it was some herbal concoction. Wouldn't have been her first choice.

"Can't sleep?" she asked the wing riders.

"We were just catching up on things without snooping ears," Lora said.

What were they keen to keep away from the rest of the Reinaleader's wing?

"I assume that's why you're just getting in as well?" Blaise asked.

"Maybe." Meilene crossed her legs.

"Leave it alone," Lora said.

Blaise scoffed. "Not like it's a big secret around here but sure. Let's just pretend we didn't know what went down."

Lora sent him a disparaging look. "Did you have a chance to look over those reports I sent you and Ryland?"

"I did. Thanks." She blew on her cup. "How long have you known Ryland for? You two seem to be close."

Blaise scoffed from his end of the table.

"Don't mind him," Lora said. "He's just upset that his application for commission down by Telaw was declined."

"Trying to leave already?" Meilene asked. "Most people would kill to be in the Reinaleader's wing."

"No offense, but I've been trying for a while. It's hard for an independent to pick up work around here."

"Which is why he's so grateful for Ryland to help us out in the meantime with a position on his wing," Lora said pointedly. "So he doesn't end up cast out on the streets, like Tork."

Blaise scrunched his face but didn't respond.

The red-headed rider smiled and stirred her cup. "But to answer your question, no, never like that. Ryland and I bonded with our dragons at the same time and were placed in some courses together."

"And how was that?"

"Terrible. The classes, that is. The company was good. It was nice to get away from home." She looked down at the table.

Meilene paused. She didn't want to pry, but curiosity overtook her. "Why?"

"Our parents were miners in a nearby village." She nodded at Blaise. "I . . . also was taken down there to help pay my way. It was not the best of conditions." She touched a hand to her throat. "Blaise would have been, too, if we didn't bond with our dragons."

"How?"

"Our father traded with the Fordde on occasion. He took us for a visit to the dragon rider's home one day and then . . ." She trailed off, staring at an unseen memory.

"It didn't go over so well, if that's what you're wondering," Blaise said bitterly. He refused to look at his sister.

Meilene nodded. "I know the feeling."

"Anything was better than that place," Blaise said.

"Even though you're already trying to run from here?" Meilene asked sharply.

"I'm tough to please," he said with a wry smile.

Meilene returned her gaze to his sister. "I hated everything about this place when I first got here. I'm sure Tork had something to do with that."

"I bet he didn't make things easy. The transition can be rough for newcomers. Those classes were built for a certain type of rider, I guess."

"Hopefully, that'll change soon." Meilene gripped her cup in both hands. It was nice and warm to hold.

"If you can convince those oldies to even consider it," Blaise added. "Trying to get those guys to change is like trying to lift a dragon on your own, with one hand, which was repeatedly stomped on by a dragon."

"I definitely know that. They'll change their tune eventually," Meilene said with more confidence than she felt. Maybe Namail was getting to her.

"Hopefully." Lora narrowed her eyes. "What do you plan on changing?"

"Nothing major," Meilene said quickly. "Some changes that make the most sense. I don't want any riders or queens forced into anything in the future."

This was something she thought about many times before. There were so many changes she wanted to make to improve life at the Fordde. She'd have to be gentle about it, as riders may not like seeing a foreign Reina changing things.

It was all to help the Fordde, but she would have to tread carefully.

Tork hated it when she brought up any small suggestion for change. He had always dismissed her and said that she didn't understand their ways.

Lora nodded. "That will be nice to see."

"If people allow it," Meilene said.

"They will. Things have changed constantly over the past few centuries, especially as new queens come in. It comes with the job, I guess."

"I guess." Meilene tapped her cup. Blaise looked unconvinced. "It's late. I'm going to head to bed."

"Same here. Will see you in the morning."

Meilene made sure to stop and bid goodnight to Aletzia first. After giving the sleeping Maleth a brief graze, she went to focus on her golden dragon. She scratched the sleepy dragon along her jawline, taking pleasure in the way her dragon hummed and leaned into her.

Are you feeling better?

"I don't know anymore."

You are worried about the riders?

"Among other things." She stopped her scratching and rested her forehead against the golden scales.

Everything felt so simple when they were together. Why couldn't things feel that way all the time? Aletzia was her partner, and they were meant to be. It was hard to decipher her own feelings some days.

You worry about the other one?

Dragons usually struggled with names. Meilene knew she meant the Reinaleader. "Not worried, no. Upset. Confused maybe?"

What will happen will happen. I am not worried. You shouldn't be either.

"I want whatever makes you happy, Aletzia."

You will be happy, too. I would not allow anything less.

"I don't know what makes me happy anymore."

You will.

"I thought I knew what to expect. I thought taking over from Tork would be easy after the mating. I realize now that he was right, and I know nothing about running the Fordde."

You are Reina. We are Reina. We are where we are meant to be.

"I'm glad you think so."

Maleth stirred. Meilene quickly made her way inside so she didn't wake the sleeping dragon and he would wake his rider.

After carefully settling into bed and without waking her sleeping mate, Meilene stared up at the ceiling and ignored the empty hole in her stomach. Ryland's snores punctured the silence as she tried to will herself to sleep. Judging by that bottle she saw left on the table, he would be hurting in the morning.

The next day, she decided that she would read more of the queens' journals left for her. Hopefully, something in there would help her make sense of things, both with the Anvers and within her own Maise.

The last journal she read had no tips on how the queen dealt with her mate and how they worked together. The first Reina Mara was only ever friends with her mate, even though she wanted more. They parted ways after her dragon stopped mating with no reason given. The senior queen, Cathlene, changed mates every match for ten years, and Reina Torianne made several mentions about how her mate was the love of her life.

There was no pattern and no reasoning why.

Meilene sighed and curled herself against the sleeping Ryland. He didn't move. His body was warm and comforting.

How did they know?

Chapter Thirty-Three

RYLAND

When he cracked an eye open, the sun was halfway across the bed. He had never been so thankful for a day off before. It had been well over a month since he last had time to himself that wasn't filled with his new duties around the Fordde. Not to mention, it felt like he was dying.

The light from the window felt as if it pounded against his skull. A headache was coming on. He shouldn't have imbibed with Raphael so much the night before.

The empty spot beside him was still warm. Where was Meilene?

Their quarters were deserted. She must have gotten an early start to her day.

With a groan, he pulled himself out of bed and got dressed in the first outfit he could find. A glass of water was left on the table which he gladly gulped down.

Are you not well? Maleth asked with a chuckle.

Ryland did not bother gracing him with a response.

Both Maleth and Aletzia still lounged outside so he knew that Meilene couldn't have left the Fordde. The sun was at its peak and hitting them perfectly. They wouldn't move for a while unless forced to.

Outside in the main Maise, most of the wing was up already. Raphael, Blaise, and Lora were talking at the dining table, while Royce and Damon sat in a pair of high-backed chairs, going over some flight plans. The work never ended for some, even with a day off.

Alistair was nowhere to be seen. He must have been sleeping still.

"Oh, good. You're alive," Raphael said cheerfully as soon as he saw the Reinaleader. He got up and grabbed Ryland a plate of food. "Better eat up if you're going to make the flight today."

Right. That was today.

Ryland held back a groan. *Someone* decided it was a good idea to fly out to the shores for their day off. While it was lovely out there and bound to be warm, he didn't know if he had it in him for the three-hour journey.

"What's wrong?" Lora smiled. "Not feeling so good?"

No, you are not.

"Most definitely not," he said bitterly. "Where's . . ." He trailed off as he spotted the Reina in the corner of the room. As usual, she was reading next to one of the fireplaces with Maeve. A finished game of Callavan lay underneath their books.

Lora twisted in her seat. "I asked her if she wanted to come. She declined."

Not surprising. She always preferred her solitude.

"If you're not up for it, then you don't have to come today," Raphael said carefully. He nodded toward Meilene. "The winds are pretty turbulent today."

"I don't feel like waiting for you to hurl every twenty minutes," Blaise said.

"It would be like junior years all over again," Lora added.

I'd love to fly with you today, but I know the Reina needs you. Our time together can wait.

Ryland contemplated his words for a minute. "I think I'll catch up on a few things. I wouldn't want to hold you back now."

"Perfect." Lora downed the rest of her drink and stood up. "I'll tell the others we can leave and don't have to wait for our annoying Reinaleader."

"We'll be gone all day," Raphael said as he clapped his shoulder. The movement was not good for his stomach. "Maleth can let Kono know if you need anything."

"Will do. Be safe."

I shall be soaking in the sun if you need me. I will require a bath to help with some of the mud from our flight the other day.

"We can do that later. When I'm feeling more up to it."

Ryland rested his head on the table and listened to the sounds of his riders readying for their journey. Lora and Raphael chatted about the shops she wanted to visit on their way, and Damon shoved supplies into an old rucksack.

Why was everyone so loud this morning?

Eventually, the chaos died down, and the ringing in his ears dissipated. The wing must have left by now. He pulled his head up and was glad to see the Maise nearly deserted. The only two people left behind were Maeve and Meilene.

Meilene. The one who had ignored him all week.

When he approached the Reina, she had a pained expression on her face. Her face was buried in her pages, while Maeve casually flicked through a journal.

As if against her will, she finally noticed him, shut the journal she was reading, and slumped back into the plush couch.

"Mind if I sit?" He gestured at the space next to her. The Reina had taken a liking to this corner of the Maise, along with its soft velvet cushions and privacy from the rest of the inhabitants.

Meilene gave a non-committal shrug.

Maeve stood up. "I'll go check on the kitchens." She shot Ryland a warning look as she left.

He settled beside Meilene on the couch, giving her plenty of space. "Doing more research?" He nodded at the journal in front of them, next to a package. She had spent hours poring over those old journals. What was she searching for?

"Trying to see if there's anything more that's of use in these things. I'm not coming up with much." Her eyes glowed as she stared into the fire beside them. "Lots of entries from Mara about how her sister annoyed her. She had a queen, too. I've never heard about her before."

"Same here. I wonder why?"

"The journals are pretty sparse about her, but there was some sort of falling out between the two sisters. There wasn't much else there but plenty of pages on how heavy the cloud cover was that day. Nothing useful."

"Same from the Reinaleader at the time. He barely even mentioned Mara and focused on his patrols. Kind of surprising, considering how long they were together. There was also a large time jump in entries with years missing."

"That is interesting."

"There were quite a few mentions of the sister, now that you mention it."

Meilene scoffed. "Maybe he had a thing for the sister."

"I'm sure that would have ended well, given everything we know about dragon bonds. We'll find the answer, I'm sure of it."

"Really?" She pushed the book across the table. It teetered on the edge. "Because it seems like nobody else believes that."

"It's still early. You need to give it time, and everyone will come around. Some of the rougher commanders are already talking about how well you delivered during the last ceremony. The one with that wing lead from the islands was particularly gracious in his feedback."

"I doubt it." She ran her fingers through her hair and twisted it back.

"You're a great Reina. Don't let anyone tell you otherwise." He shifted his gaze down. "And . . . I'm sorry if I made you feel like I wasn't on your side. I just wanted you to know you're not alone in this. I didn't realize . . . I didn't think it would diminish what you were doing."

"It's all right."

"No, it's not," he said. "I don't . . . I don't know what I'm doing here."

She gave a bitter laugh. "None of us do, it seems. You had good intentions, at least."

"I am trying my best here."

So was she.

"I may have . . ." She sighed and pinched the bridge of her nose. "Said some unnecessary things and . . ." she trailed off, mumbling.

Ryland had to hold back a laugh. She was a stubborn one. That was as close to an apology as he would ever get.

"How was your flight with Aletzia yesterday? I heard the weather was great by the villages."

"She loved it. The warm season was her favorite . . . and mine, too." She focused on the burning embers. "You could come again next time. I know Aletzia loves flying with Maleth."

Ryland froze and tried to keep his emotions in check. "We'd both like that."

Maleth rumbled in agreement. He had always liked flying with Aletzia and loved it even more so when both their riders were there. He'd been asking Ryland when they could go out again with the Reina. It was hard for him to understand why they couldn't go together.

"You can come anytime you want," she added.

"We'll try to not slow you down." He chuckled.

"Maleth is fine. He's not an issue to fly with . . . you as well."

"He says to pass on his thanks." He leaned forward in his seat, careful not to get too close to her. "What's that?"

Its presence on the table in front of them had been bugging him since he sat down. He nudged the black bundle with his foot.

"Oh, that." She scratched the back of her head and wouldn't meet his gaze. "It's from the quartermaster."

"Are those the new reins for Aletzia?"

"No. Not those." Meilene threw the bundle on his lap and shifted back in her seat. He'd never seen her so uncomfortable before.

"What's this?" he asked.

"Just . . . open it." She shuffled in closer as he unfolded the black cloth, clutching her hands together.

It was a new riding jacket. He took great care in unfolding and inspecting the piece. He ran his hands along the smooth material. It was light, yet felt more durable than his usual riding gear.

There was a gold stripe on the arm, similar to Meilene's riding jacket, and a small dragon stitched on the front. His name was sewn into the inside label.

It was the first article he had that declared him a Reinaleader. Undoubtedly, the most expensive thing he'd ever owned, judging by the materials.

He raised his eyebrow. "Did you?"

"Definitely not," she was a little too quick to say. "It's from Quartermaster Gaelen. I was asked for input and suggested a design like my own."

"Well." He closed the gap so that they were right next to each other, knees touching. "It's not exactly traditional."

"And you are very traditional?"

"No . . . Please tell the *quartermaster* I love the new jacket. He's got impeccable taste."

"I'll be sure to pass that along if he's still speaking to me after our last exchange of words. I don't think he's too happy with me right now." She rolled her eyes. "Something about unrealistic expectations with the new consignments."

"If it makes you feel any better, I overheard Commander Calenth saying how they should bring in several choice candidates for the next mating, so they don't end up with another uncultured junior in charge."

Meilene snorted. "That sounds like something he would say."

"So, by those standards, you are doing much better than I am."

"That's not hard to do against someone who failed their final tests three times." She nudged him.

"Ouch." He put on a mock indignant expression. "Sounds like someone reviewed Namail's files in detail. We didn't all have a personal tutor helping us every step of the way."

"It's way more annoying than it sounds."

"I'm sure." He carefully placed the jacket back on the table and clasped his hands together.

She studied him closely. "Why didn't you go with the rest of them today?"

"Maleth was feeling a little lazy today and wanted some extra attention, so I thought I'd stay behind."

"I'm glad he did." Meilene smiled and scooched in closer to him. "So, do we have a truce?"

"I think we do," he said. She rested her head against his shoulder. Her body was a warm and comforting presence against him. "I like it better when we're on the same side."

In a move that would have been daring a few days before, he pressed his lips against the side of her head, just above the cheekbone. She didn't freeze or move away from him. That was a good sign.

If only this was meant to last.

Chapter Thirty-Four

MEILENE

The golden wing stretched and shook, spilling liquid all over the floor of the private wooden bathing room. There were only so many big enough to fit a Reina and her mate. It was luck the quartermaster was able to clear one out for them at the last minute.

"Stop moving, Aletzia, or you'll splash me," Meilene scolded for the tenth time.

But it feels so good when you get that spot.

Aletzia lowered the wing so Meilene could continue massaging the sore muscles. She knocked over a bucket of water, which splashed Ryland's boots.

"Hey!"

"Sorry," Meilene said. "She's being difficult. How do you get Maleth to stay still so nicely?"

"We have a good system after years of practice." He hopped over a trail of water and ducked under Aletzia's neck. "And years of threats that I'd never help him again if he didn't learn to stay still."

After opening his new riding jacket and settling down for lunch, Ryland suggested the two go bathe their dragons. Meilene agreed, as Aletzia was overdue for a good scrubbing since the attack near the villages. She was also keen to leave before Namail undoubtedly would show up with more work for her.

Ryland mentioned he had never used the private cleaning rooms before and was more than happy to take advantage of them now. It was strange having another rider there that wasn't Namail.

Then again, barely anything normal has happened since Aletzia mated.

Don't stop. Aletzia nudged her partner's shoulder. Beads of water glistened like jewels on her golden scales.

"She's a bit demanding, isn't she?" His eyes were trained on the golden dragon curiously.

They were both drenched from their efforts. His shirt clung rather nicely to his muscles.

As if catching herself, she attempted to fix her hair by tucking it into a tight bun but was certain she only made everything worse. She was rather aware of how much of a mess she must have looked.

"Only a little bit, but it's worth it." She grabbed a new cloth and scrubbed along the side of the golden torso.

"It's always worth it," he said with a smile. "Do you want to try some oils that I use with Maleth? It helps to keep them clean for longer in between baths."

Meilene paused with her hands on her hips. "Why didn't I know this before?"

"It's a trick I learned when I was sent to the Red Bay Fordde for a few months of work."

The number of new things Meilene continued to learn about dragons never ceased to amaze her. "Let me have that."

"Here." He threw a jar of liquid at her.

She poured a generous amount of oil into her hand. "Aletzia, stay still. Stop squirming."

"Here." He hopped over a bucket of water and ducked under Aletzia's tail. "Let me help you."

"You sure?"

He grabbed the jar from her hand, touching hers longer than he needed. "I'm finished with Maleth. It's not a problem at all. She seems like a handful."

You tell him I am only the amount of work that I am, and he should be happy to be in my presence.

"I'm not going to tell him that."

His arm froze mid-application, and he cocked his head. "What's she saying?"

"Nothing important. She's being her regular charming self, a regular old nuisance."

He smirked, having caught her lie.

Aletzia turned around and huffed, blowing a stream of warm air on the pair. She flapped her wings haphazardly, scraping the roof and sending debris of dust and wood shavings falling on them.

I am not a nuisance.

"Hush, Aletzia. Unless you don't want any more scrubbing today."

The dragon settled down and tucked her wings into her side. *Fine. Continue, please. My left wing joint itches terribly.*

Meilene smiled as Ryland brushed the dust out of his hair, then quickly busied herself so he didn't catch her staring. She attacked a spot on Aletzia's back while Ryland went after the joints under her wing. "Want to help me with some of the old entries after we are done?"

"Absolutely." His eyes lit up and he closed the gap between them, studying her face intensely. "Anything in particular you are looking for?"

She blushed and returned to cleaning her dragon with vigor. She did not like how her dragon hummed with pleasure or the way her stomach fluttered.

"Just—anything that can help. We lost so much knowledge over the past century. I feel like we shouldn't be so far behind and I want to know more."

"I'll help you find it." He turned back to the bulk of the golden dragon in front of him and clicked his tongue. "But first, we make sure Aletzia leaves this place utterly sparkling."

"Absolutely."

After scrubbing both of their dragons until even Namail would be satisfied, they left the bathing chambers with plans of lounging for the rest of their evening.

Before they barely even stepped foot outside of the chamber, the sound of several footsteps put them on alert. Ryland tensed up and stood in front of her. He relaxed upon seeing the pair of Fordde guards around the corner.

"What is it?" she asked.

A chalky rider ran up to them. "You're needed back in the command center. Something is going on."

"What is it?" Ryland jumped at this.

Almost as if catching himself, Ryland moved to make sure she was not blocked out of the conversation. She wondered if he had done that on purpose.

"It's better you come down. Both of you," the rider added. There was a hint of nervousness in his voice that sent chills down her spine. What happened?

Ryland gestured for her to lead the way.

When they arrived at the command center, it was complete chaos. On any good day, it was busy, but today was an exceptional amount of mayhem. A dozen wing leads huddled around a map with Namail and Commanders Calenth and Jian, while several others were running around the room.

"Ryland!" Alistair popped up beside them. "We had reports of another sighting."

"What? Where?"

"Didn't you go with the others? What are you doing here?" Meilene asked.

The Reinaleader's second was wearing his riding uniform, as if he'd been there for hours already. She thought he went with the rest of the wing to the shores.

Apparently not.

Naturally, Alistair ignored her question. "About twelve hours' flight away from here. Some scouts said they had a sighting there less than an hour ago."

"Where were you this morning?" Ryland repeated. "I thought you went with the others?"

"I came here," Alistair said slowly, "to make sure we were good for the rounds next week, especially since some people thought it was a good idea to take the day off. You should be thanking me for alerting you so quickly."

"You were also supposed to be off today," Meilene said. "You shouldn't be in here."

"I'm the Reinaleader's wing second. I can go wherever I want."

"Alistair." Ryland put his hand on his brother's chest to move him back a foot. "Let's talk about this later. Show us what happened for now."

The wing second looked disgruntled but quickly rearranged his facial expressions. "Absolutely, Reinaleader. Over here."

Ryland put his arm around her shoulder and steered her toward the nearest map that Commanders Calenth and Jian were still gathered around. She glared at the wing second as she passed.

"A wing lead near Brightyn had reports of a creature attack," Commander Calenth said.

"We're still investigating," Namail said. "It sounds legitimate, though."

"We have to go on the counteroffensive," Commander Jian added. "We can't risk losing any more territories."

"Sir," a wing lead said. "We calculated their next landing. It should be past the city of Belum if they continue on the same trajectory—"

"Send a half dozen wings," Alistair said. "We shouldn't wait on anything." He turned toward the rider and tried to lead him away.

"I think that's a bit premature," Ryland said. "I don't feel comfortable—"

"Send them out, and we can adjust later," the wing second said with a dismissive wave. "We can't afford to wait as the journey is so far."

"That's a lot to send without any thorough confirmation," Meilene said. "We can't leave the Fordde without—"

"Just send the wings," Commander Garett said. "If we don't, those territories will revolt."

"We can't—" Ryland started.

"Agreed. Send them out and report back," Alistair said.

"I don't think that's the best—"

"Let's also add a battalion to the southern contingent, so it's fully supplied," Jian added.

"The southern lords are basically rising against us," Commander Calenth said. "We can't afford an attack in that area."

"It'll be better for everyone after the wings arrive," Alistair said.

"I checked the flight patterns and—"

"Let us handle this, Reinaleader, it's not a major concern."

"But I really need to—"

"Not now. We have to investigate—"

"Stop," Meilene's voice was dangerously low, but there was something about it that stopped the wing second immediately. "The Reinaleader and I need to speak alone." Alistair and several of the commanders looked like they wanted to object. "Now."

Meilene grabbed his sleeve and dragged him into her own office. His eyes darted around the place.

When she thought of it, Ryland had never entered her office before. He'd kept his distance ever since the mating, including staying far away from her private offices. Maybe he wanted to give him a place of her own that wasn't taken over by her dragonmate.

As soon as that door was closed, she turned on him.

Chapter Thirty-Five

RYLAND

Ryland tried to keep his wits about him while taking in the new surroundings. This place always felt off-limits. He was usually too afraid to enter, especially while the fearsome Reina was in them.

The Reina offices were larger than his and much brighter than the decor Tork had originally commissioned. Her seatings were a light velvet color and more inviting than he was accustomed to seeing throughout the Fordde. A healthy fire roared at the far side of the room.

Meilene slammed the door shut behind them and rounded on him. "We need to talk."

"What—"

"You have to deal with them," she hissed.

"Who?"

"Your brother." She waved her arms. "The commanders. This must be dealt with. They are trying to overrule you and this leadership."

"I don't—"

"You don't see it," she stepped in front of him, "but I do. We can't be weak in front of them. This is why they don't listen. This stops now."

"I'm trying to keep everyone on the same—"

"No!" There was a fierceness in her eyes he'd never seen before. "They are not in charge. You are. We are. You wanted to help, then help *me*."

"They're not listening to us."

"We have to make them."

You are Reinaleader.

Even with Maleth's encouragement, he struggled with himself. These were their riders. "I—I don't want to make the wrong decision. There are so many riders. If something happened—"

"Something will happen. If not today, then another day. You can't keep every single one of them safe and need to come to terms with that."

"But—"

"This is a part of leading. *Someone* has to make the tough decisions, and we are that someone." She pointed between them.

"I don't." He ran his hand through his hair and searched the room, as if someone would pop out to save him. "I don't know what the right decision is. I can't make the wrong choice. I never even wanted this in the first place."

"Neither did I. This is the last place I thought I'd ever be, but here we are." Meilene wagged her finger in his face. Barely inches away from his nose. "You have two minutes, and you will pull yourself together, and we're going to go out there with a decision."

"I can't—"

"I don't know what the answer is. You decide and stick with it. We both do. Together. This changes today. They're going to listen to us."

Something must have made the Reina finally snap. She had a look of determination on her stubborn face.

Did the other Reinaleaders feel this way in the beginning? If only he knew how they made it through unscathed.

Have faith in yourself, Ryland. We are a team together, as you are with the Reina.

"Okay, we do this together."

Meilene smiled and nodded.

He rubbed his temples and stared out the tall windows at the gloomy grounds below. He could spot Maleth laying on a large boulder below. Several young dragons dipped in and out of the clouds, their young wings struggling against the harsh winds. The journals of leaders of old always mentioned the cloud patterns.

Meilene stood beside him. "What do you think?"

"I think I have an idea."

"Pull up those weather reports we got in from the patrols," Meilene barked at the nearest rider as they rejoined the others in the command center. Ryland was in awe at the authority in her voice as she commanded the riders. "Especially Brightyn and the surrounding towns."

"Should we send the wings?" The rider asked as he pulled up a list of the cities and their maps. They'd been having the different cities report in each morning since Meilene took over. "There haven't been any irregular weather patterns sent in, and the winds have cleared up by Brightyn. We'll have good visibility if we send them out now."

"What's the next closest city?" she said.

"Anil." The rider shuffled through several sheets to find the report from the wing there. Nothing out of the ordinary was listed. A few of the commanders joined the table. The balding Commander Garett's face was set in a frown.

"Next."

"Yanver." Another village nestled at the base of a large mountain. "What are you—"

"Not that one. No."

"Lionth is a bit further away from that area but here." He pulled up the map and pointed at the larger settlement.

The town of Lionth was a larger settlement, known for its farming lands. Ryland remembers visiting there once or twice while on patrols. It was about a ten-hour flight from the Fordde.

Meilene exchanged a glance with him upon seeing the weather patterns listed from the wing lead there.

"It's like before," he said. "Same cloud cover and irregular wind currents."

"They must prefer traveling on the high currents," Meilene said. Her eyes were still fixed on the map in front of her. "That's where they attack from."

"Are you certain?" Namail asked as he joined the group. He stood behind Meilene, watching over her shoulder.

"Absolutely. We don't know why yet, but it's definitely a pattern." She looked pointedly at Ryland.

"Divert the two wings already on their way from the south Fordde to Lionth," Ryland said to the commanders. "No more than that."

"I'd like to make sure it's some of our more senior ones with combat experience," Meilene said.

"But—"

"Divert the two," Ryland pressed. He glanced down at Meilene to make sure she was all right with his intervention. She gave him the smallest of nods. "Let us know when they get there."

"And the other cities?" Alistair asked. "What do you want us to do about them?"

"They have their stationed riders if anything should happen," Ryland said. "We can't afford to send riders everywhere and need to be smart about where they'll hit next."

"Trust us," Meilene said.

"Are you certain?" Alistair asked pointedly to him.

Meilene took a step back to look him up and down. "He's the Reinaleader, and you shouldn't question him."

His brother opened his mouth as if he had something to say about their plan. He hesitated for a moment and glared at the Reina. "I'll get right on it."

"I'll help with the orders." Namail and the Reina exchanged a look before he followed behind close on his tail.

That was good. Ryland knew Namail would ensure their orders were carried out if any of the riders balked at them. Sending more experienced riders would help ensure they stayed calm in the face of any upcoming dangers.

Ryland made a note to talk to his brother the next chance he had. He needed his brother on their side.

Kono says they head back within the hour. I told them what happened, and they turned around.

"Thank you."

"Was that Maleth?" Meilene asked.

"The rest of my wing should be back soon. Guess there's no time to rest today, after all."

"No, there isn't. They can help with the rest of the plans."

She squeezed his arm. The contact was brief, and she immediately took her hand and shoved it in her pocket.

"What now, Commander Garett?" she snapped as the bald rider approached.

Ryland had to bite back a smile. At least they were making some progress.

By the time the two retired for the evening, the rest of his wing finally returned. He hadn't seen his brother since sending him off to help with preparations, not that he was complaining.

It was good to have some space from Alistair, as he could be overbearing at times. He also knew the wing second made Meilene uncomfortable at the best of times. His brother tended to rub people the wrong way with his love of the rules. Thankfully, Ryland never inherited his brother's overwhelming desire to follow every instruction given.

"How was the relaxing day off?" Ryland asked as they came upon the wing unpacking in the Maise.

"Oh, it was lovely." Raphael threw a bag through the open door to his room. "I'll clean that later," he added after seeing

Lora's scandalized expression. "We barely made it there before figuring out we should head back."

Lora flopped onto the nearest couch. "Kien was upset he didn't get to chase any of the large fish from the seas there. He says you owe him."

"Tell Kien we appreciate him making it back so quickly," Ryland said. "I didn't expect you back for another hour or two."

"Well, Maleth made it sound serious," Raphael said with a nod in his and Meilene's direction. "Sounds like we worried for nothing, and you two handled it on your own."

"Commander Calenth says the wings they sent to Lionth managed to intercept the Anver and drove it back east," Meilene said as she sat across from the pair. Ryland joined her. "There shouldn't be any other attacks today."

"That's great," Raphael said approvingly. "Nice work."

Lora nodded at his side. "You'll have to show us the patterns you found tomorrow. Sounds like you two made a good team."

"Thanks." Meilene smiled. "I think so, too."

"Well." Raphael slapped his knees. "I'm exhausted. Lora. Let's go to bed . . . not together," he added scornfully when she sent him a dirty look. He steered the redhead toward her quarters with a passing glance back at Ryland and Meilene.

Meilene turned back to him with a serious look on her face. "Thank you for today. I don't think I would have known about the weather patterns if you hadn't noticed it first."

Ryland shrugged. "It was a lucky observation, and all thanks to those journals you've been digging up."

"Still, I didn't catch it." She scowled. "Sometimes things pass me by because I haven't been living among riders all my life."

"Hey, it's not your fault." He grabbed her chin, gently, and turned her head to face him. "It's not. Did you ever think that because you haven't lived in a Fordde all your life is the reason *why* you were chosen?"

"What do you mean?"

"We've fallen into such terrible leadership for years now. So many have taken advantage of the dragon laws, and we haven't been able to do anything about it. They've used the blood bonds to their advantage, Tork most recently. Maybe we needed someone new. Maybe you were the perfect person to be Reina. Plus, you know so much about the lords, and we've always struggled, keeping them on our side."

Meilene scoffed. "I couldn't even keep my own father on my side." Her eyes glazed over. "He couldn't wait for me to start taking over from him and learning how to run his kingdom. I don't think either of us expected this."

"Have you . . . have you heard from him since?"

"Nothing," she said bitterly. "He didn't like that I chose Aletzia over him. I don't think he could ever understand the bond a rider has with their dragon. He thinks I abandoned him."

"I'm sorry."

"Me, too. I wouldn't change anything, though. If I could go back and do it all again, I'd choose her every time."

"Yeah." He nodded. "Our lives tend to take us the farthest away from what we planned." He nodded toward the den, where the pair of dragons slept peacefully. "Sometimes, I really do think they know something we don't."

"Some days, I almost believe that myself." She looked around the room, now empty of the other riders. "Hey, I've been meaning to ask you . . ."

"Yes?"

"Do you fancy playing a round of Callavan?"

Ryland scoffed. That game was the worst. He hated it. Absolutely terrible. Boring. Tiresome.

But as he looked at her staring hopefully with those big brown eyes, he couldn't refuse his Reina.

Chapter Thirty-Six

MEILENE

"**W**hat do you mean I'm *not allowed to go*?" She tried and failed to keep her voice calm in the face of her stubborn mentor. She clutched her riding gloves at her side and stared at a line in the slab of the stone wall across from her to try to calm down.

Thankfully, they were in the privacy of the Reinaleader's office, where others couldn't overhear. Ryland had yet to redecorate from the disgraced Tork's peculiar embellishments. He favored intimidating red colors and had weapons adorning the walls. At least Ryland had the good grace to take down the old arrows and blades that once filled the place.

Meilene turned up her nose. It was as if she could still smell Tork in here. She should have made them tear this place down after he left, but then Ryland wouldn't have anywhere to work.

"With the recent sightings, the commanders don't think it would be a good idea to venture so far, Reina," Namail said. "They are unwilling to budge, and we don't want to set them off."

"Remember what happened the last time?" Alistair said pointedly. He leaned against the dark oak desk as he watched the scene unfold in front of him. Thankfully, their argument was limited to only the four of them.

Meilene ignored him. "It's because of those sightings that I have to go."

"If I can have some time," Namail said, "I think I can get their support for you to attend to the lords."

"Tell them that it'll help calm some of the villagers and show we have this under control."

"Barely," the wing second said under his breath.

"It shouldn't be up to them, should it?" Meilene spoke directly to Namail only. "The villages have to know they have the backing of their Reina."

"Of their Reina?" Alistair said. "You've barely met with them before."

Namail opened his mouth but wasn't quick enough.

"More than you, I bet. What have you been doing lately? Making up more stringent rules to replace Tork's absurd ones?"

"Better than throwing out everything we've done for centuries on the whim of a foreigner."

"Alistair," Ryland cried. "Watch yourself, please."

The wing second glared at his brother but kept his mouth shut. Good. She was done with his incessant comments.

"As I was saying," she continued, as if nothing happened, "I'd like to visit a few of the nearby villages. We haven't been yet. They need to know their Reina and Reinaleader are here for them and will keep them safe when the time comes."

"I know what you're saying," Namail said. "And I understand your reasoning. Any other time, we would have already brought you there. These are—"

"Unprecedented times," she finished. It was hard not to roll her eyes at him. "I know. I understand what you are saying, but it doesn't matter."

She glared at Ryland. Why was he so quiet?

"I don't know," he said. "Maybe we should wait . . . only a couple of days," he added after seeing her expression. "They were just spotted on our lands."

"That doesn't mean anything." She placed her hands on her hips and swiveled her head between the three.

She held back the scream wanting to be released. That would get her nowhere.

"Should we try talking with the commanders?" Ryland asked. "I think they can be reasoned with."

"Doubt it," Alistair said.

"Get their permission to leave. No. We don't report to them." Something clicked in her brain. Meilene let out a long breath. "Fine. Let's wait it out and see how things shape up."

Namail's head snapped toward her. Ryland narrowed his eyes.

Alistair nodded vehemently. "Good choice."

"You two are dismissed," she said.

"But . . ." Namail started.

"I can handle this from here," she said pointedly.

Namail's face changed from one of confusion to that of shrewd understanding. "Whatever you say, Reina." He backed away with a brief bow. "Alistair, let's gather the commanders to review our next agenda ahead of time. It may take a couple of hours."

Meilene smiled. At least they still understood each other.

"Are you sure about this?" Ryland asked hesitantly as their two confidants left. He looked worried and the tiniest bit suspicious. "What's with the sudden change? I know you wanted to go."

"Why wouldn't I be sure? The commanders say it's not safe and that we shouldn't go, so what would you like me to do?"

"What are you planning?" He narrowed his eyes and followed her back into the command center. Namail was already gathering the commanders together. "I know you're hiding something."

"Nothing. We should get back to the Maise. Aletzia said that Maleth was feeling a little sick this morning."

"No, he wasn't," he hissed. "Maleth isn't sick." Ryland scrambled to keep up with her as she scurried out of the command center. No one looked their way as they left. "Meilene, wait."

As soon as they entered the threshold of their Maise, she stopped and turned on him. "We're going."

"I thought we just agreed on waiting."

"There was no agreement there. The commanders are not in charge of us, as much as they think so some days."

"We can't—"

"We are." She threw his riding jacket at him and paused. They weren't alone in the Maise. Royce and Raphael both sat at the long table, frozen, watching the exchange with interest.

Raphael seemed to be paused in the middle of eating a rather large sandwich.

Meilene pretended like she didn't see them. "I'm going, and so are you. Don't act like this is the first time you've snuck out of the Fordde. Don't forget that I've read all of Namail's files on you and your *prior* activities. Besides, the lords don't only want to meet me, they would like the Reinaleader there as well."

"What? How?"

"I've already sent a messenger ahead, and they are expecting us. Namail knows. We can't keep them waiting."

He sputtered an incoherent response.

"So, the only time you think it's fine to sneak out of the Fordde is for illegal racing, then? That's an acceptable reason but doing our duties as leaders of this place isn't?"

Raphael choked and coughed. Damon thumped his back.

"Should I go alone with Aletzia, then?"

No!

"Absolutely not."

It would be too dangerous.

"I can't do this alone. I need your support on this, Ryland. Are you with me?"

"You know I have your back," he said resolutely. "I'm going with you. We'll do this together."

"Thanks." She smiled. "Get dressed. You two," she barked at their small audience, who still hadn't moved from their place at the table. Damon jumped. "Are you coming, too, or should we *really go* alone?"

"Oh," Raphael said slowly. He placed his sandwich directly on the wood table. "We wouldn't dream of missing it. I'll get my jacket."

Meilene pointed her finger at them. "We leave in five minutes. If either of you tells Alistair, or the commanders, I'll stab you in the eye."

Raphael smiled, and Damon went wide-eyed. He looked as if he fully believed her and nodded fervently.

"Never."

"I absolutely won't."

"Thank you." She grabbed Aletzia's saddle, which the quartermaster dropped off after some repairs. "Ryland," she said sweetly. "Can you help me get Aletzia ready?"

"Absolutely, my Reina." He took the saddle and gestured for her to lead the way. "We should probably take a small escort, at least. I doubt these two will be of use if anything happens."

"Hey!"

"Good call," Meilene said. "I have an idea for some riders that won't cause suspicion leaving the grounds."

Ryland said. Looked intrigued. "Sounds like something that's going to get us in even more trouble, I hope?"

"Your brother is going to murder you!" Raphael shouted as they walked out of sight. "I take no responsibility for what happens when we get back."

Chapter Thirty-Seven

RYLAND

From the moment they touched down outside of Lord Opet's massive stronghold, Ryland knew it was not going to end well for himself.

The beady-eyed lord waited with a contingent of workers behind him and immediately greeted the Reina with a simpering smile on his face. The man, dressed in flashy robes, didn't even look in Ryland's direction as he went about complimenting Meilene and her dragon.

Contrary to what Meilene said, he was certain this man had no idea who the Reinaleader was or that he was in attendance that day. Ryland could have been one of her escorts for all he knew.

"And how was your ride in today?" Opet asked in a silky voice, his eyes fixed on the Reina.

Maleth grumbled at the lord's attention, but Ryland pushed his dragon's thoughts far from his own. These weren't riders, and they weren't used to rider customs, he reminded his dragon.

"It was pleasant," Meilene said simply. She peeled off her gloves and handed them to Damon. "Glad *we* could make it in person." She motioned for Ryland to step up. "I don't believe you've had the pleasure of meeting our new Reinaleader, Ryland Lewes."

The lord's gray eyes flicked to Ryland, then back to Meilene. "Pleasure," he said curtly.

The mask of aloofness she wore did not break under the lord's gaze. The way she handled herself in the presence of the ostentatious lord was impressive. She was clearly used to this from her years in Valchar. Ryland tried to not let his attitude rattle him.

"We're very interested in discussing how to improve our relationships over the next few years," Meilene said. That fake smile remained plastered on her face.

"Absolutely," the lord gestured toward the entrance. "If you'll come inside, I have a table prepared with some light refreshments as we catch up." He held out his arm, the silk robes billowing in the wind. "May I?"

Meilene's mask slipped as she stared at his offered arm, a hint of disgust sneaking through.

"Let me," Ryland said. He slid up in between them, and Meilene curled her fingers around his arm. "We also have a few ideas that we think you'd be interested in hearing, my lord."

Meilene squeezed Ryland's arm in thanks, or was it reassurance? The lord chattered away as he led the small group into the building. Raphael caught his eye and winced. This felt like being sent into a griffin's den just before mealtime.

"That went splendidly." Ryland covered his eyes as the bright sun beat down on them.

Finally stepping foot out of the stuffy manor, he breathed a sigh of relief. He didn't think he was going to make it through the entire proceedings in one piece. Meilene was more comfortable entertaining patronizing lords and chiefs like this.

"That wasn't as bad as I thought it would be," Meilene said cheerfully. She took the gloves Damon handed her and clapped him on the shoulder. His poor rider looked exhausted. "Lord Opet wasn't half as bad as the reports mentioned."

"He was fine with you," Ryland said. "He barely even acknowledged my presence. Here." He put his hands out to help her mount the golden dragon.

Behind him, the large stone building stood equally as menacing as when he first viewed it. On the outside, it was a regular manor for a lower lord, but inside it was decorated ostentatiously, as if Lord Opet had something to prove. Ryland wasn't a fan of the bronzed decorations filling every void in that place. He thought it was tacky.

What did he know?

"The lords are more comfortable with their own kind," she said. "Not that I've been in those circles for years. They believe I'm one of them. On their side. It's fun to let them think so as long as we keep their support. Thank you, Oksana."

The rider passed Meilene her gloves. At first, Ryland was uncertain about Meilene's suggestion to take some of the younger riders with them. The half dozen students were nervous at first when asked to come along, but managed to keep up as satisfactory escorts for the Reina and Reinaleader.

This group wasn't beholden to a particular commander and would keep their silence. A few seemed familiar with Meilene and were eager to help when asked. No hesitation at all about sneaking their Reina out of the Fordde. Plus, with Aletzia keeping high in the clouds, no one at the Fordde shot a second glance at seeing the group of seeming youngsters take to the sky.

This group would prove strong and reliable in the years to come.

They will be.

Ryland smiled as he mounted Maleth. He was continually surprised by how cunning the Reina was. Tork did a disservice to the Fordde, keeping her away for all those years.

"Shall we head back?" Raphael asked. "I'm sure we are missed."

"They'll discover we aren't at the feeding grounds soon," Meilene said. "I'm not inclined to rush back into that battle with the commanders. What do you say we stop by that nice river Lord Opet mentioned and give the dragons a little break?"

"What do you think?" Damon asked from atop his green dragon Tenna.

Ryland thought of how angry Alistair and the others must have been and of the dressing down they would get upon arrival. Their escorts and young dragons would undoubtedly be tired after their journey, and the break would be perfect for all involved.

"I think that's a great idea," he said.

Meilene sent him a radiant smile and signaled to the riders. Without a second glance, she took off with Aletzia.

Maleth scrambled to take to the air, with Kono and Tenna close behind him. He could feel Maleth's elation to be back in the air and not having to head back to the Fordde.

The young dragons scrambled to join their leaders in the air. Eventually, they made it to the skies.

They were in the air less than sixty seconds before landing at the large riverbank. The lord mentioned it was deep enough for the dragons, and the currents were good exercise for them to play in.

Ryland helped Meilene dismount Aletzia. He removed both their dragons' reins and saddles while the Reina settled onto a soft spot along the bank. She removed her jacket and laid on it to soak in the sun.

The six youngsters chose a spot further down the river, giving the Reina and her mate's wing their privacy.

"It's nice here," she said.

"Yes." Raphael finished undressing his dragon and sent him splashing into the river with the others. "Great suggestion from the lord. We'll have to send our thanks."

Raphael joined Damon on a flat rock a distance away from Meilene. He removed his jacket and watched the dragons with a cheerful expression.

Ryland sat cross-legged next to Meilene. The grass was soft and smelled wonderful. The only sounds that punctured the silence were the bubbling of the water, along with splashes from the dragons dashing in and out of the water.

Further up the river, a few of the youngsters removed their boots and waded into the shallow rocks with their dragons. Ryland wished he had a better dragon lord when he was young. It would have helped him settle in better with some good mentorship. Maybe he wouldn't have struggled to find a wing to fit into as he did before.

Ryland picked at the blades of grass. "You were amazing back there."

"Oh, yeah?"

"Definitely," he said confidently. "You'll have all the lords on your side in no time."

"We'll see. At least it's a first step."

"You're a natural at this."

"You, too."

"Doubtful."

"You never seemed like one to follow the rules. Neither am I." She closed her eyes and smiled. "Thanks for coming with me today."

"Anytime." He flopped onto his back and stared up at the cloudless sky. It was so rare to get such a warm day this late in the season. Meilene must have been thoroughly enjoying herself. It was nice to see her so relaxed. Unguarded.

"This reminds me of a lake we have back home," Meilene said. "It had a large river spilling into it, with the perfect whirlpools. I loved the smell of the fresh brooks and watching the fish jump out of the water. It was perfect. My mother used to take me when I was small, before she passed."

"I'm sorry."

"It was a long time ago," she said. "Where are your parents?"

"They're both gone now." He frowned. "My father in a flying accident and then my mother soon after from illness."

"It's a shame they will have never seen you today. Just like my father, even though he's still around. I may as well be dead to him for abandoning my people—or so he sees it."

Ryland couldn't find the right words to say, but Meilene didn't seem to need a response.

"Ryland." Meilene was on her elbows again. "Why didn't you tell me that you were the guard that night? I knew that I recognized you from somewhere."

"I didn't think you'd remember me. First bondings are an emotional and confusing time. Who told you?"

She nodded to the rock where Raphael sat. "You should have told me what happened to you. I didn't know you got in trouble because of us."

He smiled. "I'm always in trouble. I didn't want you to feel bad for something you had no control over. Plus, there's nothing to do about it now."

"I hate that man."

Ryland knew she meant Tork. "Me too . . . It was worth it, though."

They laid in silence, soaking up the sun and allowing their dragons to enjoy the currents. The young riders had taken a break and were drying themselves on the bank upstream. The playful sounds of dragons filled the air.

Swali asks where we are.

"Tell him we'll be back shortly," he said.

"Your brother?" Meilene asked without opening her eyes. Her serene face turned into a frown.

His rider asks where we are again.

"It's none of his concern."

He wants to come to us. Should I tell him we are at the river? I'm sure he would love to join us and stretch his wings.

"No. Tell him to stay at the Fordde and wait for us."

He will listen. I will make certain.

A pit formed in his stomach when he thought of how angry his brother would be hearing the command to stay behind through his dragon. Try as he might, Alistair would never be able to get his dragon to disobey Maleth.

Would that, too, disappear when this was all over?

Ryland never liked it when the chain of command was forced through dragons and knew his brother had struggled with their new change in dynamics. This wouldn't help, but he'd have to learn.

They were in no danger here, and there was nothing to worry about. He'd never let anything happen to her.

No, we wouldn't. Ryland was shocked at the fierceness in his dragon's thoughts. *Should we get out to dry soon?*

The breeze picked up, bringing the scent of flowers from a nearby field. Meilene was on her elbows and looking at him expectantly with those bright brown eyes.

"Take your time," he said to Maleth. "There's no rush."

When she smiled at him, it was the most brilliant sight he had ever seen.

Chapter Thirty-Eight

MEILENE

M eilene threw herself onto the couch with a loud sigh. Every muscle was so sore that the thought of removing her riding gear seemed impossible.

I am not tired.

"Count yourself lucky."

"Aletzia?" Ryland asked as he threw his jacket over a large dresser.

The last ten days were insane. It was surprising she hadn't pulled her hair out from the stress of it all. It was hard to believe that two months before, her biggest worry was whether or not Aletzia would rise to mate this season.

After she absconded with the Reinaleader to visit the village of Delia without a *proper* escort, Commander Garett and Alistair were beside themselves with fury.

Garett and Namail had a shouting match on the concourse until the commander finally relented. It was hard to disagree when a large golden dragon placed herself inches away from his face and threatened to eat him.

He begrudgingly agreed that the Reina was able to do whatever she wanted, and he was only here to advise her leadership. Meilene couldn't forget the look of cold fury mixed with fear on his face.

The wing second was more difficult to deal with. After berating his brother and the Reina for putting themselves in danger, Ryland finally stepped in and had to remind him who was the Reinaleader. She'd never seen someone so stunned. Alistair wasn't used to being spoken to like that.

After he recovered, Alistair decided the best recourse was to ignore his brother for days after. While Meilene was glad to not have to talk to him, that tactic hurt Ryland more than anything.

Eventually, Namail helped convince the commanders that they should continue visiting the close villages, as long as they brought along three wings as an escort and senior riders, not one's barely past their first years of lessons.

Such overkill. Meilene preferred the company of younger riders, as they were less condescending than the commanders.

The wing second eventually decided to come along for the rest of their visits to make sure the Reina and Reinaleader were safe. He'd been insufferable to deal with in the villages and even worse since then. It was better when he was ignoring them.

There were seven new Anver ambushes along the southern part of the countryside. With the cold season in full force, and the weather being so off, it seemed the perfect combination for an increase in attacks.

Both she and Ryland had spent time reassuring the people there was nothing to worry about. This was the first time she'd traveled on official business as Reina. It was exciting, even if most were not thrilled to see the youth of the new leaders in charge.

Hopefully, everyone would change their perspectives after seeing the two handle the Anvers—if they ever got an opportunity.

"I am exhausted." Ryland stretched out on the couch next to her and rested his feet on the table. He used his boot to move aside the Callavan tiles Meilene had forgotten to clean up from earlier that day.

Meilene tried teaching him how to play properly. He did not have the patience to sit through the hours-long game and tended to get distracted too easily. She'd force him again, as she needed a new partner to play with.

Namail usually won and had a poor attitude if he lost, and it felt like Maeve tried to lose every time. Meilene wanted to test her skills against another adversary.

Tonight she was too exhausted to think about the game or attempt to clean it up.

"Me, too." She closed her eyes and rested her head against the back of the couch.

They both retired early for the night. Neither wanted to put up with his surly, overbearing brother or her anxious mentor anymore. No one dared to disturb them in their private quarters.

It was nice to be Reina sometimes.

"So glad the predictions don't have anything for tomorrow," he said. "Hopefully, that means it'll be a quiet one."

She raised an eyebrow. "Hmm. What is that even anymore?"

"I'm not sure. I think that means I'll only get yelled at by the commanders twice instead of three times and that maybe we'd be allowed out for a relaxing flight."

Meilene scoffed. "Yeah right. We're going to the training rooms tomorrow to talk to the new wings if it's not busy. Did you forget already?"

"Just wishful thinking, I guess."

"You're not thinking about abandoning me tomorrow." She elbowed him in the side. "The head trainer hates me."

He grinned, his eyes dancing. "I'd never dream of it . . . and I'm sure hate is a strong word."

"Still, you better not."

"If we have time, I can help you with Aletzia again. I heard she was complaining to Maleth about her wing joints itching."

"Don't let her guilt you into anything, or you'll never hear the end of it. That dragon is insufferable."

Never!

"She's not done fully growing, so it is fair that she requires a bit more attention right now. And I don't mind helping you." The last part he added was so quiet that she barely heard it, "I like helping you."

She ignored the way her stomach flipped at his words. Instead she said, "Don't encourage her."

Tell him my wings are almost larger than all the others now. Tell him they need more attention than those weakling dragons. Tell him!

Meilene smiled and relayed her message to Ryland.

He chuckled and it made his eyes crinkle in a cute way. "I'll keep that in mind, Aletzia."

Thankfully, someone—probably Maeve—had the wonderful idea to start a fire, which was already roaring hot. Meilene peeled off her gloves and rubbed her hands together.

They just came from inspecting the junior wings outside and watching their formations. It was one of their more pompous duties all about the pageantry. At least the riders enjoyed showing off for their Reina and Reinaleader.

She reached across him to press her hands closer to the flames. Three years ago, the old Meilene would have grimaced at the sight of her calloused hands. But those things didn't bother her anymore. She would trade all the callouses in the world to ride with her Aletzia.

I love riding with you, too.

"We'll find the time to ride tomorrow." When she spoke, it was to both Ryland and Aletzia.

The closeness of her spot on the couch to Ryland didn't bother her, as it may have weeks prior. She even enjoyed it. His presence was comforting as of late.

Aletzia favored Maleth's rider, and it was hard for Meilene to not feel the same. It was nice having another beside Namail on her side, even if he fumbled around while trying to do it. She'd never seen someone so ill-suited for the job of Reinaleader, but people probably thought the same of her, too.

After a moment, she realized she had been staring at him. She coughed and rubbed her hands together as a distraction.

"Cold?" He grabbed her hands. "Let me."

He rubbed her hands in his rough ones, which were surprisingly warm. It heated her instantly. He stared at her expectantly with those bright blue eyes. She lowered her own as her stomach started doing flips again.

"Did you enjoy yourself with the young Fordde students today?" he asked with a smile "They sure loved Aletzia."

"She's always happy when the Fordde habitants want to give her some love. Apparently, she's starved for attention, according to her."

Ryland's smile turned into a smirk. "Poor dragon. Someone should have a word with her rider."

Meilene scoffed. "Maleth seemed to enjoy himself on the flight to Luwin today," she said in a shaky voice. The crackling of the fire was so loud.

He massaged the back of her hand with his thumb, tracing patterns into the skin there. "He did. I wasn't expecting him to take us for a dip in the stream. Some days, they just do what they want."

The memory brought a smile to her face. "Nothing dries you off quite like the force of winds flying through the pass or the dreadful hours entertaining that abysmal lord from Luwin."

"He did drone on. At least he didn't mention how much he missed the old dragon lord every two minutes."

"It was a nice break." She was intensely aware he still held her hand in his. "The flight was enjoyable. Such lovely fields to see and great herds for a snack for the dragons."

"Mm-huh."

The intensity in which he stared made her cheeks flush. She didn't know what to do so she continued rambling. "We made good timing, too. Namail was glad we made it in time for the inspections."

"I'm sure he was," he said in a smooth voice.

Why do you hold back?

She pulled her hands away and tucked them neatly on her lap. "They're warm now."

"You sure?"

"I think I can tell. And remember." She nudged his shoulder. "I wasn't the one whose dragon took me for a swim."

He shook his head and laughed. "That's right. You only encouraged Maleth by suggesting he should make sure to get both sides fully soaked."

I wanted to go in, Aletzia said wistfully.

Meilene ignored her. She crossed her legs so that one rested slightly across his. He smiled at the contact. "I don't recall that happening at all."

"Terrible memory you have." He picked up her hand again and played with the tips of her fingers. "Were you perhaps given too many sweets as a child? That can affect your recall."

"Pretty sure you were the one whose mom had to hide the stash from for years. I don't think that was me."

"Hey," his voice was full of mock indignation. "I told you that in confidence."

She allowed him to pull her closer to him. Their faces were inches apart. She sensed Aletzia's pleasure at their closeness. It was hard to separate her own feelings, but she didn't care about that right then.

All that she cared about was the beat her heart skipped when he smiled at him and the way her stomach had stopped fluttering as soon as she decided to embrace these new feelings.

"Wouldn't want to let some ruffian run about depleting our stores. Lora would have a fit, and you know she's already stressing about the accounts."

"I'd never." He put on a face of mock indignation.

"I'll be sure to keep any temptations out of your reach," she said.

"Not too far, I hope." His eyes wandered down to her lips.

Meilene's breath caught in her chest when he brushed his palm against her face. He ran his hand through her hair and settled it at the back of her neck.

He waited. He waited for her to decide.

"Never," she breathed. Her heart was so loud. Could he hear it from there?

"I don't know why it's me, but I'm glad you chose us this mating, Meilene." The way he said her name sounded like a gentle caress against her soul.

"Even after all the trouble I caused you with Tork? All of those punishments?"

"I wouldn't trade these past weeks for anything. Troubles and all." The intensity in his voice told her he was sincere, and Meilene had never been more glad.

Knowing he wouldn't do it himself, she closed the gap and pressed her lips against his.

They were surprisingly soft against her own. At the contact, she felt a twinge of something pleasant in her stomach. After a second, he pressed her closer against him as the hand on her neck wandered through her hair. Meilene pushed herself closer, wanting to have as much contact as possible, and he deepened the kiss.

It felt like she was drowning in a sea of pleasure as Aletzia's feelings molded into her own. All that Meilene could feel was an overwhelming sense of wholeness. This felt right and nothing else mattered.

The warmth of his wandering lips against her neck and shoulder was comforting. He smelled like lumber and the rivers back home. She curled her fingers into the fabric of his shirt, needing to get closer and closer. Hungrily, she pulled his lips back up to meet hers. They moved against hers in a perfect symphony, and everything melted away beside the thought of how she couldn't get enough.

Meilene's heart was racing, her brain was racing and her emotions were screaming at her. She reluctantly pulled away to catch a breath. She could feel Aletzia at the back of her mind, but her focus was on him. He was likewise out of breath, his chest heaving up and down.

It was at that moment she had finally realized what she wanted. So she stood up.

"Where are you going?" His eyes were dark, his hair a complete mess, and his cheeks were flushed a lovely shade of red.

The worry that filled his face almost made her laugh, as if he thought he did something wrong or crossed some terrible line. It was almost laughable.

Taking his hand in hers, she pulled him to his feet. "Let's go to bed."

Chapter Thirty-Nine

RYLAND

"You two are in a good mood this morning," Raphael said from his spot at the crowded table. Sunlight streamed in from the large windows to highlight the platters of food set out for the wing. "Must have got a good night's sleep."

Maleth's laughter rumbled in his head.

Ryland hated how every head at the table turned to them at this comment. He'd make Raphael pay by assigning him to patrol duty or something equally painful and mundane.

"We called it in early. It's been a long week." Meilene tucked a strand of hair behind her ear and chose an empty seat across from the rider. "Can you pass me the fruit?"

Lora passed her a bowl of brightly colored fruit and resumed chatting with Royce. Whatever was in front of him smelled delicious. It was nice getting treated like this while being Reinaleader.

Ryland took the spot next to her as surreptitiously as possible. "What's the plan for today?" he asked Alistair. Meilene passed him a silver dish of meat. "Thanks."

Maeve popped up to pass the Reina a cup of hot tea. She looked cheerful as well.

His brother looked between him and Meilene before answering. "Namail and Commander Yannet have an update from last night's watch."

The dragons are on edge.

"Why? That was for Maleth, not you."

"I don't think it's anything pressing," Raphael said with a smirk. "No need to rush things."

Lora focused on her plate of food but didn't seem able to hold back her smile.

Something is in the air. Can we go riding today? I'd like to stretch my wings.

Well, that was vague and nonspecific. Was he neglecting Maleth lately? He'd have to make a point of taking his dragon out more.

I know you are busy. You are Reinaleader now.

He twisted his head to check their dragons' den. Both Maleth and Aletzia were absent from their stone sanctuary. That was odd, as they usually liked to sleep in until after their partners had left.

"Aletzia said they went for a loop around the Fordde," Meilene said to his unvoiced question. "She's antsy today."

"Maleth, too. I wonder what's wrong?" he mused.

"They probably want to blow off some steam," Raphael said. "It's good to do now and then."

Meilene pursed her lips.

"What's wrong?" Ryland asked.

"Nothing." She shook her head, as if trying to clear her thoughts. "I've put in another order for new uniforms for the wings. Some of the riders haven't had anything new in years."

Lora dropped her fork, and her face turned into a stressful frown. "How many did you order?"

Meilene looked up and studied the ceiling. "Hmm. Maybe a few hundred."

"A few hundred?" Lora asked incredulously. "Where am I supposed to find the money for that?"

"Just fudge a few of the numbers," Blaise suggested. "Make things magically disappear, like Tork did."

"Quiet." Lora smacked him. "I'm trying to do things the right way around here."

"I think we can move things around. Properly," Ryland said. "It's important everyone is properly geared for the upcoming season."

"Yes, but the *money*," Lora whined.

"I can help you with that," Raphael said. "We got some funds from a western island lord—Belesby or something. Apparently, he was quite taken in with the Reina during his last visit and decided to pledge additional fundings."

Meilene smiled. There must have been more to the story. He'd get it out of her later.

"That's great to hear," Ryland said. "Hopefully, there will be others."

"Especially if we keep spending like this," Lora said. "This is going to be a nightmare to fund."

"Running the Fordde isn't cheap," Ryland said pleasantly. "There's a lot of dragons and their riders."

Lora scowled at him and returned to her meal.

"That wing we sent to Swom must have returned by now," Meilene said. "We should meet with them for a firsthand account."

That group had encountered a smaller Anver near the southern border towns. Thankfully, they had senior riders who were able to work together to kill the creature. Ryland was relieved to hear the riders were slowly figuring out how to fight back based on their encounters with the Anvers so far.

"Agreed." Ryland helped her with a tray of bread. "I know they had injuries, so it'll be good to check on them."

"Excellent idea to boost morale." Alistair nodded to himself. He was in a better mood and talking to him, at least. That was some progress.

"I'll get one of the wing leads to arrange for the visit," Raphael said. "Anything else you'd like included in your day?"

Meilene exchanged a glance with him.

"Hmm, that's it for me. Want to check in with Namail?" he asked her.

Alistair cut through his meat with relish. "I think you and I should go to the armaments. We were supposed to do that yesterday, before some people got tired." He glanced in Meilene's direction.

Okay, his brother hadn't forgiven everything yet.

Alistair had spent three solid hours telling him how irresponsible he was for going with Meilene to the towns without telling him. He accused Ryland of pandering to the Reina and trying to keep on her good side.

What did he expect Ryland to do? Ignore Meilene and continue living around each other as strangers?

That was no life, and he wasn't prepared to do that.

Alistair blamed Meilene for making the Reinaleader go against his wing second's counsel. If it were up to his brother, they'd work nonstop from the moment they woke. He needed to learn how to let loose and to keep some of his comments to himself.

"How's your breakfast?" he asked Meilene quietly.

"Quite delicious, thanks."

"Do you want to take Maleth and Aletzia for another flight this afternoon? After our meetings, of course."

"That'd be great. Hopefully, it will help Aletzia calm down a bit. I feel like I've neglected her lately." She focused on her plate.

"I doubt she sees it that way." Ryland shrugged. "It could be the change in weather today. It puts them on edge."

"Maybe we should all go," Raphael said cheerfully. "If you want us, that is. Kono and the others love flying with the Reina queen. He won't shut up about it."

"That would be lovely," Meilene said.

Raphael sent her a winning smile and resumed attacking his meal.

"Aletzia thinks her clutch will start hatching soon," Meilene said casually.

"Really?"

"How does she know that?" Alistair asked curiously.

"No clue," Meilene said. She resumed her meal and refused to look at him.

Ryland knew she was as unhappy with his wing second as he was, maybe more. He never thought he'd meet someone more stubborn than his brother . . . That was until he met this Reina.

"Think she's right?" Alistair asked Ryland. "What does Maleth think?"

"I can't see why she wouldn't be . . . and Maleth has no clue about any of that."

"Would be good to mark in the records if she's right." Raphael grabbed another roll and stuffed his face. "Seems that the queens tend to know a lot more than we thought before."

"Good idea," Ryland said. "The records we have now are terrible at best and half of the time missing key details or pages."

"I'll have Commander Jian make the additions if it's true," Meilene said. "We'll wait and see what happens with the eggs."

"Speaking of the commander," Raphael said. "Did you see those reports he sent from up north?"

"Yes, I don't think it's anything of concern," Ryland said. "If things change, we can send a wing of riders to check it out."

"We should also go over the numbers from the smaller Ford-des," Lora said. "And with the commanders who served under Tork. I've found a few discrepancies there that—"

Whatever she found in the books was drowned out by the deafening sound of hundreds of dragons roaring at the top of their lungs.

"Maleth, what is it?"

We are under attack.

Chapter Forty

MEILENE

Time froze in the Maise as the table registered the words from their own dragons. Raphael still held a roll inches away from his mouth as he processed the warning. Then, as if a spell was broken, everyone rushed to get up.

Ryland jumped to his feet and helped her out of her chair. Lora rushed around, trying to find her jacket, while Alistair shouted at the nearest guard. It was hard to hear over the thunderous cries of the dragons.

Raphael rushed up to talk to Ryland, but all Meilene could hear were the dragons. Between Aletzia screaming in her mind and the Fordde dragons' howls reverberating throughout the building, Meilene could barely even hear herself think.

It was hard to focus on the discussion in front of her as Aletzia sent her image after incoherent image.

"Ryland," she called out, hoping he could hear her.

Ryland nodded. He held his hand out and pulled her with him out of the Maise. Alistair followed close behind.

As soon as they got through the door, Namail was there. His birthmark was shining red, and a bead of sweat dripped down his face. He must have run all the way there. "Good, you heard."

"Of course, we heard. Everyone in the entire Fordde heard." She clamped her hands over her ears. "Aletzia, you need to stop!"

Within seconds, all the cries were silenced.

"Finally." She removed her hands gingerly. "I can hear myself think again."

"It's Prael," Namail said. "The riders out there are calling in reports of Anvers."

Meilene felt her stomach drop. That town was less than twenty minutes south of here. She turned to Ryland, who looked equally worried.

"Why didn't we have any prior warning?" he demanded.

"We didn't see anything until now." Alistair ran up to their group, along with another rider she didn't recognize. "Must have come in through the mountain pass. The updrafts there are perfect to sneak through."

"How many?" she asked.

"At least a dozen."

"A dozen," Ryland repeated in a hollow voice. There had never been that many together before.

"We don't have enough riders." She turned to face Ryland and was not happy with the look on his face. "No!"

"We need more riders," he said.

"Don't be ridiculous," she said.

Alistair rubbed his hands together. "Normally, I would agree with the Reina, but we need everyone we have. We have to go."

Two full wings struggled to take down a single Anver. They'd have to send every fit rider they had. She just didn't want to accept it. She was loath to place her dragon in danger, but she was the Reina.

I am not afraid of them.

"Me neither, love." She was ready for this. "Somebody get Aletzia's harness ready." She turned, but Ryland caught her arm.

"Meilene," he said softly. "I think you—"

"Don't you even say it. Don't you dare." She pointed her finger in his face. He didn't seem afraid. Rather, he looked at her kindly, which only infuriated her even more. "Namail—"

"He's right," her mentor said. "You should stay here. Help rally the riders and direct from the command center."

"The commanders need someone to lead them," she said. "Ryland should stay."

Ryland scoffed. "That's not happening, and you know it."

"We have to go," Alistair said.

"Why don't you go with Namail, and he can keep you in the loop?" Ryland said. "It would be too dangerous if you went."

It felt like the walls were closing in on her. She'd never felt so powerless before. How was this happening again?

None of them would even meet her gaze. She'd been mad in her years at the Fordde but never this furious. She could strangle Ryland.

"Same for you." She struggled to keep her voice steady. "Can I speak to you for a moment alone, Ryland?"

"We don't have time for this," Alistair said. He pointed down the hall toward where the riders must have been getting ready on the concourse.

Ryland waved him off. "Help get Maleth ready. I'll join you in two minutes."

"No, you will not." Meilene grabbed his arm and dragged him off to the side. "Have you gone insane?" she hissed. "If I'm not allowed, then you definitely shouldn't go. You're the Reinaleader and can't—"

"I won't put our riders at risk for something I wouldn't do myself. I'm the Reinaleader. I have to go."

"Then, I'm coming—"

"You can't."

"It's for the same reasons you just said."

"No," he said firmly. "You're too important to the Fordde, to me. We can't lose you. I know you want to come, and I know you can handle yourself . . . I have no doubt that you two would be a fearsome duo out there, but you need to let me take care of this for you."

I would never let any harm come to you.

"I can't—"

"You know you have to stay behind. If something happens, then you and Aletzia can defend the Fordde. Someone has to lead from here and not just the commanders."

Meilene scoffed.

"Help guide the commanders through this. Show them how great of a Reina you are. Remember the first day I met you at the hatchery? There was nothing anyone could do to stop you from getting to that egg. You were unstoppable that day. Be unstoppable today."

"You promised," she said quietly. Her Reinaleader's face was set, and there would be no convincing him. She grabbed his jacket. "You're so stupid."

"I know."

"I hate you."

"No, you don't." He cupped her face in his hands and rested his forehead against hers. "I don't regret any of it. Not the punishments for being there that day in the hatchery and getting to be a part of that with you and all the troubles you've caused since then. I'm honored to be a part of your story for however long you have me and Maleth in it." He pressed his lips against her forehead.

Reluctantly, she let go and pushed him away. "Don't let him be stupid," she said to Raphael, who was waiting for him against the far wall, jacket in hand and a grim expression on his face.

"I wouldn't dream of it." He passed the Reinaleader the black riding jacket Meilene had made for him.

Ryland took it reluctantly. "I'll be back soon. It'll be all right."

Namail appeared at her side. She couldn't even look at him. "I'll take care of her for now. The Reina will keep things safe from the ground. You handle the skies."

Ryland nodded and followed Raphael toward the concourse. Meilene was left in the hall with Namail. Alone, once again.

"I'm sorry, my Reina."

"Don't even."

"We should—"

"Shut it," she said. "I've had enough of being told what to do."

"I know." Namail tilted his head. "You are the Reina."

Chapter Forty-One

RYLAND

The main concourse was complete chaos. Riders ran around, searching for supplies, and wing leads shouted orders to their riders. Fear and panic were visible on every face he passed.

They were all his riders. It terrified him to think about what he was leading them into.

Maleth was on the edge of the chaotic grounds, high on a rock ledge. His head swiveled as he watched the dragons below, and his wings were extended, as if he had expected to take off without him.

I am ready. We lead them together.

When he was close enough, he noticed Maleth had his saddle and reins on. Perfect. His brother had Maleth ready for him. He ran up to him, trying to get his arm unstuck from his jacket as he did so.

"Everyone should be ready to take off in five minutes," Alistair said. "We've hit a snag with a couple of the older wing leads."

"Let me guess," Ryland said dryly. "They don't want to take orders from the new Reinaleader."

Alistair looked at his boots. That was confirmation enough. "I tried talking to them, and they wouldn't have it. Maybe they should hear from you and Maleth directly."

"How many?"

"Three wing leads: Gari, Raka, and Eddie. The rest are fine." He made a face, and his voice had a slight hitch to it. "Mostly fine."

"What is it?"

"I think it's nerves." Alistair looked around to make sure no one was close enough to overhear. "We sent away a lot of the senior wings to help with the earlier attacks, and this is the first time this group has faced anything like this. They're used to light patrols, maybe a small scuffle here and there. Not much more."

"They just have to remember their training and follow their orders. The dragons know what to do."

"Oh, the dragons are on edge, but eager to go. They can't wait to get up there." He changed his tone as Raphael returned with three riders with wing lead stripes on their arms. "And these are the wing leads that wanted to speak with you, Reinaleader."

Unseen by the newcomers, Alistair rolled his eyes at them and backed away.

"Is there a problem, riders?" he asked as pleasantly as he could. He threw his hands in his pockets and studied them.

The three wing leads were familiar to him from his years at the Fordde. Recently, they had been vocal during key meetings when they didn't like new plans put forth by the Reina or himself.

The thin-faced Raka had the strongest opinions of them. He was on the path to becoming a commander under Tork, so naturally, he was not pleased with the displacement of the old dragon lord.

"Our wings are not going anywhere near those things," Raka said. "The dragons have never fought them before. They don't know what to do."

Ryland grit his teeth and kept a level head. "Everyone's gone through the same tactical training based on what we know. We're all dealing with the same thing."

"This isn't what we signed up for," Gari said. The bearded wing lead had been given special privileges by Tork when it came to keeping the lords in line.

Eddie, an older rider who was known to shirk his duties, did not speak and only nodded fervently. Ryland recognized him from his old days at the dragon races. The man refused to acknowledge him directly.

"What you signed up for?" Ryland asked incredulously. "None of us signed up for this. Yet, here we are. What do you think dragons are for, if not defending these lands? Just fun pets to fly around on?"

"We're not going," Raka repeated. He stepped up, so he was inches away from Ryland's face, even though he was nearly a foot shorter. He must have thought that he looked threatening. "You can't make us."

"I can't, but Maleth or Aletzia can. Your dragons can't ignore an order from them, even if you want to."

Raka opened and closed his mouth like a fish unable to produce any sound.

"I'd rather not have to do that." Ryland closed the gap between the two. "If you want to stay, then stay. Your dragons will join the battle without you. You'll be immediately removed from the Fordde and forfeit all your commissions and your entire wing's commissions, if we manage to make it out. If we don't make it back, then you'll still have to deal with the Anvers, as they're coming here next."

"But . . . but . . ."

"We have to work together if we all want to make it out alive." He looked the lead up and down. "I look forward to seeing your dragon in the skies, rider. I hope you're with him."

Without checking to see if they moved, Ryland turned on his heel. He was fuming. This was the last thing he wanted to deal with.

The nerve of those riders not stepping up to their duty. How did Tork manage to let things slip so far?

"How'd that go?" Alistair passed his gloves over.

"They should be joining us," Ryland said. "They don't have a choice."

They approached their dragons. Maleth flexed his claws and shifted from leg to leg. Looks like someone was itching to go. Ryland checked his harness and straps to make sure they were good and tight. Anything less could prove fatal today.

They will fly with us today. I will make sure of it.

"I know you will." He thumped his dragon on the side. "I don't think you'll have to enforce it, though."

Their riders will not leave them to face the Anvers alone.

"Good work back there." Raphael joined the pair. "I've never seen Raka backtrack so quickly."

"Just find what motivates them," Ryland said with a smile. "Is everyone ready?"

"They are. Let's do this."

"Remember to go for the wings or their abdomen."

"Not that hard to forget." Raphael raised his hands as he backed toward Kono. "Even I can remember that."

"Alistair." He grabbed his brother before he could leave. Things had been off with them, and he didn't want to leave on a sour note. "I'm sorry for snapping at you earlier today and for everything else before that."

"It's all right." He shrugged. "I deserved it."

"I need to count on you guys to listen to Maleth today. Can I trust that?"

Alistair had looked confused at first, then his expression changed to one of understanding. "I was trying to help you. I may have overstepped a bit before."

"Just a bit?"

"I have to learn to let go a bit. I will."

"I need you to." Ryland grabbed his brother's elbow. "For today, though, I need my stringent wing second by my side."

"I know you have this. I trust you, Reinaleader." His eyebrows furrowed. "Tell Maleth to keep you safe out there today."

I always will.

"You can't be that reckless rider anymore."

"Hey!" Ryland said. "Those days are behind me now, re-member?" He thumped his brother on the back and jumped onto Maleth's leg. He settled onto the sleek saddle on the ridge of his back. They had always flown as one, and today would be no different.

We are one.

Ryland looked around to make sure the rest of his wing was ready. Raphael was seated on his white, Kono, and Alistair was settled on Swali. When everyone was seated, he raised his arm and gave the signal to take off.

It wasn't only his wing he signaled to. It was all the wings in the Fordde. Today, they were all his responsibility, and he had to keep them safe.

Chapter Forty-Two

MEILENE

By the time she made it to the command center, Meilene was beside herself with fury. After everything he had promised about being partners and working together, Ryland went against his word and left her.

He worries about you, and he worries about the commanders.

"I don't care. You there," she barked at a short rider who jumped at being addressed so brashly. "Where are the commanders?"

The large room was usually bursting with commanders hoping to give her direction. Where were they all right then?

"Calenth is helping the wings prepare to leave, and Jian returns from a flight. Yannet left in search of you. He mentioned a strange report he wanted to talk about."

Elio's rider wishes to talk with you. He said it is urgent.

Elio was Yannet's dragon. If what he had to say was so urgent, then where was that rider? Whatever it was would have to wait since he decided to wander off at such an inconvenient time.

"It's only me so far," the balding Commander Garett said. He was bent over a map by the large stone wall. "What do you need?"

"Perfect," she muttered under her breath. "We need to keep in constant contact with all the wings. I want to know where they are at all times. Have their dragons checked in, Garett?"

"All of my wings are ready, save for three. I can brief you in your office, as there are a few delicate matters I'd like to review first."

"Of course." She nodded at Namail. "Can you find Yannet as well? He should be here. I don't know why he isn't."

"Must have been sent away. I'll find him at once." Namail backed away and called a rider to help his search.

"Commander, this way, please." She gestured for Garett to lead the way into her offices.

When she shut the door, she was thankful for the silence that filled the room. The confusion of the command center felt so far away.

"It's good and quiet in here," the commander said. He ran his hand along her thick desk and looked around the bright room.

She walked to the large windows where the wings of dragons could be seen taking off. She spotted Maleth among them. Kono and Swali flanked his sides.

They would protect him. Keep him safe.

If only there was a way to join them and fight like the queens before her. The commanders would never let her get close. The first Reina Mara would never let anyone stop her. Meilene was weak.

"You had some new reports in?" she asked the unusually quiet commander.

A Reina's journal was open on the table by her desk. She flipped through Mara's notes until she landed on the page with two queens in the air. The other queen belonged to her sister, one that she had many problems with. Whatever happened to her?

"Reports, yes," the commander said. "Not necessarily new."

"Is it Commander Yannet? Where did he go?" Hundreds of dragon wings carried the riders away until they disappeared into the sky.

"I sent him away. Same as the others." The desk creaked as he leaned against it. "Yannet wanted to talk to you about a new report on Tork's whereabouts. I told him you were by the stables, helping with the preparations. I assume he must be somewhere around there."

"Why would you tell him that?" She whipped around.

Garett still examined the artifacts on her desk with a curious expression.

"Did you know that Tork had well provided for many of the commanders, including some comfortable retirement plans with lands he received from some of the lords?"

"I did not know that."

"And a lot of those payments were not fulfilled when you took over."

"Is that so?" she said as casually as she could. Her heart raced as she tried to process his words.

Meilene called to Aletzia and received no reply. She must have been busy listening to the other dragons and helping with the attack.

"Yes." He stood up, and his hulk of a body blocked the path to the door. "I was supposed to receive one of those lovely packages, but now . . ." He shrugged.

"I'm sorry if you feel like you were cheated somehow, Commander, but those lands should never have belonged to the riders. Surely, you realize that now?"

"Maybe. Maybe not. That's not the problem." He stepped closer to her. "The problem is you . . . and what you've done to this place. We both agreed that things were better without you around. Maybe the next Reina will be more compliant."

"*We?*" Meilene's heart sank at his words. She looked at the door and back at his face again. A vein in his neck pulsed. There was a noise outside, and the commander broke his gaze.

This was her opening. She tried to rush past him to the door, but he grabbed her arm and threw her against the desk.

Pain erupted from every inch of her body, but she pushed past that and swung wildly. She pushed him away from her. Instead of pursuing her, the commander withdrew and returned to blocking her only exit.

A man stepped out of the shadows in the corner, and all the breath left her body.

How could she forget that surly face that haunted her for so many years?

"Tork," she gasped.

Tork Streno had lost even more of his blond hair, and his uniform was patched and dirty as if the past few months were hard on the ex-dragon lord. Not surprising, given that she last heard he was on the run from an angry southern lord.

Those dark eyes bulged. He was beyond crazed. "You," he said. "You ruined everything for me."

Aletzia! She cried out in her mind with all her might.

A faint reply came.

"I worked so hard to get where I was. Then you come along with your queen and think you can change everything and take everything away from me. I won't let you do this to the riders."

"Don't do this, Tork." Meilene searched for something in the room that would help her. There was nothing. "It's not my fault the dragons chose me over you. You need to move on."

"You—you did something to bond her to you. You must have figured out a way. That's the only explanation. You and him—you planned this together from the beginning."

"I barely knew anything about dragons back then. How could I have? I just wanted to go home."

Tork looked beyond reason. "You knew what you were doing," he said breathlessly. "I took you for a fool, but I was misled. Not again."

Meilene tried to step away from the desk, but he moved forward.

"I have to help the riders," she said. "They need a leader."

"You're not a leader, not one of them. You're nothing and would be nothing without her. You should never have been chosen to lead them. I've been trained to lead my entire life and you come in to take everything away claiming to be one of us."

"They are my people." She was surprised by the conviction in her voice.

"They never will be!"

"Namail," she screamed with all her might.

Tork lunged for her and was quick. She tried to push him off her, but he was too strong. His hands wrapped around her neck and squeezed.

Meilene!

Black spots filled her sight as she clawed at the hands clutching her. All she could hear was her own heart desperately thumping and the man's heaving breathing. Her mind raced around, trying to understand what was happening.

It couldn't end like this. She wasn't ready to give up.

Meilene grasped at the cool table underneath her, desperately reaching for something that would help her.

Her hand found a hard, cool object. An ornament of sorts she received from that Lord Belesby after the mating. She grabbed it, and with every ounce of strength, she struck the ex-dragon lord with it.

As his fingers released her neck, she pushed away, and her vision blurred. Several voices shouted before it turned black for a second.

Rough hands pulled at her and shook her.

"My Reina. My Reina. *Meilene!*" She recognized the voice of her friend.

"Namail," she choked out, clutching at her mentor.

"Are you all right?" She had never heard such worry in his voice before.

There were noises all around, and it was hard to focus. Commander Yannet and several guards struggled with a man on the ground, his long silver hair flying around. A Fordde guard lay unmoving next to them.

"Where is he?" She looked around wildly. Where was Tork?

"He must have used an entrance we didn't know about. I'm so sorry."

"He's gone?" she repeated, as if she couldn't understand the words that came out of his mouth.

"I promise he won't get far."

Meilene leaned against the desk and poked at her tender neck. How could she have ever thought he would go quietly? Stupid.

Commander Yannet approached her, looking pale as ever. "We should take the Reina someplace safe."

Namail's worry was replaced with fury. It was all over his face. "Maybe that"

"No!" she yelled with a force she'd never had before. Commander Yannet backed away. "No more hiding." Her blood was boiling, and Aletzia wanted flesh. She shouldn't have let the other leave her behind. Tork knew she'd be vulnerable.

Meilene was done letting others tell her what to do.

Chapter Forty-Three

RYLAND

Maleth and Ryland soared through the air. Beneath them, grass waved like a sea of green against the wind. His wing trailed behind in a close formation, along with all the other riders under his command.

The weight of his responsibilities had never truly hit him until that moment. Seeing hundreds of dragons follow him into the skies, into battle.

The Fordde shrunk beneath them as Maleth took him into the clouds. For a moment, he allowed himself to clear his mind. He was always at his calmest while flying with Maleth—maybe that was why he entered them in the races. That . . . and the money was good when they won.

Today, they didn't fly for fun.

Today, they flew with a purpose.

They flew in silence for several minutes with nothing but the sight of white mist all around. Just as Ryland started wondering if they were close, Maleth started rumbling.

"What's wrong?" he asked as they nearly crashed into Swali.

Something is wrong back at the Fordde. Something has happened.

Ryland's stomach dropped. "What is it?"

The silence dragged on. Maleth must have been talking to Aletzia.

Aletzia is worried for her rider. Something happened to the Reina.

"What?" He nearly fell out of his seat and grabbed his reins to pull himself upright. Alistair signaled to him to check if he was fine. Ryland waved him off.

Aletzia is panicked. She is angry. I am not sure what happened.

"Then, ask her!"

A moment of silence that stretched forever. *She says her rider is fine now.*

"And she wasn't before?"

No. She was not.

"We have to go back." He looked wildly around, as if the others could somehow hear him over the rush of wings. Alistair still watched him closely.

We cannot. She is fine now, and we must stay with the riders. We are close.

"Are you sure she's all right?" He had to know what happened.

The others will keep her safe. We must keep the Fordde safe.

As much as Ryland longed to go back, Maleth was right. He had to trust Namail would keep her safe and trust in his dragon. He couldn't abandon his riders. He'd never gain their trust back.

You are Reinaleader and must lead. We must lead them, just as the Reina wanted.

"You're right. We have to stop this now." He clutched the reins and squeezed his eyes shut.

Meilene would be all right. She was tough, headstrong, and resilient. He had to focus on the task at hand and trust she was fine. He held on to that belief as Maleth continued their flight into danger.

The journey to Prael, even though less than twenty minutes total, felt like hours. They could see the smoke and dust clouds long before they could see the village and long before they could see *them*.

We are here.

At least Maleth's intuition was better than his own. His dragon felt the presence of the Anvers long before Ryland had ever seen or heard them.

Hold on.

With a deep roar Ryland had never heard before, his dragon climbed high into the air. The rest of what happened unfolded in a hazy blur. There was a sickening growl, just like he'd heard once before, and a blur of black around him.

The reports were wrong.

There were more than a dozen Anvers. At least more than twenty. The screeches that met his ears were deafening. There was a large black beast just in front of them, and Maleth went for the creature.

Mine.

Ryland wasn't sure who that was meant for, but Maleth dove at the creature with his claws outstretched. A memory came to him of Aletzia grabbing ahold of that one Anver's wing and tearing it off.

Maleth understood. He dove to the side when the creature turned and went for the junction at the base of the wing. With a horrible ripping sound, the membrane went flying below.

There was a terrible squeal from behind them, and a force hit into Maleth hard. Ryland barely remembered what came next, as he was forced forward and slammed into Maleth's brown scales.

Ryland!

Darkness overtook everything else.

When he came to his senses, Maleth was still screaming at him. It took a moment for him to remember where he was. How long had he been out?

You're awake.

Something warm dripped down the side of his face. It was warm to the touch. Blood.

Are you all right?

"I'm fine." He focused on a set of brown scales in front of him to keep from retching.

The coarse disks protected the soft hide below. It had always seemed odd, so many small pieces working together to create an impenetrable shield. On their own, it was easy to pluck off, but not as a whole. Just like the dragon wing formations they flew in.

Ryland!

"I'm fine." He pulled himself upright. It was hard to keep from swaying. "Where are the others?"

After a minute, he was finally able to see more than a foot in front of him, and it was pure chaos. It was good his saddle was on so tight, as it kept him from falling hundreds of feet to his death. He had his brother to thank for that.

Dragons flew around, dipping and diving at black creatures. He recognized the white Kono, and the brown Swali, both trying to fend off a nearby Anver. Lora and her blue, Kien, were helping a wing with their own duo of creatures.

All he could see was a jumble of dragons and Anvers. It was hard to tell which one was which from here.

It all felt lost. The cacophony around him came in shrieks and whorls of sounds that threatened to overwhelm him again. How could they win against this?

We need more help. There are many of them, and these dragons are not used to fighting this way.

"There's no one else to call. Watch out!"

Maleth dove at such an angle that Ryland was nearly ejected from his seat.

Red claws came from nowhere and nearly hit him. Maleth turned on his side, so the claws sank past his scales and into his dragon's flesh.

The new sound frightened him. His dragon's pain was his own, and he wasn't sure if Maleth screamed or if it was his own voice that called out. The creature turned on its wing and made to go for them again.

Another growl came from nearby. A war cry.

Not an Anver. This was an eardrum-shattering roar he recognized.

Where did it come from? Below? To the side?

Without dislodging himself from his seat, he twisted his head to look behind him. Cutting through the clouds and sending a group of Anvers scattering was a gleaming gold dragon.

Chapter Forty-Four

MEILENE

Aletzia dove out of the sky with a deafening bugle and made straight for the Anver attacking Maleth. With a movement so fast, Meilene barely had time to register. She sunk her claws into its skin and bit at a spot on its neck. She twisted and threw it to the side as if it were a buck she had plucked for dinner.

The black creature plummeted to the ground.

"That was a close one, Aletzia."

It was no match for me.

Aletzia lowered herself, so she hovered next to Maleth. The two flew in circles around each other, so the Reina could get a look at his injuries.

Thankfully, Meilene was already on her way when Aletzia got the call to help from Maleth. Something was wrong with his rider, so he reached out to his mate. Ryland seemed fine now. He was covered in blood, both from himself and Maleth, but looked otherwise unharmed, albeit a bit surprised.

From this distance, it was hard to tell if his face was filled with confusion or anger. Maybe both?

That would be something to deal with after. She was already here and not going back.

It took about ten minutes after the commotion with Tork and Garett to get Aletzia saddled up. Jian and Yannet wanted her to stay behind, where it was safe, but the look of fury on her face was enough to quiet them.

They finally understood who was in charge.

Namail would take care of things in her absence. She always could count on him.

As he sent her off, she saw the pain in his eyes, knowing he'd trade anything to be able to ride with and protect his Reina. She told him she needed him protecting things back at the Fordde. They both knew now was the time to take charge of her destiny. She was Reina and wouldn't sit behind while the others defended their home.

Leave the others to deal with Garett. She trusted Namail to continue the hunt for Tork and keep the Fordde running smoothly.

Today the Reina and her dragon were out for blood.

She rubbed her tender neck. How had she not seen beyond Garett's pretenses before? She was a fool to ignore the signs but wanted to see the best in her riders.

No matter where she went, the remnants of Tork's reign were still around. How long had Garett been working to undermine her? Since the beginning?

No one else will dare touch you. The venom in her dragon's voice surprised her.

Aletzia was beside herself and demanded they bring her the commander so that she could eat his head. It took a few minutes to calm the dragon enough to get her geared up to fly.

They had as much right to be there and had to help their mate lead them through this. If there was one thing she had learned from the old journals, it was that queens were at their best alongside their mate, as they were supposed to be.

Besides, Aletzia had already laid the next Reina egg, so any of their reasons for *preserving the bloodlines* didn't count anymore.

The other dragons are pleased to see us.

The grounds below were covered in a red haze. Was it blood or fire? It didn't matter. They would repair it all later.

Was Ryland all right?

Maleth and his rider are fine for now. The others need us.

Meilene held tight to her reins as Aletzia dove to the side, leaving the pair behind. All she could hear was the rush of wings and something sharp ricocheting off her queen's thick hide. A dark mass whizzed past her head and barely missed scalping her.

A creature fought two blue dragons below her. Meilene had never gotten a chance to fully see one before. She was usually too busy being attacked.

The black creatures moved similar to dragons. The way they dodged and clung to drafts of air was reminiscent of how her own Aletzia moved.

From above, she spotted two large Anvers flanking another lighter one. The trio disappeared into the foray.

That was strange.

They usually moved independently of each other, but this trio was different.

While they had flown as a group sometimes, they had never fought together. Anvers didn't flank each other the way this group did. Meilene didn't remember reading anything about that from the old journals.

Another thing the old queens had failed to tell her.

It didn't matter. Meilene was the one here today. She was the one flying against the Anvers and not them. Aletzia and her could do this on their own for their fellow riders.

Aletzia burst through the clouds and felt the dragons rallying around her, around their Reina. It was as if they were given a second chance and came together in formation again.

These were her people now, and she had to lead them into victory.

Drops of rain fell heavy and weighed against them. Usually, she hated the cold. Instead, she let it fuel her, fuel them. Together, they were unstoppable.

The drums of war reverberated in her skull. Was it from actual drums or just in her head? It was like an ancient call reaching out to her.

It was hard to separate herself from her dragon. She didn't want to.

Aletzia flew, defiant in her glory, for surely, there was nothing that stood in her way. She was born for this. So was her partner.

The first Anver, she tore through easily. She remembered the old queens and how nothing could stand in their way. Aletzia dug into her memories from the first Anver she had ever seen and remembered slicing into that deep, dark flesh.

They swayed back and forth against the wind. It pushed them to the side, then down again.

Meilene was nearly thrown from her seat. "Aletzia!"

Do not worry. I will take care of you.

With a mighty pump of her wings, Aletzia led the dragons against the creatures, hunting for the one they protected.

Maleth was close by her side, never letting her get too far away. His worries were ill-spent, as the Anvers were nothing against her mighty claws. Queens were built for speed and agility and were voracious protectors of their dragons. Nothing could stop her.

Then she saw it. The Anver that stood out. It was a different color and built leaner than the others.

It led this group like Aletzia did the dragons and their riders.

Mine!

Aletzia must have spoken to the other dragons, as they backed off. A wing of red and black dragons took down the two that flanked the light-colored Anver, so their path was clear.

Aletzia circled the creature carefully to survey it. The others kept the rest of the creatures away.

This one is different from the others.

"I think this one is like you."

It is nothing like me.

"I mean, it leads the others somehow. It could never be like you. We have to stop it."

With one giant swoop of her wings, Aletzia closed the distance. Queens were quick and agile, so was the one. Its claws were sharp and long, and the scales were twisted but similar to Aletzia's own. The way this one moved reminded her of Aletzia's flight patterns.

Could they be some distant relative of dragons?

Never!

Meilene was surprised by Aletzia's venom. They dove at the creature, but it dodged the Reina easily.

"We have to go higher."

As much as Aletzia refused to admit it, this thing reminded her of a queen. Of a twisted, demented queen.

Meilene remembered a mention in the old Reina's journals of the death of a queen rider. Could it have been Mara's sister? Something terrible had happened to her and her dragon. Something so awful that they'd removed it from any of the history books and kept all knowledge away from future queens.

Could her dragon be related to these distant creatures? Were the age-old enemies of the dragon rider born of dragons?

How could a dragon have fallen so far? That was a question she'd have to figure out later. For now, she needed to stop it.

Aletzia turned on her wing and pumped to take them above the clouds. They would have trouble seeing here but so would that thing.

With a growl, the creature dove at them. Aletzia whipped at the Anver with her talons and kicked it away.

"Higher, Aletzia."

More?

"Keep going."

These creatures liked the damp and the clouds. They needed to get above them. Aletzia sensed the updrafts and took advantage of them. She allowed them to power her wings.

Aletzia took them higher and higher through the turbulent vapors until they burst through the sea clouds into the warmth of the sun.

The air was thin up there. Meilene took long breaths to compensate.

Streams of light reached out and caressed her face. It energized her and gave her new hope.

They couldn't afford to let this one go, especially if it was anything like Aletzia. If their lead dragon went down, that could turn this battle in their favor.

Meilene held up a hand to block the sun from her eyes. Perfect.

They would use the bright orb to their advantage, just like they were taught in all those lessons and battle drills where she pretended to not pay attention. But Meilene always paid attention.

When the creature emerged through the clouds, Aletzia dove outwards from the cover of the harsh light.

The creature hissed in surprise at their sudden appearance and couldn't move quick enough. Instead of going for the wings, Aletzia attacked its exposed throat. She tore apart the flesh and splattered dark blood everywhere. The creature tumbled below the white floor of clouds below.

Meilene could sense Aletzia's triumph fill her body as the Reina let out a victory bugle. Unseen dragons returned the sound below.

This was what they were born for. Both of them.

Aletzia joined with her mate's wing, and as one, they attacked the few remaining Anvers, now lost without their leader.

One by one, her sharp claws tore into their weak flesh until there were none left.

After the last creature was taken down, Meilene searched the skies for Maleth and Ryland. She found them and locked eyes with her Reinaleader. He looked relieved and maybe even a bit proud. He nodded and signaled for the wings to land.

Smart. They needed to tend to the injured and see what fatalities there were.

As soon as Aletzia touched the ground, Meilene hopped off. She ran to where Maleth landed. He shifted his weight off his hind leg and crouched in a strange way.

Was he injured?

He says it's nothing serious.

That was a relief. His rider tried dismounting and slipped at the last step. Meilene ran up to Ryland and helped him straighten up. She buried herself in his chest, and they fell back against his dragon.

"I was so worried about you," she said against his jacket. She breathed in the smell of leather.

"I was worried about you," he said in a shaky voice. His arms were tight around her. "Maleth said you were attacked."

"It was nothing I couldn't handle."

Well, nothing that Commander Yannet, Namail, and a few Fordde guards couldn't handle. He didn't need to know that yet.

"Are you sure you're all right?" he asked.

"I'm tougher than I look."

Everyone is down safely. There are quite a few injuries. I will ask about them and let you know.

"Thank you, Aletzia." She brushed back his matte of hair so that she could see his face fully. Was he truly all right?

"My Reina!" A young rider ran up to the pair, doubling over to catch his breath.

"What's wrong?" Meilene asked. She felt a pit in her stomach at the sight of the rider. Ryland froze beside her.

"It's the eggs," he said breathlessly.

"What?" Did Tork remain behind to cause more destruction? There was no way he could have gotten close to them. Namail promised he would post extra guards.

"It's nothing like that." The rider straightened up. "They've started hatching."

"Already?" Ryland had a mixture of relief and amusement in his voice.

"Namail thinks it was the close presence of the Anvers. Ten of them bonded at the same time, and we've been dealing with that. It's been complete mayhem back at the Fordde."

"It's been a tiny bit hectic in the skies as well," Ryland said.

"Thank the skies, that's all," Meilene said. She turned to Aletzia. "Why didn't you tell me?"

It was not important at the time. I knew they were well taken care of.

"I'm sure they're all fine." Ryland rubbed her arm. "It's nothing Namail can't handle. I'm sure he's being perfectly pleasant to those nervous young riders and welcoming them in as we speak."

She wrapped her arms tighter around Ryland. Relief filled every part of her body. After everything she had been through, she finally understood why the dragons chose her as Reina.

It could never be anyone else.

Chapter Forty-Five

RYLAND

SIX MONTHS LATER

"Do you prefer this, or the red one?" Meilene twirled around for what was surely the hundredth time. She ran her hand along the silver fabric and picked up the ends of her dress to examine more closely. "Maeve thought it complemented my eyes more."

Ryland barely lifted his head off the bed and made a non-committal noise. He had flopped onto this spot after about the fifth or sixth option, fully dressed and ready to go in the new suit Meilene picked out for him, just like he had been for the past hour.

Kono wishes me to ask how much longer you will be.

Ryland laughed.

What a coward. Was he that afraid of coming in himself?

Outside, the brown and gold dragons lay draped over each other without a care in the world. They didn't have to get dressed for any stupid parties that night.

Lucky dragons.

"Tell them to go down without us," he said bitterly.

Meilene raised an eyebrow and adjusted her dress. "Is that your brother?"

"Raph."

"I don't know why he's so excited to go down."

"You know him. He gets antsy if he's even a minute late. And he'd never pass up an opportunity for some drinks and socialization."

"People can wait," she said with a smile. "So, this one?" Now that she had his attention, she spun around once more. "Or should I go back to that lovely black one? Maybe the red?"

"I think they're both fine. Same as the last dozen or so."

"What's wrong?"

"Nothing. You look perfect in everything, so I don't know why you're making a fuss."

"That's what it is." She crawled on the bed next to him and traced a finger along his shoulder and down his arm. "Still thinking about the next mating? Worrying isn't going to help anything."

Easy enough for her to say. She wasn't the one who had the potential to lose everything with the next mating.

Ever since their victory against the Anvers, it was easy to embrace the dragon bond and grow closer to his mate. The thought of what may happen after Aletzia's second mating frightened him to his core.

They never talked about what happened next.

It seemed like talking about it would make it more real. Just like that night was another step toward making it real.

He turned on his side and rested his head in his hand. His fingers flinched. They were tempted to run through her dark locks but knew he'd pay if he ruined her hair. He was warned about that ahead of time.

"I'm just not excited for this pre-mating tradition of parading the Reina in front of all her potential mates and all the nearby lords. I feel like I'm in a race against hundreds of other dragons trying to catch a phoenix. Impossible."

The last thing he wanted was to spend his evening entertaining the masses that had descended upon the Fordde in advance of the Reina's next mating. The new season was about to start, and naturally, everyone wanted to be there for it. It didn't help that Namail and the commanders sent the invite far and wide in the hopes of some *new blood*.

It was hard to not be upset by the prospect of the next mating. He knew how strong his feelings had grown but was unsure if Meilene would feel the same when the time came.

The past few months had gone by in such a blur, and tonight made everything seem more real. He thought they had more time.

She brushed his hair back. "If you don't like it, then think of how much I hate it. It's going to be full of hundreds of riders—"

"Absolutely terrible."

"Trying to figure out how to get Aletzia to mate with their dragon."

No!

"Ugh."

"When I'm not busy being chased down by potential riders, I'll have to entertain all those snooty lords—"

"Dreadful."

"Who do nothing but ogle me the entire time or ask ridiculous questions about what a dragon eats or how long is Aletzia or trying to get me to describe in detail what happens during a mating."

"Sounds like a horrible time all around." He pushed her onto her back and hovered over her. He was careful not to press his full weight onto her. "We should skip it." He pressed a kiss along her neck, and she closed her eyes. "You hate all those people." He kissed the other side. "We could go for a flight with no one to stop us." He trailed along her jawline and made his way to her lips, hovering millimeters away from them. "Find a cozy place in the countryside to sleep under the stars."

"As lovely as that sounds." She ran her hands along his chest. "We have a duty to fulfill." She pressed against him and pushed him off. "Plus, it'll be the first event for those riders from Aletzia and Maleth's clutch. You should be there to support them. We. Are. Going."

He rolled onto his back with a groan. "Do I have to? I don't remember signing up for this. I'm fairly sure it's called the queen's ball, not the Reinaleader's ball."

"Yes." She jumped to her feet, lithe as always, and grabbed his hands. "If I have to, you have to. You can't leave me to those vultures. Maybe I'll find someone I like better . . ."

With a sigh, Ryland allowed her to pull him to his feet.

"If I must. Only for you, though." He pressed his lips into hers for a lingering kiss, only separating when she broke it off. "And I want you to know I'm going to hate every single minute of it, though."

"Your sacrifice is appreciated . . . and remember that you won't be the only one hating it." Her eyes clouded over as her dragon spoke to her. "Aletzia said she doesn't understand our human traditions."

"Tell her I don't, either."

"I will." She intertwined her fingers in his, bringing them up to her eye level, as if to examine them. "Should we head out?"

When she moved to leave, he pulled her back by her hand. He hesitated.

"Before we do," he said. "I have something for you."

"Is it a present?" Her eyes lit up with excitement as he brandished a small box from a nearby drawer.

"Just something I had made for you. It's nothing big."

Except it was. He spent almost all his commissions on it, against his brother and friends' advice. They thought he should have saved his Reinaleader's commission, since who knew when he'd get a money influx like that again if Maleth didn't mate with Aletzia?

There it was.

The thought that caused his stomach to drop. He shouldn't have worried about it, but it was constantly there, nagging at the back of his head. He had never thought his feelings could grow to this. A dragon bond was something they could never prepare you for.

It was also something they didn't prepare you for losing.

What will happen, will happen . . . but I am faster than all of them. Aletzia says she is older now and will not be caught so easily this time.

Would the bond just sever and break, as if those feelings weren't his own? No. There was nothing to break.

Would her feelings change? Would she forget him easily?

His Reina took the box into her delicate hands and opened it. Sitting inside and resting on the velvet fabric was a shining necklace. It had a fine gold chain and large black jewels, which he was told were from the northern mines.

It was single-handedly the nicest and most expensive item Ryland had ever bought.

"Do you like it?" he asked.

Meilene took the piece and held the largest jewel up to the light. It was hard to read her expression.

Her silence worried him. "I know you didn't get to keep much from before the Fordde, and I wanted you to have something nice." He checked her face for a sign. "If you don't like the colors, I can get a new one made. Whatever you want."

She reached out to caress his face. "It's perfect. I love it." She spun around. "Can you help me put it on?"

Ryland unhooked the expensive piece and wrapped it around her neck. As soon as it was clasped, she allowed him to examine how it looked on.

The necklace settled perfectly along her delicate collarbone. The dark jewels glistened in the light and brought out the sparkle in her eyes.

"See?" she said, letting him admire it closely.

Meilene crossed the room to a long, silver mirror and surveyed herself. Her hand shot up to the necklace, and she frowned.

"What's wrong?"

"It's gorgeous, but it doesn't match my dress." She gestured at the silver fabric. "I know what to do. Let me try that gold one on again."

Ryland groaned and flopped back onto the bed in defeat.

Chapter Forty-Six

MEILENE

Another wing lead swaggered away with annoying confidence. Meilene squeezed the arm she was holding on to. Ryland's face had set into a frown since they arrived. The festivities were in full swing, and she'd had to exchange pleasantries with nearly twenty riders.

The great room was decorated quite nicely, thanks to Meilene's intervention. She hated the old, drab curtains that ordained the stone walls and opted for a bright blue instead. Strings of lights twinkled above, as if they were stars in the sky. It reminded Meilene of the nights she used to sleep outside with Aletzia before everything changed.

A group of young riders had imbibed too much and were causing a raucous near the dance floor. Hopefully, someone would deal with them soon, or else she'd make Ryland step in. He had been so patient with all the preseason proceedings. Surely, he'd love the chance to berate the rambunctious riders.

Namail sent a glare from his spot among the lords and commanders and downed the drink in his hand. She sent back the brightest smile she could muster. Her poor mentor was not happy when they showed up over an hour late.

What did he want her to do? Show up half-dressed like a slob?

No. She was Reina, and they could wait on her.

After trying on a few other styles, she finally settled on a cute, form-fitting black number that showed off Ryland's necklace brilliantly.

"I heard you frightened away the two potential riders Namail found for your wing," Ryland said in a playful tone. "We haven't had a single one make it to moving into the Maise yet."

Meilene made a disparaging noise. "Don't remind me."

None of them could keep up with me.

"One day, you will have to find a rider you can at least half-tolerate. Namail is going to lose his hair by the time he finds even one permanent rider for your wing."

"I'm only a little picky. It's not my fault he hasn't found anyone good. I guess I'll have to continue riding with my mate's wing until then."

Ryland turned to face her. "I don't know. You're starting to weigh us down. You may need to find someone else to ride with."

I fly with whoever I want. I am Reina.

"Good luck with that." She grabbed his shoulder and turned him back to the crowds. A familiar pair of red-haired siblings passed by, both with full glasses of wine in each hand.

"I have half a mind to give you Blaise to deal with."

"Pfft. Trying to punish me now?"

"He needs a change . . . and maybe not having a dozen others in the wing to fight with may be good for him. Give it a thought."

"I'll see. He's a stubborn one, though."

He nudged her shoulder. "Just like someone I know."

A short rider in a tan suit approached the dais they were on, trembling from head to toe. When he was merely feet away, he let out a squeak and backed away without a word.

"Did you see the length of that one's hair?" Ryland whispered.

Meilene scoffed. "Better than the one dripping with sweat. Why bother coming if you're that nervous?"

"They're terrified of you." He poked her side. "You're quite the force to come across."

"Who? Me?"

"Unquestionably. Why else do you think I took over assigning the patrols with the juniors? They were all too afraid of you to point out any inconsistencies, and half of them called out sick from nerves the last time you came."

"Hey." She hit him playfully. "I just like things the way I like them."

"Some people would call that difficult."

"Some people would prefer to use tenacious or determined." She tried to look as threatening as possible in her sparkling dress. "If you know what's good for you, you'll do the same."

He smiled at her threat, knowing it was empty. She had to use humor. It was the only thing getting her through this whole thing.

This evening brought her back to the days before Aletzia's first mating. The new riders. The stares. The whispers.

The all-encompassing pressure to meet everyone's expectations. She didn't miss that feeling of dread.

Ryland was worried but put on a brave face. If only she had the words to reassure him. She couldn't even calm her own fears.

Alistair passed by, talking with another wing second, Myles. He nodded at her. Whatever problem there was between Ryland and his brother had passed in the last few months.

Perhaps Alistair had finally gotten used to the idea he was not the one in charge, or maybe he was hoping the next mating would change things.

Never. I am not a fan of Swali as a mate . . . and his rider never greets me as he should a Reina.

Ryland trusted his brother with his life. She knew better than that and preferred to keep an eye on the tumultuous wing second.

"You're lucky you have such a patient Reinaleader," Ryland said.

"Extremely lucky." She gripped his arm again and groaned as a pair of South River Fordde riders approached them, looking as nervous as ever. When would the night end?

"What do we have here?" Ryland whispered. "More victims for you."

After that pair, a flood of riders approached, including Raka, the supposedly reformed Tork loyalist. Ryland was willing to give him a second chance. She still hadn't forgiven him and his wing for nearly deserting them at the attack on Prael.

They needed all the loyal riders they could get for the battles to come, especially if the Anvers regrouped quickly. Killing that lead Anver kept them at bay for the time, but it wasn't over with those creatures.

If they were like dragons, then that wasn't the only queen of their kind. They must have more.

Meilene was determined to get to the truth of their origins, something the history books tried to keep quiet. They had to know more about what could turn a dragon into something so cruel and twisted. Perhaps that could help them destroy the Anvers once and for all.

The old dragon lord himself was difficult to track down, but Ryland had assigned Damon and Royce from his wing to help with the search. She'd never seen him so furious as when he found out about her attack. If he hadn't been so worried for her safety at the time, she thought he may have taken off on Maleth in pursuit of Tork.

As long as Tork was still out there trying to rally support, she wouldn't be able to rest and couldn't fully trust those who were once loyal to him.

After a while, a well-dressed lord in red silks caught her eye and made his way toward her, accompanied closely by a pair of aides. She stiffened when she recognized his face. She hadn't had any contact with him for four years.

What was he doing here now?

"Who's that?" Ryland said.

"Father," she stammered out.

"Father?" Ryland furrowed his eyebrows and turned toward the newest arrival. "Lord Eoibard."

"Meilene, or should I say, my Reina." He bowed his head at her and ignored Ryland's greeting.

"What are you doing here?" Meilene winced when her voice cracked. She rubbed her hands on her dress. "I mean . . . I'm glad to see you here, my lord."

The lord of Valchar took her hands in his and pressed his right hand over his chest in the usual show of fealty to a queen. Meilene was too stunned to move.

He was the same as the last time they were together, except for a few more gray hairs on his head and lines under his eyes.

"I wanted to come and show my support for the new Reina."

Meilene narrowed her eyes. Ryland's hand was on the small of her back, supporting her. "Your support?"

"I came today to pay respects to the Reina and to see if we can come to an arrangement to renew Valchar's support to the Fordde. If it pleases the Reina, I will send an aide over with the details of our support tomorrow."

"You want to help the Fordde now?" The sudden change of heart was oddly suspicious.

"Naturally. I think we can find a new arrangement to work for both our people," he hesitated. "If that's all right with the Reina?"

Her heart skipped a beat. "Of course, my lord. I can arrange a time to meet tomorrow."

"That would be lovely. I'll take my leave of you then, my Reina." He bowed his head and backed away.

She felt a familiar warm presence beside her as Ryland grabbed her hand and squeezed.

"Are you all right?" Ryland asked.

"I don't know what I feel right now. Years ago, the sight of him would have made me weep with happiness . . . Now, I don't know."

"I heard he was at one of the villages but didn't want to say anything. I didn't know he would be here today. Is that okay?"

"That's all right. I'm glad to see him again, even though I'm uncertain what his motives are."

The relationship she had with her father was always a complicated one, even before she bonded with Aletzia. He had never been a man of many words, and the fact he was willing to come to see her meant so much. Was it weak to hope he didn't have a hidden agenda and was truly here to see her?

"Will you come with me and Aletzia tomorrow? When we meet with my father, that is."

"You know I wouldn't miss it for anything."

Meilene did not leave Ryland's side all night, much to the chagrin of her mentor. Namail and the commanders wanted her to socialize to meet new potential mates. They still held on to a hope for someone new with more experience and had been throwing new riders at her at every second she was alone.

While she promised Namail she'd keep herself open to options, that didn't mean she had to entertain every last simpleton who thought they had a chance.

An open mating would continue to give the option of the best leader, and Ryland fully supported her decision. They both wanted what was best for the Fordde.

Meilene knew what was best for her and the Fordde, or rather, who was best. She was confident Aletzia felt the same.

I will mate with whoever is able to catch me.

"Care to dance?" Ryland asked, breaking her out of her reverie.

"I'd love to." She took his hand and let him guide her to the dance floor.

The pair settled on a spot in the far corner, away from curious eyes. They passed Raphael and Lora, who were paired up and dancing ostentatiously in the middle of the floor.

Ryland placed his hand on her back and pulled her close. They swayed to the music together, forgetting about all else. This was better than standing on that dais and making small talk with the masses—anything was better than that.

Thankfully, one of their commanders had removed the rowdy group, creating calm throughout the ball.

After a while, she looked up into his blue eyes and felt safe. She pressed herself into his chest again. He was her rock and had been in the past few months. He was always so unsure of himself and didn't want to do the wrong thing.

Ryland was worried about the next mating. She understood and had the same uncertainties. As much as she had grown to like him, the weight of the Fordde's future weighed heavy on her shoulders. It wasn't just about her anymore.

Would it always be like that every mating?

It was always so comforting in his arms. He wouldn't let anyone hurt her and that he'd do anything for her. All her troubles seemed to melt away when she was with him.

Within days, Aletzia had her second mating. It was all a blur, just as the first time. She watched through what felt like her own eyes and soared high above the clouds while the others followed in their pitiful pursuits, calling out and attempting to lure the dragon in.

The next morning, she woke up with a start. Suddenly, being torn away from a sweet dream was jarring. Thankfully, a comforting hand came up to pull her back down. She settled into the crook of his shoulder and stared up into the face of her match. Her mate.

How could they have ever been worried before?

When she stared into Ryland's blue eyes, for the first time in a long time, she was home.

THE END

Book 2: Fall of the Dragon Queens

In this sequel to Reign of the Dragon Queen, Meilene's saga continues as she struggles to balance the burdens of leadership, navigating the birth of a new queen, and keeping those closest to her safe as two wars wage against her people.

Order on Amazon

Note From the Author

Thank you for following Meilene and Aletzia's journey. I hope you enjoyed reading it as much as I did sharing it with you. Reader feedback is always welcome and appreciated. If you have a moment to spare, please share a review with your thoughts.

Sincerely,

Cadence

Printed in Great Britain
by Amazon

24107176R00215